Petr Zhgulyov

The RETURN

Don't wait for miracles.
Make them happen!

IN THE SYSTEM BOOK #6

Magic Dome Books
in collaboration with 1C-Publishing

In the System
Book #6: The Return
Copyright © Petr Zhgulyov 2023
English translation copyright © Sofia Gutkin 2023
Cover Art © Vladimir Manyukhin 2023
Published by Magic Dome Books in collaboration with 1C
Publishing, 2023
All Rights Reserved
ISBN: 978-80-7693-136-7

THIS BOOK IS ENTIRELY A WORK OF FICTION.
ANY CORRELATION WITH REAL PEOPLE OR
EVENTS IS COINCIDENTAL.

In the System LitRPG series
by Petr Zhgulyov:

City of Goblins
City of the Undead
Defending Earth
Overlord of the Dungeon
Sovereign
The Return
The Choice

TABLE OF CONTENTS:

Chapter 1. An Uninvited Guest....................................1

Interlude No. 1. Mistress of the Pack 23

Interlude No. 2. A War Stratagem 30

Chapter 2. Suicide...34

Chapter 3. Relocation..53

Interlude No. 3. The Strategist 76

Interlude No. 4. The Sacrifice...................................82

Interlude No. 5. The Offensive 92

Chapter 4. The Wait 100

Chapter 5. The Wall 120

Chapter 6. Spiritual Sword Embryo 136

Chapter 7. Bait 159

Chapter 8. The Trap 174

Interlude No. 6. Dan 188

Chapter 9. A Quiet Place...190

Interlude No. 7. Escalation 209

Chapter 10. Sabotage 230

Chapter 11. The Meeting Place 253

Interlude No. 8. The Extermination 273

Chapter 12. Running Man.............................281

Appendix. Factions and Characters.............301

Chapter 13. The Return Attempt...................315

Chapter 14. The Perimeter 327

Chapter 15. Check.......................................345

Epilogue. Consequences..............................363

Addendum. Character Table........................364

CHAPTER 1

AN UNINVITED GUEST

WHAT WAS I FEELING right now? The traditional range of emotions, I suppose: fear, determination, a little excitement, mixed in with relief. We initially thought that players would return to the goblin world after a month, but it had taken three and a half times longer. So much had changed that it felt like a lifetime ago. I joined the state service, received weapons and equipment, healed hundreds of people, completed dozens of local missions and was a hair's breadth from death more than once, captured the *Dungeon* and created a *Minor Altar*, helped to create the Guild, and became stronger. All for the sake of today…

Level: 21 (319/420 System Points).

Things had ended badly with Eva, but sometimes you have to do what you think is right, even if you're not going to like the consequences. I don't know why she was so desperate to go on this mission, but I didn't want to see her dead. She must be so mad right now! Well, if I died a heroic death, I guess she'd appreciate it someday. Or not, if our world fell. The goblins were in a similar position, so it looked like I'd have to hate someone else this time.

Time remaining: 59 minutes and 56 seconds.

These thoughts took bare seconds, not hindering my movement at all. We were given an hour to prepare, which allowed some room for maneuver. According to publicly announced agreements, the majority of players would teleport at the last minute. The target of the mass attack would be the fortress, the site of Quel's _beacon_. Alas, I'd have to miss the "party" since I had another task, and I didn't want to waste any time.

I took the raven out of the _Ring_, together with a lighter I'd previously taped to him with blue duct tape. I could have thrown him into the bag alive, but then he would have occupied one of the slots. After passing a flame over the body, I left the raven to hatch out and forgot about him for a while.

Activate combat form!

The department's players had received special armor for this mission, combining elements of medieval and modern equipment. It was quite light, didn't restrict movement and protected more from bladed weapons than firearms, as well as from undead claws. Lastly, I lowered an almost weightless, open-face helmet over my head. The _Ring_ also contained a heavy version, but it made it difficult to see and was intended for combat, not reconnaissance.

Time remaining: 53 minutes and 27 seconds.

Not bad, I had gotten everything done in six and a half minutes.

Legion took off and landed on my shoulder, where special fasteners had been installed for him.

"Caw!"

"Caw indeed." I removed him from my shoulder and sat him on one of the bags. "Perch somewhere else for now."

Time was running out, but I spent a couple of minutes inspecting the divine gates. All were closed, but the sixth one belonging to Shiva looked darker and was covered in numerous cracks. Had he really died then? I'd had no time to panic since all my attention was focused on the upcoming teleportation, but now, I could imagine the consequences.

If Shiva wasn't the traitor as Hera suspected, then Earth was currently being protected by five gods, not six. Hera had called this number critical for deterring enemies. This meant that the stakes were higher once again. I reached out, touching the cold stone.

Attention! Insufficient access rights!

Would you like to open the gate to Shiva's domain by force? (100 SP)

Yes(1%)/No(99%)

Attention! The gate is damaged.

An attempt to open it has a 99% chance

of causing its destruction!

The chance of success was small, but considering all the players, there had to be thousands of such gates scattered across the personal rooms. And, if the "break in" wasn't a rare bonus, someone could potentially get into the domain while the owner was dead. Although I doubted the gods would look kindly on such an attempt.

In any case, I was interested in the gate for a slightly different reason. It was difficult not to draw a parallel between Shiva and the Great Y, who had suffered a similar fate. Initially, I'd planned to fight my way through to the temple, but the idea seemed naive now. Capture the Altar? I really doubted that such a valuable object would be located in the center of an ordinary city. Unless Sar itself was a divine domain, but this seemed very unlikely. I'd bet anything that a projection would be waiting for me in the temple, like the one that the Golden Monkeys had created. It would be a kind of door that one had to open somehow.

Judging by how easily I'd struck a deal with Hera, the gods believed I had no or almost no chance of pulling this off without their help. At least it explained why I was allowed to remain independent. As usual, it was all assumptions, guesses, and theories. Time went on, but nothing changed — I'd have to figure it out as I went along.

Time remaining: 52 minutes and 39 seconds.

I'd checked everything I wanted here, so it

was time to wrap up. I went back to the scattered bags and, sighing, began loading them onto the motorcycle. They were so full that, despite the reduced weight, I could only carry them all for a very short time. Unless I just threw them into the portal? Bad idea. Okay, it was time to check out the Mission Gate and get down to business.

* * *

Global Task No. 3
Type: *Conquest*
Information:
*This is the heavenly city of Sar, which once belonged to the **goblin nation.** Their **gods** lost and were defeated. Although the enemies have retreated, a curse hangs over the city. The center of the city is controlled by the **undead**, while the outskirts are pillaged by the surviving goblins. Once allies, the living and the dead come together in the fight for the Altar.*

Additional information:
Earth is in danger! The enemies are strong and numerous. The only chance for our world to survive is to seize the Altar of the Great Y, a fallen goblin god, and dedicate it to one of Earth's gods. This is the only way for our world to become strong enough to face the threat on equal terms!

Destroy the enemies, whoever they are, and then fight your way to the Altar! Hurry or you might have nowhere to return to!

Global objective:
Difficulty level: A.
— Capture the Altar of the Great Y and dedicate it to a new owner.
Reward:
Variably, depending on the choice.
Allies:
— Players (13,000/ 13,000).
Anticipated enemies:
— System creatures.
— Undead.
— Goblinoids.
— Traitors.
— Followers of foreign gods.
Local objective:
Difficulty level: C.
— Survive for 1,000 days.
Reward:
— Return to Earth.
Penalty for failure:
— Death.

Nothing had changed since last time, except the number. Thirteen thousand people. No one had managed to kill themselves yet by jumping through the portal without waiting for the others. It was a huge number of players, but, on the other hand, it could have been more. We'd lost 2,000 soldiers before the campaign had even started. Even if they were newbies, it was still upsetting.

Select a destination:
— Random.
— Quetzalcoatl's beacon.

Both *beacons* were working, so I didn't need to change my plans. The raven perched on the motorcycle's handlebars, shuffled his feet, and cawed. I wondered if this could be considered an ominous omen.

Attention! You have selected Inti's beacon (Heresy)!

The portal glowed, opening the way, and I saw a dimly lit room. It had been a sheer wall the first time, only vague outlines visible the second time, but now it resembled a *window* — not perfectly clean, but quite transparent. I touched the *Spatial Ring*, releasing the ghost.

"Check the other side. If it's safe, appear in front of the portal and wave your tentacles. You know what to do..."

Sending the ghost to a place with towers designed for their capture was slightly risky, but the prison was located inside the area controlled by the tower I'd destroyed. Plus, the towers weren't active all the time, so I doubted anything would happen.

"Yes, boss!"

Bri dived through the portal and reappeared thirty seconds later, waving its limbs uncertainly. Apparently, it wasn't sure about the exact location of the *window*. Well, at least there was no undead in the immediate vicinity, which was all I wanted to know.

Activate Invisibility!

"Legion, you go first. Tell Bri to get out of the

way."

The raven took off obediently, leaving the personal room, and Bri also disappeared from view. I pushed off with my foot, steering the motorcycle and winced in advance.

*   *   *

The difference in height was slight, but the drop was accompanied by an ominous screech. Fortunately, the ceiling held, so I didn't end up plunging to my death. Rather, the motorcycle, since I would have managed to avoid such a stupid death. I stopped and turned off the engine. Although it was designed to work silently, and most of the undead were deaf, I doubted that I could drive it out of the room. If I didn't have the *Spatial Ring*, this could have been a problem.

Activate Search for Life!

The wave passed through the building, showing a single flare outside the room. Bri, most likely. As practice had shown, the skill reacted to the ghost, despite its name. I strongly suspected that the search revealed creatures with a sufficient energy reserve, rather than abstract "life". It ignored insects and grass yet showed large trees.

We assumed that the undead tracked not only their victims, but also each other using this skill, so I hadn't obtained some kind of "Search for Dead". The more skills one had, the harder it was to navigate, and who knew if there wasn't an overall limit? It was unlikely, but even the raven couldn't give me a clear answer. Checking behind me out of habit, I saw that the portal had closed e, leaving only a sensation of goosebumps down my back. I hate the undead.

Deactivate Invisibility!

"Nobody here, boss! We're on the third floor! No enemies detected!" Bri reported and added, glancing at the raven, "Or crystals!"

"Well done."

Now I needed to go down to the first floor. I stood up holding the *Slaver's Bag (S)*, and was heading to the window when I was flooded...

Attention! You have received 1,000 SP! (1319/420)

You've reached Level 22! (899/440)
You've reached Level 23! (459/460)

I fell to one knee, struggling with the overwhelming pleasure. If I had been as weak as I was when I'd left this place, so much energy at once could have easily, if not killed me, then knocked me out, making me easy prey. I understood where the flow of energy had come from immediately and felt cold. I'd done it now. My *beacon* had just been used by someone willing to pay the price that I'd set as a joke. This someone was within 77 meters of the installation point.

"Son of a... Legion, go out the window and search for the enemy! Bri, to me!"

The raven understood the situation at once and left the room. The ghost wrapped its tentacles around me, clinging to my back.

Activate Invisibility!

I was hidden again a second later, but I wasn't sure this would help. If I'd scanned my surroundings as soon as I arrived, then my opponent had probably done the same. The flow of experience could have also hidden an additional effect from me. I had nothing left to lose.

Activate Search for Life!

The wave passed through the building again, catching only the raven. It would be dumb to expect my uninvited guest not to have their own disguise. Now what? I rushed to the window and jumped out, slowing down my fall by flying. Nevertheless, the landing wasn't pleasant: the heavy bag made me spend too much mana. I couldn't leave it though, for thirty soldiers slept inside. Should I release them? Only as a last resort, since they would be nothing more than cannon fodder. They were trained to fight the undead, and I'd bet anything that the enemy following me had divine protection. Ordinary people couldn't help me right now.

"I hate..."

I popped a capsule in my mouth, since it was no time for scrimping. Nothing was going according to plan. To be able to pay 1,000 points in one go, the being must either have a high rank or a very high level. Hard to say which was worse. The minimum level would be a D-ranked creature with Level 23. We might be technically equal if I considered our levels, but one got more points for each level as the rank increased. Not to mention other advantages, such as learning more powerful skills.

Without wasting any time, I ran along the wall, inspecting my surroundings as I went. I had to ignore the risk of being exposed. One enemy had arrived at my *beacon,* but what would I do if ten more followed? Rejoice at the levels unexpectedly showered upon me? Only if I was an idiot. Unfortunately, I couldn't adjust the settings remotely.

"Was it here?"

I stopped at a window and tore down the rusty grate with a few blows of the sword. The divine blade coped even without *Split.* I took a running jump inside, admiring the combat form as I went — this trick would have been much riskier in a real body. And painful. A second later, the blade was in my hand again.

Activate Search for Life!

Nothing, not even the raven this time. He must have risen too high. And no sign that someone had come to confront me. Perhaps the enemy ran away, not wanting to hang around the landing site? I would have already spotted someone like a Leviathan or even a Disaster — by the crash of the collapsing houses, if nothing else — and a large group of players would be too hard for any other creature.

The ground floor greeted me with emptiness and dust. I usually hate dust, but now it could help me spot the enemy. Unless they could fly, of course, like I could. Remembering this possibility, I flew five meters and rounded the corner. Then I ran again. Caution was all well and good, but speed was more important. I had to fix my mistake. Phew.

Inti's Beacon (Heresy of Cain)

A ghostly banner with the infinity symbol. The *beacon* stood before me, but I still took a look around, checking that the dust of recent months hadn't been disturbed by anyone. Only then did I take the last few steps.

Would you like to change the access restriction?

Yes/No

Going into the menu, I closed the *beacon* to everyone, and only then took my time, changing the settings to more acceptable ones. Access was now free but closed to everyone except members of Hera's faction and my own cult. Or a System group. This way, I could count on the arrival of allies. As long as the enemy wasn't strong enough to kill us all. Or did they flee without waiting for the cavalry to arrive? I needed a decoy to make sure.

* * *

Armet accepted his role without complaint. He seemed to be getting used to this already. Although, considering that he was a follower of the Great Izur, his formal ally could well be lurking outside. Or allies — a high-ranking player almost certainly had a pocket army. Damn, why was I such a pessimist? Or was I being realistic?

In any case, ten minutes of waiting produced

no result. No one tried to take the bait or make contact with the traitor. If it weren't for the two levels, I would think I had imagined it. But I couldn't forget about what had happened. The stranger wasn't going to disappear, and who knew what they could do? And it would be all my fault.

"Legion, find the one who came after us!"

A mental order wouldn't have reached him, but a tiny earpiece had been fashioned for the raven, allowing us to stay in touch within a certain radius. He couldn't answer, but he could hear my commands. This was somewhat unnecessary, since I could send messages through the Heresy interface, although it took more time. Not very convenient during a fight, and I'd gotten used to not revealing all my trump cards.

"Can I help too, boss?"

"Check the building again, but don't fly too far. If you do spot someone, don't engage."

The ghost was a huge advantage against lowly undead and goblins, but posed no danger to a high-level player with *True Sight*. Simply a sentient cloud of mana, which could be easily injured with System weapons or magic.

I sighed and returned to the building. I couldn't carry the bag containing the assault squad and their equipment even if I wanted to. Even in combat form. The bag weighed well over fifty kilograms.

Would you like to retrieve Oleg the Prophet from the Slaver's Bag?
Yes/No

"Have we arrived?"

"Yes, take up a defense position and check the cargo. A strong enemy... a player, I suspect, has been spotted nearby. I'll try to catch and destroy them, but you should wait for our allies to arrive."

"We can help."

"We're in undead territory right now," I shook my head. "You will only attract attention, so keep your head down. I'll be back soon."

"And if not?"

"I've reconfigured the *beacon,* so you'll be under Diva's command. We have an alliance, and she'll take care of you."

Unlike the players, the soldiers didn't speak the System language, but everyone knew English, and some even knew French. Diva had even purchased a *Russian language* card. I was sure they could make themselves understood.

"Got it."

If I didn't have assured resurrection, I wouldn't have dared to pursue an evidently stronger opponent but, as I'd already said, one had to recognize and rectify one's mistakes. I had to try so I could later say, "I did everything I could". And I could always escape if things went badly.

"I'll leave the bags, including the main one, and you're personally responsible for them. Deploy the antenna, we'll keep in touch."

The *Slaver's Bag* wasn't bound to me. This not only allowed others to use it, but also increased the risk of theft, but I had to accept the risk. Otherwise, the plan to transfer troops and cargo from the *Dungeon* would go down the drain. I had started something dangerous, but there was a chance I could use the *beacon* again if I died. So, the valuable artifact had to remain here, and not on my mutilated corpse. The *Ring* would provide enough storage for me.

*   *   *

Searching for someone invisible was like searching for a needle in a haystack, but even *Invisibility* didn't mask physical traces. The chance was very slim, but luckily, Legion spotted the direction in which the enemy was moving. If he weren't a raven, he would be Hawkeye.

I had the Tracker skill, in which I now invested 60 points, raising it to the second *(439/460)*, and then to the third level *(399/460)*. My current target allowed me to learn on the go, picking up more and more details...

Tracker (F, 3/3)

I couldn't go any higher—the skill card had been dropped by a goblin and didn't have more levels. To some extent, it was a waste of experience points, but I was in no mood to be stingy right now. I was finally tracking my alleged enemy. Literally. The tracks of my potential victim were... humanoid. Larger than a human's, but within the scope of the combat form. This was encouraging. The enemy might turn out to be a fellow two and a half meters tall, but I was quite capable of killing someone of that size. In theory, because a *human (E)* had to be above level 50 to use the *beacon.*

"What am I getting myself into?"

While I had been lucky the first time, the enemy eventually stopped hiding and moved right down the road. I kept coming across new tracks—unique enough not to lose the trail. However, the likelihood of us meeting was very unlikely, since I would prefer to kill them in the most "dishonest" and safest way possible. I just had to figure out how. Contrary to my suspicion, the enemy was heading for the outskirts, rather than into the center of the city. It was difficult to say whether this was an accident or part of a plan—the stranger was unlikely to have been in these ruins before—but if they were hurrying towards the temple, then they weren't looking to escape. On the other hand, information about the goblin city wasn't a secret among the players, and the enemy gods had plenty of informants. Let's assume that they're not tough enough to solve the problem directly. This was encouraging...

For a change, I wanted to believe in something good and bright for once. For example, that the enemy would stumble on a horde of undead, and I could admire the mutilated corpse from afar.

* * *

"Come in, where are you?" came Diva's voice. It meant that our allies had arrived.

"I'm following an unknown player. Most

likely, a follower of one of the other gods. They came through the *beacon* using a loophole. The tracks are slightly larger than a human's, and are heading towards the exit from the third ring."

"Then it's not our problem anymore. You should come back."

It was a tempting suggestion, but I was in no hurry to agree. There was too much at stake. Or was I just being stubborn?

"I'll track them to the edge of the ring. If they pass through it, I'll come back. Follow the plan."

We were supposed to lie low immediately upon arrival, since the analysts thought that rushing into the city center, as I had originally planned, was suicide. There was a chance of success, but it hardly exceeded a couple of percent. Not enough when so much was at stake.

"Suit yourself, you've a big boy." Contrary to my expectations, there were no further objections. "Good luck."

"Thank you. Over and out."

*   *   *

Activate Search for Life!

I thought the enemy player might be somewhere nearby, so it was dangerous to use scanning, but moving blindly ahead was even more so. Maintaining constant *Invisibility* consumed too much mana, so I had to hope that their mana regeneration didn't allow them to pull off such a trick. The only question was who would spot whom first. Besides, a sudden flock of Bone Chimeras could certainly ruin my mood. There was a weak flash in one of the houses this time.

"Bri, check the ground floor. Come back if there are any undead."

The ghost detached itself from me and dove through the window. I didn't even have to stop as the scout immediately returned, confirming my guess. A skeleton warrior was "sleeping" inside and didn't pose a danger unless I broke into the area he was protecting. I wanted to avoid encounters with the sentient undead most of all, but so far, I'd been surprisingly lucky.

"Caw!"

An agitated and disheveled Legion landed on the sidewalk a little way away and gave me a careful look.

"Well, did you find something?"

"I... I..." the raven stammered. "I demand more crystals! This work is more dangerous than I thought!"

"If you found them, you'll get a crystal."

"I..." To my surprise, Legion didn't argue. "I found them. But let's move more slowly, okay? You don't really want to catch up with this monster, do you? He spotted me and almost knocked me down, even though I was flying very, very high up. This precious body, whose bloodline I worked so hard to awaken, was almost cut to pieces. Moreover, my soul could have been injured too!"

"Tell me more. Don't worry, you won't have to

go near him anymore. I'll handle the rest myself."

"If you die…" the raven paused, his gaze glued to the crystal in my fingers. "Fine, but I warned you! I warned you twice!"

* * *

When you have an idea of where your opponent is heading, you can easily, if not overtake them, then at least arrive there a little earlier and find a suitable observation post. By the time I climbed onto the roof, my opponent was approaching the gap in the wall. They didn't bother to disguise themselves, even though the passage was blocked by piles of bones.

Iris. Player. Archon. Rank: D. Level ??? Patron: Unknown.

Attention! Additional quest available: Liquidation (D)!

Description: Destroy the follower of a hostile god! Reward: Unknown, variable.

Penalty for failure: None

The name was more feminine than masculine, but it was impossible to tell the player's gender due to the combat form. I saw something like a spacesuit studded with spikes and claws, and with tentacles on the back. It resembled, very slightly, the Queen of Blades from an old game. But this form was meant for combat, not for fanservice and attracting a bunch of excited fans. It could even have been a man, for the creature was large enough.

Around her—I'd assume the gender for now—swarmed about thirty monsters. High-level *Hellhounds (D)* and even a pair of *Cerberi (C-)*, although it was unclear why they were called that when the evolved form had just one head. Only the size, rank and abilities had changed.

Hellhound. Rank: D. Level 33.

There was no way I would have missed such a horde, which meant they had been released quite recently. If they'd come from a bag, this was important information since there could be other players inside, not just monsters. Had I been lucky... or had my "guest" used the *beacon* by accident? This group could be considered a small army, yet the enemy gods could have sent someone much stronger.

I gazed at Iris's back through the scope of the rifle and was struck by a bad feeling. The bullets for this rifle had been cast from System metal, but they weren't weapons, and I didn't know if they would pierce her suit. Okay, let's wait...

As the enemy group approached the passage, the bones began to move, and their way was blocked by a horde of undead. My old friend Einstein stood out among the crowd. Apparently the Bone Horror hadn't left after my escape, remaining to guard the passage and await my return. I should have named him Hachiko.

The two armies clashed, but it quickly became clear that the living would win. The undead had greater numbers, but the difference in strength was too significant. Skeletons and chimeras struggled to penetrate the chitinous armor, while the hounds acted in unison, protecting each other.

"What the hell?"

Despite the clear advantage, events were developing in a strange way. Iris attacked only the weak monsters, ignoring their leader. Why? Did she want to capture him "alive" or... did she want to attract the attention of the true masters of this dead city? Even if they didn't arrive here in time, the raid would cause her competitors a lot of problems in the battle for the Altar. Our squad, first and foremost. Otherwise, it was hard to explain why she had started this skirmish at all. She could have passed through unnoticed, and since that didn't happen...

"Two bullets, only two..."

My sight shifted slightly higher and to the left, to where the commander of the undead army sat on a stone. Perhaps a large-caliber rifle couldn't penetrate a player's divine protection, but the god of the undead had long been out of the game. I pulled the trigger gently and a shot rang out. The bone sphere protecting the *magic heart* was strong, but it couldn't withstand a bullet, and shattered into pieces. The Bone Horror who had once almost killed me shuddered and crumbled to pieces. I'd gotten my revenge.

"You will die, you will die, you will die."

I had been tempted to test the player's protection, but now I didn't hesitate and jumped off the roof. It was about ten meters to the next building, but *Flight* allowed me to do the impossible and land safely. The roof I'd left a second ago collapsed, and I wasn't sure that the ceilings inside had held up. Moreover, half the pack rushed over there, apparently to make sure that I was well and truly dead. If I'd been caught in the attack, I would have hardly been able to escape even if I'd been resurrected.

Cassandra fell silent, but I jumped further, moving on to the next roof and thus leaving the possible impact zone. Like a damn ninja. I was more likely to avoid a chase this way, since I assumed the hounds had an excellent sense of smell. And sharp teeth. I wasn't going to tempt fate any further—sometimes, one needs to critically assess one's strength and retreat. If I was allowed to do that.

INTERLUDE NO. 1
MISTRESS OF THE PACK

IRIS, MISTRESS OF THE PACK, was an archon. A strong player who had lived for over a hundred years and survived countless fights. The Great Izur was considered a worthy ruler, and mostly left his faithful followers alone. A personal mission from god always carried more risk, but there were plenty of followers, so one rarely received this dangerous honor. Losses among the Chosen were high, but the families of the fallen received decent compensation. Those who returned victorious were exalted.

Those who completed ten divine missions received an *Indulgence*, a seat in the Senate, and the status of *Free Player*, allowing them to choose their own missions. Not everyone benefited from such favors. Many great warriors of old became mired in idleness and debauchery, but for the rest it remained a cherished dream. Together with the Eternal Youth card, which allowed one to live forever without leveling up... at least until one was killed by enemies.

When Iris found herself among the Chosen, she accepted it joylessly but with dignity, using the remaining hours to finish her business and say goodbye to her family. The siege of a new world was always accompanied by heavy losses, but she had been lucky. Where other players were intercepted by enemy gods or annihilated by the weapons of an enemy civilization, she invariably returned. Sometimes she lost the pack, but Izur was generous, and made up for the losses. After all, a whole world in his empire was set aside for *Hellhounds*.

However, luck tends to run out. A jump using the incomplete coordinates of a global mission was utter madness. They'd basically been written off in advance. Not belonging to the world of the Call, most archons ended up nowhere, appearing in outer space, landing on lifeless planets, or burning up in the flames of the local sun.

She had been lucky to guess the direction correctly, lucky to slip through a gap in the barrier surrounding the star system, but she would have missed the world itself if not for the *beacon*. Iris had accumulated a lot of sacred energy over the past few months, planning to spend it on a high-level skill. But she had spent almost all of it to buy her life. Hundreds of players had stepped into the portal created by their god, but only a few reached the goal. Perhaps she was the only one who had succeeded. Not the strongest or the worthiest, but the one who could be sacrificed for the ghostly chance of success.

Once in the goblin world, Iris performed the standard actions, camouflaging herself and scanning her surroundings. She even spotted an enemy player, thought for a moment about eliminating the pipsqueak, but decided not to risk her very important mission. An enemy army could arrive at the *beacon* at any moment, and she was no Titan or a Demigod to deal with thousands of players. Even a hundred could pose a problem.

Even if Earth was inhabited by nothing more than *people*, destined to rise or become slaves of a higher race, she had to admire their achievements in technology and weapons. The *beacon* ought to be destroyed so that the followers of other gods couldn't use it, but the owner would surely do so himself. He should have enough brains to guess where the free energy had come from and close access to others. He was human after all, not a monkey... the archon actively disliked her official allies.

A thousand Sacred Points! Resentment flared for a moment. A shame to spend so much, although she could get it all back later. She didn't even have to do it directly. Iris simply turned around and headed out of the city. Perhaps she could have fought her way to the temple, but the archon wasn't certain of success. The Altar Guardians may be weak, but first she needed a

Key, and the goblins would have several.

It was better to approach the problem comprehensively. She didn't have to venture into the temple herself, just stop her competitors from getting ahead of her, then open the way for her Master's legions. Or make sure that one of the human allies reaches the Altar. The Great Izur trusted his servants, giving them free reign. Or, came the heretic thought, wrote them off in advance, trying for the sake of form. The bet was on the traitors, but the prize was too great to leave everything to chance. Iris understood this.

At some point, the archon turned off *Camouflage* since it was quite pricey to maintain even with her regeneration. The *Search Wave* didn't find anything interesting, but a warrior's habit made her check the sky as well. Her eyes turned red, and she saw a bird. A raven! Such birds were found on Earth, but were rare on other worlds. Due to their older cousins and their rather bad reputation, the rule "if you see a black bird, kill it" had become very common.

Unfortunately, even she found it difficult to reach the creature at such a height. She tried anyway, throwing up air blades. The carcass of a bird that hadn't awakened its pedigree had no special value. She missed. The raven seemed to sense the threat, swerved to the side, and the air distortion flashed by without hitting the vile creature. Abruptly folding its wings, the bird dove down to hide behind the houses. Damn. "Oh well..."

Iris continued onwards and soon reached the gate. An ancient map dating back to "before the fall" had been accurate. She'd come across weak undead before, and while she preferred to avoid it, the situation was radically different this time. A huge mound of bones, identified as a Bone Horror, was definitely guarding this place. It could certainly signal the others, provoking the true owners of the city to take decisive action. This was a great opportunity to make life harder for her competitors and repay for the lost experience points at the same time.

Iris came out of *Invisibility*, summoning the Elder Pack from the bag as she did so. Twenty-eight high-level *Hellhounds* and two newly reborn *Cerberi*. While the *Hellhounds* were already in combat form, the *Cerberi* needed time. Time, mana, and flesh. There were no enemy corpses nearby, but pre-prepared meat worked just as well, and she could carry it in an ordinary *Spatial Ring*.

"Onwards!"

The undead stirred, rising to their feet. However, only their leader represented any kind of threat, and even that was more theoretical. Iris could have killed the clumsy creature at once, without raising an alarm, but this went against her plan. On the contrary, she was going to give it plenty of time, and a reason to report the situation... Therefore, the first explosions scattered a dozen warriors but not the commander. Obeying a mental command, the pack rushed forward, easily dispatching the low-level skeletons. *Bone Blades* couldn't penetrate the pseudoflesh, and the weight of the skeletons wasn't enough to stop these live battering rams. Human machine guns probably could, but the pack was protected even from this by divine protection. A pity it wouldn't last for long. Iris had the highest one, which wouldn't disappear until she spent all her energy, but the protection of the hounds would only last a day.

She felt a prickling at her neck, as if someone was about to attack. However, before Iris could pinpoint the direction, the hostile gaze disappeared. A second later, the Bone Horror twitched and broke into pieces, and his horde lost its unity. A sniper! It wasn't difficult to figure out what kind of weapon was used. The archon had studied the enemy's world from the inside.

"Bastard!"

Iris turned, not holding back this time, and *Izur's Rage* rained down on the building where the enemy was supposed to be, breaking the roof and ceilings. It was hard to say whether the strike was successful, for her initial anger had already disappeared. Even if the *worm* had dared to attack her, strong emotions were the mark of lowly beings. Therefore, she limited herself to showing the possible observer the middle finger—a sign of contempt in their civilization—and gave an order to one of her pets.

This would be enough. If the player's death didn't bring her any experience points or help her reach her goal, a proper hunt was pointless. And if the Bone Horror had managed to send a message, this place would soon be swarming with the undead. It made sense to be away when that happened.

Let the enemies slaughter each other, while she observed them from the sidelines. The chance to strike would present itself, and the archon had no doubt of her success. Her *Intuition* was all the way up to 20, and she believed that fate was saving her for great deeds. What deeds could a corpse achieve? The Great Izur was merciful, but he didn't forgive failure in such matters. Yet the reward for success would be more than generous!

INTERLUDE NO. 2
A WAR STRATAGEM

ACCORDING TO THE PLAN, the players were supposed to appear together a minute before the timer ran out, but the closer you were to the top, the more opportunities you had. Bill Michigan arrived first, not remaining in the personal room for a second longer than necessary.

He was lucky with the location, for the portal opened on the dungeon's roof. He had a great view of the entire fortress. The goblins had returned to the stronghold after the humans had left, and even placed a large garrison in it. Very lucky...

Release Nameless Unit No. 1 from the Slaver's Bag?

Yes/No

Thirty Navy Seals soon appeared, ready to carry out any order. Bill's faction currently had three such bags, so they could deploy up to 90 professionals. A good chance for America to get ahead of the competition. However, their help wasn't yet required...

"Stay here and protect the bags."

The Swordsman approached the edge of the roof and jumped, pushing off an invisible step each time. *Air Steps* wasn't flight, but the skill worked even better, not only allowing him to overcome obstacles, but also granting unprecedented mobility in battle. Ten jumps and he was there, beside the ghostly *beacon*.

Quetzalcoatl's Beacon
Would you like to change the settings?
Yes/No

Bill wiggled his fingers as if typing on an invisible keyboard—he'd had to write a lot of reports lately—and the interface readily responded to his thoughts.

Attention! Access to the beacon is limited to 40 minutes!

The beacon is only accessible to followers of Quetzalcoatl.

More than enough time for his faction to gain a strategic advantage, while the rest still had time to use the *beacon*. Mission command had considered not letting anyone into the fortress at all, forcing the other factions to use random teleportation, but common sense prevailed. It would be considered betrayal by the other leaders of what was now the Guild, stripping Bill of all his allies at once. Even if the officials had given such an order, he would have told them to get very, very lost. The fate of the world was at stake, and he still had people to protect. Even if his daughters had been turned into heroes and received powerful skills, so they could now hold their own.

Level: 19 (320/380).

"Here we go," Bill said, checking his watch. "Provide cover. Don't interfere with the players, your task is to capture the commander of the fortress or one of the officers."

Captives were needed to assess the situation, and he ought to do it himself, but his subordinates would manage just as well.

"Yes, Captain Michigan."

Bill had been promoted again before the mission, and the surname, once taken from the name of a lake where his life was supposed to have ended, became real, migrating to official documents. As far as he knew, many had done the same, including Vasily. It was possible that even his name wasn't real.

Attention! You have gained 6 SP! (326/380)

Quetzalcoatl's regard has improved!

The sentry's head flew off his shoulders. A slightly pretentious blow, but it allowed Bill not to waste time on freeing the blade. As for the blood, there was no longer a need to hide. Portals were opening all over the fortress, releasing trusted players...

The goblins reacted quickly, but there was little they could do. Perhaps the Earth gods were weak, but they had successfully adopted the enemy's tactics and provided divine protection to some of their followers. Even if only for a few hours for most people, but during those hours, they were like superheroes from comic books. Arrows fell, unable to pierce the skin, and swords bounced harmlessly off them. Only System weapons and possibly magic could injure the "chosen ones".

Attention! You have gained 2 SP! (328/380)

"Sir, we've spotted Alexander. Sulu is here too."

The Swordsman chuckled, for he had expected the other leaders to arrive. The others were bound to be here too—except for the ones who had decided to use the second *beacon.* Great minds think alike, and even if someone wasn't particularly intelligent, they were supported by countries and gods. Unsurprising that many didn't wait for the official deadline and took advantage of the short window before Bill closed access to the beacon. So be it, but the followers of other gods would come too late, and the lion's share of the loot would go to his faction.

"These are allies, watch them, but don't interfere in their work. Complete your tasks!"

As the commander, Michigan was supposed to lead the whole operation, but his involvement wasn't really necessary. The soldiers would take control of the gate, preventing the enemies from escaping, and capture prisoners, while the arriving players had only one job. Kill, kill, and kill again.

CHAPTER 2
SUICIDE

HOWEVER, MY IMPULSE to flee didn't last long. After jumping a couple of roofs, I circled back and crouched behind the parapet. The half of the pack sent after me had split up and were combing the neighborhood but would find nothing. No matter their sense of smell, the Hellhounds clearly couldn't fly. I needed to finish the job. The monsters quickly dispatched the remaining undead after Einstein's demise. None of the undead thought to escape, for there were no other commanders capable of giving such an order among them.

Iris took her time, participating in the battle, and collecting the loot, inspecting the corpses and periodically tearing pieces out of them. She was collecting the bone swords, obviously knowing which "spare parts" were the most valuable. Oh, and the hounds also had the ability to transfer experience to their owner, so the slaughter would have been very profitable for her.

Cerberus. Rank C-. Level 1.

Identification had little effect at such a distance, so I could see only the most basic information. Although they belonged to the dog family, the hounds didn't try to gnaw the old bones. I considered checking whether they had divine protection, but even if they didn't, their armor was impressive in itself. And I'd need to hit the much smaller pilot, otherwise, there was no point.

Nothing interesting, really, and I was sitting here only to ensure that the enemy left our area of interest. Ten minutes later, the archon finished her looting, the hounds that failed to find me returned, and she began to call back the pack. Apparently, Iris bet not on the combat strength of her pocket army, but on its inconspicuousness. I bet she also suspected my presence...

"She suspects for sure," I muttered.

Once Iris was ready, she raised her hand, curled all her fingers except the middle one, and made a broad gesture. I doubted this gesture was common throughout the System worlds, and it came out too naturally. As if she'd spent a lot of time in a place where it was the norm, or rather, she'd acquired it using a skill card. She might have learned the gesture as part of a language packet.

Iris didn't try to fire at random roofs and simply disappeared into the darkness. Studying the tracks, I was convinced that she was moving towards the breach in the wall, as I had expected. The question was, did she leave any of her pets on this side? I wasn't talking about a *Hellhound,* which might have disappeared without my noticing. I think she was one *Cerberus* short. If I was right in my paranoia...

*   *   *

Five minutes of running across roofs, and I was at the agreed place. I abandoned *Invisibility,* allowing the raven to find me. I hadn't returned him to the bag, leaving him to wait for my signal nearby. After almost losing his life, Legion had no desire to get close to the archon. It was also time to contact my colleagues.

"Vasily speaking. Do you read me?"

"Dmitry speaking, over. Have you dealt with him?"

It may seem strange that a follower of Odin was using my *beacon,* but he had special permission.

"No, it's a high-level player with a whole pack of hounds. It didn't work out and I nearly died myself."

"Are you being followed?"

"I'd say no, but it's hard to be sure. In any case, the drop-off point has been spotted."

"We're getting ready to move. We'll wait for you and move out."

"Good. How are my people doing?"

"They're listening in. Just a second."

"It's all right, Commander," Oleg's voice rang out. "We haven't had any problems."

It seemed like nothing had happened while I was away. A union was great and all, but I never learned to trust other people unconditionally, and maybe that's why I was still alive.

*   *   *

My journey was much easier this time. The undead didn't like heights, so traveling across roofs turned out to be much safer. Especially if one was mindful of Bone Dragons and scanned the skies, used *Invisibility* and, well, didn't linger. Even if the undead were lurking in the next building and somehow spotted me, they couldn't climb up to the roof and reach me in time.

However, my speed dropped, and mana costs increased significantly. The combat form made me pretty good at parkour, but the distance and height between buildings varied greatly, so I couldn't always cross the gap using physics. *Flight* required heaps of mana, and if I hadn't possessed the skill, I would have never taken the risk. A reason to rest and recover turned up in the form of a dead lookout on one of the roofs. *Identification.*

Ancient Skeleton Warrior. Rank F+. Level 5.

I could see the other stats, but only *Strength* piqued my interest, which was the maximum ten. An interesting individual. The skeleton's bones shone black, and the sphere around the *magic heart* was fully formed. If I had run into him on my last visit, I would have had my work cut out for me. This time, I decided to take the easy way out and drew the *Sword of Heresy.*

The skeleton was moving fast, trying to impale me on a blade growing out of his hand, but his chance of success was purely theoretical. I slipped to the side and struck at the elbow, taking off his right arm. The enemy didn't have a blade in his left hand, so he froze for a moment, allowing me to deprive him of his other limbs. I didn't finish him off right away, having picked up the already familiar loot.

Sword of Warrior of Y (F-)

A rather useless System weapon, but worth a considerable amount on Earth. It was suitable for initiating units, and the ones I'd brought back last time had been put to use. It didn't bother anyone that the blade had once been part of a sentient being. In this case, the bones were not only very strong, but also Systemic, so the entire skeleton was valuable. However, I had no intention of carrying around a pile of bones.

"Bri, monitor access the roof. Legion, scout the place out. Check if anyone is following us."

The defeated skeleton lay motionless all this time, showing no signs of life and no interest in continuing the battle. At least he didn't try to crawl or snap his jaws in my direction. He accepted the end of his existence stoically, although it took me a little while to hack his *heart* out, allowing the crystal to materialize. It worked, but I had no idea how to get it out of its shell.

Attention! You have gained 25 SP! (424/460)

Attention! The Sword of Heresy has consumed 5 SP!

The card was yet another emptie, although I'd expected something more interesting. I didn't have much to go until Level 24, but I preferred to spend the points on something... more useful. However, the options were too extensive, ranging from raising *Sword Fighting* to Master, to continuing to remove the attribute limits or increasing the rank of skills. They were all good options, so there was no single answer. Although...

The level limit had recently exceeded 400 points, which allowed me to raise one skill to the third rank. The choice was between *Moderate Magical Ability*, *Great Healing*, *Invisibility*, and *Spear Master*. It was easier to make this choice, especially when there was a coin in my pocket. I hadn't resorted to this method in a while. The winner became clear on the second round, when I no longer wanted to flip again.

Attention! Do you want to improve Invisibility to Level 3? (400 SP)

Yes/No

I confirmed my decision (**24/460**) and decided to see the result in practice.

Attention! Connection to the Server established. Access is allowed.

Attention! Rank has increased! Skill

strength has greatly increased!

Select an additional property:

1) **Optimization.** *Allows better control of mana consumption, increasing skill duration.*

2) **Elimination of Shortcomings II.** *The field does a much better job at hiding everything inside.*

3) **Improved Control.** *Allows control of the field in a wider range.*

4) **Illusion Veil.** *Allows control of the outer layer. Ability to change/hide one's appearance.*

5) **Stability.** *The field is much harder to dispel.*

The list of extras hadn't changed much compared to last time, but I chose *Optimization.* My life would depend on stealth in this mission, and my supply of mana capsules wasn't endless. Just like the crystals.

Level: 23 (24/460 System Points).

My mana still hadn't fully recovered, and since no one had bothered me so far, I decided to distribute the points I'd received for the previous levels. I could have spent them earlier, but even the the combat form's evolution took time, and it wasn't something I wanted to rush.

Attributes:

Strength: 8/10 (100 SP) +3=11.

Agility: 11/15 +1=12.

Intelligence: 11/15 +1=12.

Vitality: 12/15 +1=13.

Stamina: 11/15 +4=15.

Perception: 10/15 +2=12.

Luck: 2/10 (1000 SP).

Race Attribute:
Intuition: 15/15 (300 SP).
Additional Attributes:
Wisdom: 15/15 (300 SP).
Spiritual Energy: 1.
Faith: 0.
Heresy: 9 (Cult of Cain).
Fame: 7.

I had another difficult choice to make, since none of the attributes required leveling up faster than others. There were several theories on development, but each path had its pros and cons. For example, I could raise one of the attributes to the limit, with a good chance of scoring a bonus for being the first. Yet the hunt for additional skills was flawed in many ways, and the further it went, the more it led to distortions in development. So...

Intelligence: 13 (+1).
Agility: 13 (+1).
Perception: 13 (+1).
Strength: 12 (+1).

I hate this. Even though I was advancing the combat form and taking breaks, the sensations were far from pleasant. If I decided to transfer them to the main body, it would be much worse. Nevertheless, it allowed me to save time and avoid unnecessary risk in the here and now.

Unlike games, where any development was a blessing, and specialization ruled, the most optimal path in the System required universality. Those who leveled up only one or two attributes gained an advantage in the short-term, but then either corrected this skew, or died a pointless death. If you leveled *Strength* up to 10, but left *Vitality* at 5, you were bound to have a heart attack. If you ignored *Agility*, you'd end up with ligament damage. Not enough *Stamina* and you'd collapse from fatigue. However, not all attributes were directly linked, and proportions didn't always work in both directions. Certain attributes could be leveled up without a problem, and a negative skew of *Strength* wouldn't result in any particularly negative consequences. In my main body, it lagged slightly behind the main attributes, but this didn't cause me any discomfort.

Nevertheless, I couldn't forget about those who'd reached the next level and decided to act according to the "usual scheme". I could also have a snack while the raven was away. *War is war, but lunch is on schedule.*

*   *   *

Attention! Connection to the Server has been lost!
Summoning a goblin is unavailable!

Here we go again. This star system and the goblin planet had protection, which, although full of holes, often blocked outside access. The connection was stable in some places, unstable in others, and absent altogether in most places. It wasn't like mobile phone coverage, where the principle of "climb up higher and catch the nearest tower" worked, but rather satellite coverage, where the grouping was close to zero, and the signal travelled in a narrow beam and at a certain time. Well, I shouldn't complain — this option was only available near the *beacons* last time, or required special skills.

Travelling over roofs might be safer, but it was tiring, so I had to descend sooner or later. If I wanted to get back to base before dark, of course. The third rank and chosen bonus allowed me to maintain *Invisibility* for much longer. About an hour and a half, even without boosts using mana pills.

"It's definitely out there somewhere," the raven warned me. "But you can easily avoid it if you're careful!"

My suspicions turned out to be correct. Iris hadn't simply left, but had sent a hunter after me. A *Cerberus*. It might seem like a trifle, but it was a C-ranked monster—the recommended weapon for such a creature was artillery. Powerful armor, unbelievable vitality, strength, speed, and stamina, and an impressive skill set that included *Invisibility*. Even though a *Cerberus* wasn't powerful enough to be considered a Disaster, it was a threat that couldn't be ignored. Fortunately, the *Cerberus* couldn't maintain constant *Invisibility*, so Legion found it without much difficulty. The raven was much more worried about the the beast's mistress being somewhere nearby, but the archon didn't try to hit him again.

The *Cerberus* moved clumsily but quite

effectively, zigzagging along my old tracks. If I had returned by a similar route on foot, it would have eventually spotted me. Or it would have stumbled across the base. And if not for my stop, I would have moved too far ahead and wouldn't have sensed the danger until it was too late. Unless we wanted a deadly monster circling us, we had to do something. Changing the location of the base wouldn't help since the *Cerberus* would follow our tracks. I decided to consider the worst possible outcome.

"What do you think, Bri? Can you take control of this doggy?"

"I'm not sure. It looks very dangerous. I barely managed that big rat last time."

"Well, what do you think, Legion?"

"I believe in junior," The raven didn't hesitate. "Bri can do it!"

I was tempted to acquire this elite mount, but the ghost looked terribly uncertain. If it wasn't already dead, I would have thought it was close to tears.

"Well, if you don't think you can, I'll take care of it myself."

* * *

The simplest thing would be to ambush and attack as a group, but simpler didn't mean better. I had a suspicion that a major skirmish would attract the attention of the undead, meaning our plans would go to hell. Well, they were already heading there...

Players remaining: 12894/13000.

Thankfully, losses among our allies were small this time—apparently, the goblins in the fortress had failed to organize a proper resistance. I supposed that most of the dead players had simply ignored the warnings of the gods and chosen a random location or... never mind.

Bang!

The bullet hit the creature, and I was surprised to find that it had no divine protection. But it had impressive personal armor. The large-caliber bullet left a spiderweb pattern of cracks but didn't go any further. I had failed to penetrate the armor. A second later, the _Cerberus_ disappeared without waiting for more.

I didn't wait either and retreated into _Invisibility_, before running to the edge of the roof and jumping to change position. Aerial reconnaissance had helped me find a great spot for this battle. I already had a plan, although it depended on a lot of variables.

Three minutes later, there was a pop in my old spot, and a pink suspension billowed into the air, outlining the monster. As expected, _Cerberus_ had identified my position and hastened to take revenge.

If I'd had a chance to mine the building, that would have been the end of it, but... Bang! Bang! Bang! I shot in quick succession without checking the result. _Cerberus_ spun around, spotted my new position, and took a running leap.

Activate Overclocking!

The world slowed down dramatically. Bang, bang, bang! I could aim properly this time, and struck the vulnerable spots: the eyes and mouth. I put the last bullet in its chest. That's it, the magazine was empty. Large caliber guns had their drawbacks. It might not have done much good—I doubted that I'd wounded it—but I was counting on inertia. The distance between the roofs was great, and after being hit by several bullets, the beast didn't reach the edge but crashed into the wall below. For a second I was afraid that the wall wouldn't hold, but the ancient building didn't let me down, and the monster plummeted to the ground.

The buildings grew taller closer to the city center, so it was a fifteen-meter drop. Certain death for a weaker creature, but I doubted that the damage would be sufficient.

"You will die, you will die, you will die!"

I know. Taking out my sword, I didn't dawdle and jumped straight after the creature, correcting my fall by flying. However, gravity was on my side this time, so I didn't try to slow down. As long as I aimed right...

The *Cerberus* lived up to my worst expectations by already getting up. Even without the pink suspension, its *Invisibility* had dissipated, and the beast wasn't in the best shape. It didn't react in time. My blade went in between its shoulder blades... a different weapon might have snapped without penetrating the armor, but this one went in and became stuck inside. *Shrapnel!*

If the world hadn't slowed down, I couldn't have repeated this trick, but right now, I managed to maintain my focus despite the pain. Landing broke numerous bones and threw me to the side, driving all the air from my lungs. Turning my head, I made sure that the sword was still sticking out of *Cerberus*'s spine. *Identification.* If I had calculated everything correctly...

Attention! You have gained 40 SP! (64/460)

Attention! The Sword of Heresy has consumed 8 SP!

Attention! Your sword is stained with Ancient Blood!

Blood of the Pack Leader — *a high-ranking monster was killed with this sword. Similar monsters can feel this, which can be both a plus and a minus.*

I remained surprisingly clear-headed even on the verge of death. *Spiritual Thread*, the skill I'd obtained when I reached Master Archer, worked this time, although it was supposed to only work on arrows. Wrapping the hilt of the sword also turned out to be easy. Cough...

"*Die! Die! Die!*" Cassandra reminded me. That's right, it was about time.

Activate Instant Death!

Attention! You have died!

The Backup ability has been activated! (5 SP)

Get ready!

Time remaining: 3... 2... 1...

I opened my eyes and stood up, wincing. The world had returned to its normal speed. The combat form had disintegrated so my clothes were too big, but the mana level was recovering quickly. I'd swallowed plenty of capsules, after all.

"Hot damn!"

It was hard to believe that I'd done it. I could have avoided killing myself, relying on *Healing* and *Regeneration,* but it would have taken too long to recover.

"Hey, Iris!" I shouted. "How about you show yourself? You think I don't know you're here?"

There was no answer, which was slightly reassuring—I preferred to avoid another deadly fight right now. There were escape routes, of course, but I wasn't sure I could use them.

Activate combat form!

I got back to my feet and straightened my clothes again, while the raven landed next to me.

"A good jump! Five crystals out of five!"

"Are you making fun of me?"

"A little. Have you gone mad?"

A fair question. At what point did I completely go off the rails and decide to pull something like this off? Yes, I had insurance in the form of *Blink,* which allowed me to get out of the way, but if I'd missed, couldn't penetrate the armor or the wound hadn't killed the monster... If *Shrapnel* hadn't reached the pilot hiding in the depths, I would have been resurrected on the *Shard.*

That was the answer, really. I knew that I

wouldn't die, so I was taking risks I'd never had dared before. If I didn't learn to control my impulses, things would end badly for me one of these days. Was that the right thought? Perhaps, but what was the use if I didn't feel like I'd done anything wrong? I'd had to get rid of the spy by any means necessary.

"Well, what are you going to say to this Old One?"

An interesting detail—the raven was calling himself that again since we'd returned to the goblin world. It was worrying.

"There's a crystal inside. A large crystal."

"Caw!" Apparently Legion hadn't considered the situation from this point of view. "Are you crazy, letting that pack go? We've lost so many crystals!"

"You're not serious, are you?" I asked.

"No, but the thought is painful. Why can't you be a little stronger?"

"Isn't that why we came back to this place?"

"Caw!" The raven turned away, not wishing to continue this conversation, and shifted to the spreading corpse of the *Cerberus*. The combat form hadn't completely disintegrated after its death, leaving behind a pile of mucus, in which floated the *true body*, as well as a set of teeth and individual pieces of armor. A kind of loot, I guess.

*   *   *

Cerberus.
Status: *Monster.*
Type: *Bronze.*
Creature Rank: *C-.*
Level: *1.*
Danger: *High.*
Specifications:
Strength: 30.
Agility: 26.
Intelligence: 6.
Vitality: 30.
Stamina: 35.
Wisdom: 25.
Perception: 30.
Instinct: 30.
Features:
— System Creature / Pack Leader / Sniffer V / Regeneration / ... / Monster IV / Combat Form III / Concealment / Forced Evolution.
Master: *Iris*

Even on the verge of death, I hadn't forgotten to replenish my "monster base" by using *Identification.* Humans had killed such creatures before, but we only had the scraps of a corpse and video recordings for research. The main list of abilities was of no interest, except for *Forced Evolution.*

Forced Evolution. *This creature had been*

forcibly moved up in rank, which has made further growth in levels much more difficult.

So, the creature was so weak precisely because of artificial growth. The higher a creature's rank, the harder it was to advance. For many creatures, the "simple" way up was closed or almost closed, so they had to look for other opportunities. Or maybe their mistress had launched the evolution prematurely, before they could level up? The result was worth it in any case, since even at Level 1, the creature was much stronger than ordinary *Hellhounds*. Yet this augmentation came at the cost of stagnation.

"Hey, are you still alive over there?" said the voice in my ear. Right, my backup option.

"The monster is dead. We don't need the ambush anymore, and I'll be there soon."

"Got it. Congratulations."

*   *   *

I didn't dig through the remains, just dumped everything into the *Ring*, took the card, and hurriedly left the battlefield. Only after I had taken refuge on the roof of another house did I finally check what I'd acquired.

Cerberus Blood Essence
Rank: *C-.*
Purity: *Very Low.*
Type: *Item.*
Description:
— *The blood essence of an ancient being,*

collected from the body of its distant descendant. Allows one to awaken the bloodline or force evolution in Hellhounds.

"What do you reckon?" I caught Legion's attentive gaze. "Do you need this?"

"This is a fire entity. Although it belongs to an inferior being, I can purify it enough to absorb and enhance my fire magic."

"Will you hibernate again?"

"No! I lit a flame last time, but I'll just be adding fuel to it this time."

Sighing, I handed him the card, from which flew out a drop of blood. It was a dirty red, as if full of impurities, but Legion swallowed it without hesitation and cawed ecstatically. I hoped there wouldn't be any problems.

...No problems arose. I even took the opportunity to finish off five skeleton warriors (**109/460**). At my current level, it was relatively easy and didn't take much time. I reached the starting point before dark. Although everything was just beginning, I was already so fuc... tired. I doubted it would get any easier.

CHAPTER 3
RELOCATION

Activate Search for Life!

THE WAVE DIDN'T REACH very far, but enough to cover the buildings on both sides of the street. I detected six sentries covering the approaches to our temporary base. It was quite reasonable since we couldn't ensure our safety by any other means at the moment. Fortunately, low-level undead lacked proper scanning abilities, however, if a "leader" appeared, we'd have to destroy it immediately. Perhaps my worries about the global connection were unfounded, but the closer we drew to the city center, the stronger the *Blessing of the Great Y.* Or the curse, depending on how you looked at it.

"Vasily here, I'm coming back," I warned. "How's the situation?"

Naturally, I had a separate line of communication with the group, in case problems arose with our allies.

"Sergeant Melkov speaking," said a vaguely familiar voice. "All clear. We've destroyed several small groups of undead and posted sentries. We're also compiling a map of this part of the city."

The others hadn't wasted any time while I was away. Several blips of undead that I'd spotted inside the buildings went out, which meant they were clearing the area around the drop-off point. This went against our original plans, but it didn't really matter since we'd decided to leave this place.

"What about collecting research samples?"

"We're working on it, Captain."

As long as I had contact with the *Shard*, the idea of looting the neighborhood seemed quite logical: any object here had considerable scientific and financial value. This was especially true for papers. Plus, a share in the loot would clearly boost morale. It didn't matter much to me, but it was important for the personnel. It was better to take charge of this than to wonder if they were carrying around a few kilos of "souvenirs". Even without the promised bonuses, all returning soldiers would become millionaires. Although I didn't think our chances of returning were very high...

"Copy that. Over and out."

Yes, we definitely couldn't stay here now. The high-level undead were sentient and didn't always stay in one place. Many patrolled the streets, and their routes could easily change. They also had no issues with their memory, so the mass disappearance of junior comrades along the way would inevitably raise questions. The more undead we killed, the easier our location would be to pinpoint. That's why we couldn't stay here, despite all the advantages. Yes, the prison was easy to defend and, according to the goblins, the place was considered relatively safe, but we wouldn't be able to fight back if we were cornered. We couldn't destroy all the undead in the city, there'd be too many bones to climb over. Which would quickly turn into Bone Dragons or something. We had a lot of bullets, of course, but not an infinite number... "And they cost money." I chuckled, stopping in front of the building.

Activate Search for Life!

There were surprisingly few living beings inside, no more than thirty. If I didn't know the reason, I might have become alarmed.

"Hey, I'm coming in!" I warned just in case. Backup was in cooldown and wouldn't be back for a while, while my combat form looked unusual. The last thing I needed was to be shot at by accident.

"Come in!" a voice shouted from inside. "We've been warned."

The ground floor was empty, but no one had bothered to hide traces of our stay. The three French soldiers guarding the entrance appeared relaxed, but kept their weapons close, and the glances they threw at me left no doubt that they would use their guns if required. The fourth soldier was from my group.

The escort group consisted of thirty military specialists, and the selection process had been very strict. Funny, most players were desperate to avoid a deadly mission, yet there were thousands of volunteers ready to go to another world, with no guarantee of returning. You couldn't blame it on naivety, either—these were healthy men, aged between 24 and 39 years. They were all in peak physical shape, excellent specialists, and nearly everyone had combat experience or had been involved in the monster cleanup. Each one had become a unit after passing the selection process, which was the minimum System status required to interact with artifacts. For example, one could only throw a non-System object or being into a *Slaver's Bag* through the opening.

The unit was divided into three platoons, commanded by lieutenants. The rest were considered sergeants — I say "considered" because there were only a few real sergeants there. Sergey, who had met me at the entrance, had been a captain before this trip, while the commanders of the second and third platoons were actually majors. Their rank had dropped significantly for this mission, but they had been promised to go up a rank when they returned to Earth. The captain, if I wasn't mistaken, could have received the next rank in the past year since he was a senior officer. But this also required an appropriate position, which was usually occupied by someone else.

Well, nothing helped a military career like war. A monster invasion worked nearly as well. He wouldn't have had to wait long for a promotion even if he had remained on Earth. I suspected the French had also sent the best of the best, so there were no random people here. Although they probably weren't all natives of France, judging by their appearance. The Foreign Legion, for example, gathered its members from across the globe.

"Welcome back, Captain," Sergeant Losev stood up. "I'll accompany you."

"There's no need," Dmitry appeared out of nowhere. Was *Invisibility* becoming more popular? "Come on, we were waiting for you."

I noticed that none of the soldiers even flinched in response to his appearance, although I wouldn't have been surprised if he was riddled with bullets.

*　*　*

"You warned them, didn't you?"

"Who?"

"The guards. Otherwise, I can't explain why they didn't put a few 5-mm holes in you. Or however the French measure it."

"They follow NATO. But you remember that, I think."

"True." I was silent for a moment. "I'm sorry to be so blunt, but... even though I gave you access to the *beacon*, are you sure you should be here?"

"I'm simply helping April. No more, and no less."

I nodded automatically. I even envied the couple. He had done the exact opposite of me. To give everything up for a girl... in books, such tales usually ended in death or betrayal. Occasionally, with a wedding.

"Your wishes may not coincide with Odin's wishes. What about his interests?"

"I'm his follower, not his slave. I have a head on my shoulders and the right to set my own priorities. I know you dislike the gods, but I don't really have anything to blame them for. It's thanks to them that our world is still holding on."

"You don't think he'll try to influence you?"

"Odin is far away, and he doesn't need to know about my role in what's happening. If we lose yet I survive, I can always say that I acted in his interests."

"And if we succeed?"

"Do you think Odin will take revenge on the husband of the High Priestess of the head of the Pantheon?"

"Husband already? Then congratulations."

So, the wedding had already taken place, and whether they would live happily ever after remained to be seen. But they definitely could die on the same day. Well, this was no reason to worry ahead of time.

"Wait." I stopped in front of a curtain made of familiar material.

We knew about the undead's scanning skills in advance, and a similar ability in some players allowed scientists to develop countermeasures, mainly through trial and error. They developed special capes that jammed the signal and significantly reduced the blip. Although you had to wrap yourself from head to toe to get a decent effect or hang several layers of fabric on the walls.

Activate Search for Life!

Now that I was close, I could feel signs of someone else's presence, but in general, the technology worked. I passed through this improvised airlock, designed to prevent us being spotted, and stepped inside. The base had been set up in a fairly large hall, and, as expected, sheets of shielding material hung on the walls. The downside was a lack of windows, so the lighting was artificial. This wasn't a problem right now, but the batteries would eventually run out. A lot of effort had gone into this base, so it was a pity that we'd have to leave soon. I noted that "my people" had taken up a separate corner, distancing themselves from the allies. This was to be expected and quite reasonable.

* * *

Those who could be considered commanders had gathered around the makeshift table. Diva, Dmitry, and I, and most of our lieutenants. Eight out of nine, to be exact. It was a hassle because simple units didn't know the System language, so we had to assign players to translate.

"Maybe you can take off your combat form?" Diva suggested. "We've decided that we'll move out tomorrow, so there won't be any fighting until morning."

"Maintaining the combat form is a kind of training. I'd recommend using yours as often as possible. It'll be bad if the soldiers shoot us by mistake."

Diva was also in the second seven, so I had no doubt that she possessed the best skills. Unlike Dmitry, who clearly didn't enjoy Odin's favor.

"That is impossible!" Commandant Labbe, one of the French officers, objected a second later. "All our soldiers have been instructed and would never make such a mistake!"

"Certainly, Jean," Diva smiled. "Vasily was simply explaining his reasons. Worrying about one's safety is quite natural. Don't take it to heart."

The priestess of Hera wasn't in the military, so the soldiers didn't obey her directly, but rather played the role of bodyguards. Of course, Diva could set them a task and define a goal, but it was the role of an employer, not a leader. Which forced her to look for an approach to her officers and could potentially cause problems.

"How are things at the fortress? Has Leon gotten in touch?"

Only fifty of Hera's best followers had used my *beacon*, while the rest chose the fortress as their landing point. This allowed us to get an inside look and be aware of the situation.

"The capture didn't go according to plan, but there were no major problems. By the time the main wave of players arrived, the goblins had already been dealt with. The prisoners have told us that the holy campaign had failed. Few survived, and Prince Ra escaped only by some miracle. Apparently, the goblins are trying to raise a new army, but there is some unrest, so they have other things to worry about. Unfortunately, there's no information about Shiva."

I wouldn't have called this good news. Given the situation, the goblins didn't pose much of a threat. Rather, they could serve as a source of experience and resources, no matter how cruel it sounded.

"What about the sabotage squads?"

"We don't have much information, but drones have already been sent to the center, and each faction has paragliders. Someone is bound to use them to try to reach the temple. If they're successful, then we can all return tomorrow. With all that this implies..."

I might have been concerned if it weren't for Legion, who flat-out refused to venture close to the first circle. He also had very unflattering things to say about the mental capacity of any player who would try to reach the temple by air. He considered it a suicide mission.

"The main assault?"

"It's hard to say, but I think they'll need a few days. It won't take long to blow up the wall, but they need to solve internal problems first. So, we have time. All that's left is to decide where we're heading."

The goblin map obtained in the last mission

had become widely available, but drone photos had now been added to it. Moreover, we had printed them out, so the images could be viewed not only on a tablet, but also as a puzzle spread out on the table. Sections of the city overlapped in places, but it wasn't hard to figure out.

Also, we didn't use ordinary drones for reconnaissance, but special ones resembling birds. Hard to say if they tricked the undead though. The undead perceived the world differently, so the "steel birds" soaring in the sky might be no different than the buzzing quadcopters.

"Have you found anything suitable?"

This was no easy feat since it wasn't enough to find a large building, it also had to have little value to the city's defenders. Information from goblins had really helped me in the past, since they had marched in and cleaned up the area close to the breach plenty of times. But the further we ventured into the ruins, the less reliable their information became. Goblins traveled along traditional routes, using the old gaps in the wall.

On the other hand, such an enormous city couldn't rely on one or two gates in the ring of walls, as this would create huge supply problems. In short, there were plenty of gates, but most were locked, and it was much easier to blow up the wall than to try to break through a gate. The magic protecting them was too strong even years later. The gates opened using keys that had long been lost. Or, more likely, had come into the possession of the undead. Consequently, the enemy had another potential advantage: greater mobility. The closed gates could reopen at any moment, releasing a horde of undead from where we weren't expecting them. We needed to find shelter away not only from current patrol routes, but also from potential ones.

"Here, here, and here. An estate, a tower, and some kind of administrative building. The drones didn't pick any activity, but we can't be sure that the undead aren't hiding inside."

"I'd choose the estate. The tower is too obvious and we'll be too cramped in there, while someone large might be hiding in the government building. Although I'll send the raven to investigate, and we'll know more by morning."

*　*　*

While I was surprised that Tatra was among the players—she wasn't one of Hera's elite supporters, it was easy enough to figure out why. Just like her desire to speak to me alone...

"What did you want to talk to me about?"

"I don't want to be a part of this," Tatra announced immediately. Some things never change. "You know I never wanted to become a player."

"Then you should have stayed in the fortress. Isn't it the safest place?"

"Do you really think someone would let cowa... people like me to sit it out? The factions are working together for now, but this is unlikely to last long. My faction has been weakened. Marcus is dead, and the strongest players are here. Without yours or Diva's protection, the others will be sent to fight in the front ranks."

"That's quite a pragmatic way of looking at things. So, what do you want from me?"

"You know that I'm aware of the general plans. Cargo transfer and all that. You still have a link to the *Dungeon*, right?"

"Let's say I do."

"Then send me there! I'll do whatever you want in return!"

"I won't even ask what you mean by "whatever you want". What's more important is... Do you remember the mission in Tokyo?"

"One doesn't forget that." She shivered. "You mean they won't let me go?"

"We'll have to check. Are you sure you want to be a guinea pig?"

"I'm willing to take the risk. I'll take painkillers, and you get me out if something goes wrong. Can you do that?"

"It's hard to say. It depends on the type and severity of punishment. You might simply die."

"I'd rather die immediately than tremble with fear for months."

Such optimism... if we failed, I doubted that we'd have these months. Things would come to a head much, much sooner. Her self-criticism was also really something.

"Besides, I've fallen too far behind the others.

How will my Freeze help against the skeletons? I doubt you have anyone more useless in your squad, right?"

Tatra's death and the subsequent resurrection had changed her for the better. Even though she was still trying to flee, it was now a more conscious decision. But her sense of self-preservation was well-developed too.

"Alright, let's try. But a little later, I need to prepare."

*　*　*

Attention! Would you like to summon a goblin? (1 SP)
Yes/No

"My Lord," the newly arrived vassal bowed as usual. "Am I in that world?"

"Yes, Uli. This is indeed Sar. I think you'll be interested in seeing it. This city once belonged to your kin."

The setting sun illuminated the streets, revealing an impressive yet disheartening picture. Unlike the ruins on Earth, this place had been alive not so long ago by historical standards. It still had a chance of coming back to life. Well, theoretically...

"How is my family doing?"

"They have already started hunting. They are accompanied by the strongest hunters, so they are in no danger."

"What about the soldiers? They're not causing

trouble?"

"Nothing you need to worry about, my Lord."

So, there were problems, but they weren't critical yet? I didn't want to delve deeper, and there was a brief silence.

"Well, what do you think of this place?"

"It is impressive. However, this settlement is a far cry from your cities, my Lord. If the inhabitants of this city had your weapons, would they have let it be destroyed?"

"Is that all you feel?"

"No, my Lord. I am pleased that goblins can reach such heights. That my people can compete even a little with yours..."

"Don't say that," I responded. "By accepting my patronage, you have also become my people."

"Then, perhaps, the Lord will take my daughter as his youngest wife?"

I snorted, aware that I had walked into a trap. This wasn't the first time I'd heard such proposals, but I'd never left myself open like this. It wasn't hard to refuse, but true unions had long been sealed with blood, not words. The blood flowing through the veins of shared offspring, and the blood spilled by common enemies.

Funny, but the thought didn't shock me. I'd seen the elder's daughter before. She was quite pretty and didn't provoke disgust. Even if she was a crocodile, this was more of a political and logical question. Theoretically, this could damage my status as a "God", but it would strengthen the alliance with the goblins, ensure my family's safety and, finally, provide me with offspring. There was no guarantee that I would leave this mission alive—the stakes were too high. And there was no guarantee that Earth would withstand the onslaught of the gods. What was on the other side of the scales? The high moral principles of a "builder of communism"?

"I still have a wife," I replied. Or would it be more accurate to say that I *had* a wife? An interesting question.

"I know there are at least two, but the Lord could have ten wives!"

Two? Oh, right, there was also Nata, whom I'd once proclaimed to be a "junior wife". So much for that joke.

"Have you ever thought to ask her if she desires such happiness?"

"Esha is my daughter, Lord. If she was stupid enough to refuse, she would have been devoured by rats as a child. There can be no greater happiness for Esha than to be chosen by you!"

"I will consider it once the current mission is over."

"How long will it last?"

"No more than a year."

"Why wait so long? The nights are cold, and my daughter could warm your bed tonight. You can send her back in the morning and, if the Vault so pleases, she will deliver a baby in seven months."

Apparently, there was no question of whether we could have offspring. I also wasn't sure that he was relying on legends in this matter, and not on the practice of recent months. Close encounters of the third kind, damn it.

"We'll discuss this later, Uli. As I already said, I have a task for you..."

* * *

"Are you ready?"

"Yes," Tatra grinned. It looked like the painkiller was already working. So much for that precaution.

"Don't waste any time, Uli," I turned to the goblin. "I will summon you back after exactly one minute... no, thirty seconds, that should be enough. If anything goes wrong, bring her back."

"I'm sure it'll work. We simply can't fail."

"Don't jinx it, please, I have my raven for that."

Request to place the player Tatra in the Slaver's Bag?
Yes/No
Attention! Request is confirmed!
Attention! Recall the goblin?
Yes/No

Uli disappeared with the bag, and I started counting down the seconds. Thirty seconds passed.

Attention! Would you like to summon a goblin? (1 SP)
Yes/No

The goblin appeared, and I could see the

outcome on his face. It hadn't worked.

"What happened to her?"

"I think she's... dead, my Lord. I brought her body."

"Take her out!"

If the cause of death wasn't a System weapon, we still had five minutes to reanimate Tatra. Had she gone into shock from the pain again?

Healing... Healing... Healing...

Surprisingly, it was enough. Tatra shuddered and opened her eyes, brimming with animal terror. After a second, she blinked, and tears ran down her cheeks. It seemed that this escape route was closed—at least for the players. This was very, very bad.

*　*　*

I spent the rest of the evening ferrying the obtained samples to the *Shard*. Although this district would have been looted more than once, the soldiers managed to fill eleven containers with archaeological garbage. I didn't bother checking what they'd gathered. All the finds were photographed, and there'd be someone to take inventory at the other end.

I didn't feel sleepy and had been performing basic exercises to develop magic for the past hour. I could do a lot already, but I wasn't a real mage, since all my abilities came from the System. It might be years before I could reproduce this level of magic on my own, but even a journey of a thousand miles begins with a single step. The goblins managed somehow, and I had much higher Wisdom. And more information. Even without my direct involvement, scientists on Earth had organized the information and created the first manuals, based on the books they had received and after talking to the shamans.

The first step was to feel mana, which was something I had no trouble with. The second step was to establish control over the flows in my body. I had gotten nowhere at the start, but had made some progress in recent weeks. True, not only the training helped, but also an overall increase in *Wisdom* and, in particular, the *Innate Control* feature. The mana flows were moving continuously, and it was important not to try to resist them, but to direct them in the *right direction*. Except this was much easier said than done, and mistakes didn't feel very pleasant.

Once I'd finished with mana, I tried to reach my qi again, but got nowhere as usual. A one in *Spiritual Power* was barely enough to feel its presence. Plus, the instructions for qi were much vaguer. I would see some progress only if I moved *Heresy* into this attribute, but I wasn't in the mood to experiment further today.

*　*　*

I had a separate tent, made of the same insulating material, so I occupied a separate room. When someone else appeared in the night, it didn't go unnoticed. First of all, by the ghost who didn't need any sleep.

"Who's there?"

"It's me," came Tatra's voice. "Please. I'm... I'm afraid to sleep alone."

"Are you serious?"

"Do you want me to go ask someone else?"

I wanted to send her away, but then I considered the consequences. Nothing good would come of my refusal. I could bet that Tatra would do something stupid.

"Okay, come and lie down," I sighed, shifting to make room. "But I won't try anything, if you were counting on it."

"You can try something if you want."

I only hugged the girl and closed my eyes. Despite my paranoidal tendencies, I didn't feel any danger. Tatra had no reason to try to kill me. Hera still needed me, while Tatra herself was too afraid of death. She was being guided by the same thing as Lisa in the past: the desire for protection in a difficult situation. Her bet on the *Dungeon* had failed, she had ended up deep in a city full of undead, and I was the most obvious way for her to get out of here alive. Perhaps the only way. Add to this the stress of another death and...

But I had no wish to take advantage of the situation. At least it would be honest with the goblin girl. How I hated all this.

* * *

The night passed surprisingly calmly, and the undead didn't come knocking. If not for Iris, we could have spent a week here. But it was too dangerous now. The raven returned in the night after checking the chosen location and confirmed that it was suitable. This information cost me *two crystals*. That's how much it took to stimulate the courage of one brazen bird.

Players remaining: 12843/13000.

Our numbers were dropping. Fifty players had disappeared during the remainder of the day and the night. The mission hadn't ended, and a short transmission from the fortress reported the disappearance of five paragliders. The attempt to solve everything in one blow had failed miserably.

"I told you so!" croaked the raven.

I ignored his boast, focusing on a new goal. Unfortunately, I couldn't temporarily transfer the soldiers to the *Shard*. Although they weren't affected by the mission restrictions, I wasn't sure if I could bring them back later. At present, the connection wasn't as stable as it had been in the first few hours, even at the drop-off point. Therefore, we urgently transferred some of the cargo to this side. We took some with us and hid the rest in case we had to return. I did have to sacrifice one of the *Bottomless Bags (F)*.

We decided to travel in three groups. I headed one, Diva—the second, and Dmitry—the third. The soldiers went back to their bags, but the players would travel on foot. With all the associated risks, such as appearing on scans, leaving tracks, and endangering themselves, including our new shelter. But what other options did we have?

"Move out."

Although my squad included all of my own players, most of the others belonged to Hera's faction. Nevertheless, my reputation was sufficient to avoid disobedience, and reconnaissance went well. I wasn't the only one to figure out the benefits of a combination of skills, and the "elite group" boasted a very impressive range of skills.

We met a lot of undead, but mostly low-level creatures. Those guarding the destroyed estates couldn't leave them, and we successfully avoided patrols with the help of aerial reconnaissance. If we couldn't, we destroyed them, eliminating the traces of the crime as much as possible. In other words, we took the bones with us. Of course, it was possible that the number and timing of the patrols were recorded somewhere, but there was nothing we could do about that.

* * *

This time, we spotted a fairly large group of undead in advance, and I decided to ambush them. A Bone Knight strode in the center of a formation of ordinary skeletons, periodically stopping and releasing a *Search Wave*. It meant we couldn't simply hide in one of the buildings and let the patrol pass us by. Not to mention the footprints on the road and the disappearance of some of the undead along the knight's route. It was easier to kill him than to risk it.

I froze, letting the skeletons pass me by, but they were walking quite freely so I didn't have to make any unnecessary movements. The *Calculating Mind* ensured that I didn't do anything stupid.

Activate Split!

The spear struck the bone sphere—*Invisibility* allowed me to aim carefully, and the flow of mana smashed the armor into pieces and kept moving...

Attention! You have gained 112 SP! (221/460)

The flow of energy wasn't that strong, yet it deactivated *Invisibility*, leaving me standing in a crowd of skeletons. However, they were not destined to avenge the death of their leader.

Blink!

I shifted to the first floor of a building and turned to watch the carnage. Although most undead were deaf, we wanted to make as little noise as possible, so players attacked the enemy with bladed weapons. It was all over before I had a chance to intervene. I went down and picked up the card dropped by the Knight, which was another *Search for Life* (E, 0/100). Not so useless, if you thought about it...

The trip went smoothly, and we reached our destination by the end of the day. Diva's squad was already here, and Dmitry arrived half an hour later. Neither team had suffered any losses.

There were no surprises inside the estate, only several skeletons, which we didn't even destroy but simply hacked off their limbs and left as insurance. A house that already had its own undead shouldn't arouse suspicion, right?

All that remained was to screen the selected rooms and get ready to wait. There was no access to the Server here, but we would solve the problems as they arose. If I explored the surroundings, I was bound to find a spot where I could summon a goblin. In the meantime, we'd wait for the fortress to make a move... or the undead.

INTERLUDE NO. 3
THE STRATEGIST

QING LONG SAT BY THE WINDOW and pondered the situation. He had already grown used to the bodyguards standing behind him, and paid little attention to them. While everyone strove to become stronger individually, he understood that the strength of one could never compete with the strength of thousands. Although the Chinese man remained a strong fighter, it would be more accurate to call his specialization as a Strategist.

The view from this spot was limited, but this didn't stop Qing Long from observing the situation as a whole. The sentries on the walls, the working groups, the newbies being trained by veteran instructors. They were much better organized this time, yet the situation was... difficult.

Only eight of the twelve members of the Circle had gathered in the fortress. Eleven, after the death of Marcus, but there was no point in counting the empty places. They weren't

Freemasons, so the maximum number was limited only by common sense. Anyone who proved their mettle could join the Circle. In some sense, the Italian man had been the weakest link—he didn't have exemplary strength, or status, or political influence. However, being in the Circle was a power in itself. A Level 7 player was nothing impressive, but a member of the Circle, Head of the Italian Branch of the Guild, and a veteran of the first thousand was a considerable status.

Players remaining: 12843/13000.

But of the 13,000 players who went on this mission, only 11,500 had arrived at the fortress. Some had died, so their location was of no interest, yet what about the rest? Many had seen Inti's beacon, but an investigation showed that no more than 200 people could have used it. In the end, it wasn't hard to assume that there was radio contact, as well as to work out the sources of the leak. The communication session revealed where three members of the Circle had gone, but it didn't explain the disappearance of another 1,000 people.

Qing Long strongly doubted that so many players would choose a random landing point. Plus, the world media had been discussing the upcoming campaign for weeks. Largely false and brimming with optimism, they contained instructions for this exact situation. In addition, the gods had warned the newly initiated immediately before the teleportation. If some had ignored the hint, there should have been plenty of veterans among the missing. Was it possible that there were more than two *beacons*? And that one of the priests was playing their own game?

"Comrade Long, I've made you some tea."

"Thank you."

Qing Long picked up the cup and took a sip. He wasn't afraid of poisoning since *Poison Detection* was one of his skills. It had already come in useful once. The higher you climbed, the more people wanted to get rid of you. He could also identify food that had gone off at a glance.

During his last visit to the goblin world, he hadn't yet become a priest but had received the position and the *Sword of Justice* after the mission. You couldn't set up a *beacon* without a divine weapon, so he had an alibi. Obviously, Qing Long didn't expect to find himself guilty during the investigation, but his allies would also draw the same conclusion.

Alexander was above suspicion for the same reason. The German man became the High Priest of Odin after his return, and even that had been a struggle. However, the winner is always the winner, no matter how small the margin. Dmitry had lost that race and joined the Priestess of Hera. Not the worst tactic.

Could it be Diva herself? The *Lightning Staff* had been found in the goblin treasury and, before returning to its owner, had passed through Qing Long's hands. She hadn't left the fortress after that. In addition, the priestess was known to have used Inti's beacon.

The story of the first priest of Inti was well known. Vasily had used the man's sword to install the second *beacon*, which meant he was also beyond suspicion. In general, it was easy enough to figure out the "apostate" trio's plan. Either an attempt to break through early on, or an attempt when the undead were distracted by the main force. Not a bad idea, but it was too obvious, so no one would help the competitors.

Who was next? *Quetzalcoatl's beacon* was located in the fortress, which automatically cleared Michigan of any suspicion.

Brahmin, priest of the fallen god? He had died at the very start last time and couldn't have activated the *beacon* in time. Many people had seen the *Spirit Staff*, and some had even held it in their hands.

By a simple method of elimination, the only candidate left was Sulu, Priest of the Great Set. Although the Somali man remained in plain sight most of the time, he could have put up a *beacon* on the first day, before everyone gathered. Moreover, his faction was heterogeneous enough to hide several hundred players.

Of course, this wasn't a crime in itself, but information about a traitor among the gods made the situation a lot more worrying. Although the gods were formally on one side, there were coalitions, which their followers had to observe. The Great Set was in league with Shiva. If the latter's death had been orchestrated by the gods to eliminate the traitor, they would have informed

their priests of the situation, which meant...
nothing. Although the Egyptian god seemed
suspicious, it wasn't enough for anything except
extra caution.

"Comrade Long?"

Qing Long handed the empty cup back
without turning his head, and the young woman
immediately snatched it up. It was reminiscent of
the old days, before his great country had
embarked on building communism, but wasn't
considered reprehensible.

The wind carried the scraps of an argument
to him, and, listening, he caught the details.
Nothing interesting—one of the players couldn't
decide on which squad to join, since his chosen
religion didn't match the territorial preferences.
Amazing. By simply sitting here, Qing Long could
track global trends, and look for ways to gain an
advantage over his competition.

The first faction consisted of the followers of
Guan Yu. As the strongest of the gods, he found
himself in opposition to the rest. Therefore, China
could count only on itself. Of course, there were
foreigners among them, but they were perceived by
most as "laowai".

The second faction was pro-American. Its
leaders were Michigan, Lisa and, by extension,
Ryuu. The United States, Britain and their
longtime ally, Japan. However, a union didn't
guarantee unity. Quel and Inti both wanted the
same thing and would work together only for the
time being.

The third faction was European. It included Diva, Vasily, and Alexander. In the absence of the first two, the German man was the undisputed leader of the united forces. Hera's faction was formally led by Leon—perhaps not the best warrior, but from the first thousand and with a truly unique life story. There were no representatives of *Heresy* in the fortress, and the few members of the Russian unit had chosen squads based on their divine affiliation. A pity that none were his subordinates... at least none of the ones in the fortress.

Well, the fourth faction was African, a union between Saud and Sulu. Both were followers of the Great Set and had managed to take charge of almost everyone from Africa and the Middle East.

Shiva's followers were supposed to join this union too, but they had stayed away. The god's death had hit his followers hard, but the Brahmin and Sahel had taken matters into their own hands and united people with the desire to resurrect the patron. They claimed that they didn't need the Altar of the Great Y, since there was no one to give it to, so it was much more important to finish the mission and return to Earth. At the last meeting, the Brahmin had apologized and volunteered to remain in the rear to guard the fortress. Minus fifteen hundred players. It was a suspicious move, no matter how you looked at it.

The last faction were the traitors—players recruited by enemy gods, identifying whom took a lot of effort. Perhaps it was finally time to act.

INTERLUDE NO. 4

THE SACRIFICE

WHO DARES WINS. That's what they say, right? Matrix wasn't a risk-taker, preferring to play it safe. But the worms in his body prevented him from sabotaging the order given by the Great Goddess. Or, rather, by her messengers, since she didn't stoop so low as to communicate with slaves. The task and deadline were set, and if they failed, the parasites would devour them from the inside. One of their comrades had served as an example of how that would happen, and his death would haunt their nightmares for a very long time...

Matrix never considered himself a coward, nor was he a hero, ready to die for some great cause. Of course, he didn't want Earth to be captured by alien monsters, but this was a problem for specially trained people. The army, navy, and air force. After all, that's what he had been paying taxes for almost half of his life. Nuclear weapons were stronger than magic anyway, right? Not that he was keen to live among radioactive ruins. He wasn't a cockroach, was he?

However, there were a plethora of human worlds, and if he completed his task, he was promised not only freedom, but also the right to settle in a safer place. A world guarded by mighty gods, where he and his children could live in peace. He didn't have any children yet, true, but the player status was akin to the highest nobility. Perhaps he could even join one of the royal families? Anyway, it was much nicer to believe in these fairy tales than to imagine himself an eternal slave of the vile insects. Or, even worse, their food and incubator. They wouldn't deceive him, would they?

They wouldn't, something whispered comfortingly in his head. Or was it his imagination? Probably one of the worms that had nested in his brain. He could trust it. Who else could he believe, if not the voices in his head?

"Stop standing there like a dolt and finish him!" Came a voice from behind him, like some kind of cultist.

"Shut up, Aini," Matrix snapped. "Accept this sacrifice in your name, Thousand-Legged Giz!"

An unnamed victim from among the newcomers—unlikely to be missed—grunted as they tried to wriggle away, but without much hope. He should have made a move earlier. Matrix swung the dagger, slicing through veins and letting the blood run down the altar stones. It had taken several hours to assemble everything required, even though there were plenty of stones here.

Finish him, finish him, finish him...

"Die!" Matrix plunged the dagger into the victim's chest, and...

Attention! You have gained 8 SP!

Like it, like it, like it...

The pile of stones was encased in a film and lit up, becoming a single System object. First time lucky? They did it! Of course, they had guessed that the world's protection would be weaker near the *beacon* but thought that they would need more victims. That's why they had prepared three.

Projection of the Altar (Thousand-Legged Giz)

Attention! You have received an additional quest – Beacon (D)!

Description: Sacrifice ten victims to open the way for the servants of your Mistress!

Reward: Freedom, and you will be able to leave the goblin world.

Penalty for failure: Variable

Victims: 0/10.

"You're filthy. I hope he wasn't sick with anything contagious."

"Help me remove the corpse!" Matrix ordered, wiping his hands on a handkerchief. However, British scientists had proven that players didn't get sick. Otherwise, viruses and bacteria would be a greater threat to our planet than monsters, who could be killed. "Would anyone object if I continue?"

"I object. Everyone needs experience, so I'm next."

"Are you sure you want to do this, Aini? Are you ready to kill a person?"

"Easy!"

"Actually, I could use some experience, too," interrupted White Eagle. A Native Indian judging by his nickname, but an alcoholic judging by his appearance. The people he had to work with!

"You snooze, you lose. Bring the next one. A girl!"

"Can we leave her until last?" Grem suggested. "I mean, can we kill the guy first? Or at least give her the last word?"

"What, you think she'll beg you to give it to her right here? Don't give me that look, I've seen you all staring at her! All men are bastards, and you lot are totally fucked up."

"Right, so capturing her and sacrificing her to the Spider Goddess is fine, but fucking her beforehand is not?" The fourth cultist intervened. "Do I understand your reasoning correctly?"

"Oh, shut up, Spike! Those are two totally different things!"

"Let's get this farce over with," Matrix grimaced. "We still need to find another eight victims, and we don't have much time. You know what will happen if this place is discovered."

The secret underground room was an ideal place for an altar, but it was also ideal for storage and utilities. The army would leave the fortress in a day or two, and they might have to join the campaign. Matrix had no desire to fight the undead. Just because there was a worm or two in his head didn't make him an idiot, right?

You're totally fine...

"I'm next, okay?"

"Hey, why are you next?"

"Accept this sacrifice in your name, Thousand-Legged Giz!"

Aini was extremely sloppy with the dagger and sprayed blood everywhere, yet she got the job done.

Victims: 1/10

"Oh, yes, I came!" she arched her back. Crazy creature. "Wow, that was awesome. Can I kill the next one? I've nearly got enough to level up."

"No, you can't. You said yourself that we should take turns."

"Shut your face, Matrix, it's not your turn. Who should I negotiate with? How about we play rock-paper-scissors, guys?"

"And then what?" Grem asked.

"The winner will give me his turn, and I will let him fu..."

In that moment, there was a knock on the door. It was a polite knock, but each cultist felt a chill.

"That's it, you virgins are out of luck," Aini said grimly. "We're done for. Can we at least finish the witness?"

"You think it will help?" Matrix asked skeptically. "I think the corpses and the altar don't leave us much chance to pretend to be sheep. What's the point in the extra deaths?"

"Am I the only one with any balls here? To your glory, Great Giz!"

The last victim had already been dragged to the altar, and the man didn't have time to react before Aini cut his throat. She was clumsy, but there was enough blood to spray not only the altar, but also everyone standing in the room. Who would open the door now? Looking like this? The altar began to shine brighter.

Projection of the Altar (Thousand-Legged Giz)

Victims: 2/10

Minimal saturation is available! Try to send a signal?

"Look, we're all goners anyway, right? So, why don't you die and give me a chance to survive?"

"Fuck off, you bitch!" Grem shouted, trying to throw off Aini, who had jumped on his back. "Get off me!"

"To your glory, Great Giz!"

Projection of the Altar (Thousand-Legged Giz)

Victims: 3/10

Aini didn't comply with the recommended requirements again and simply grabbed her ally's throat, falling with him on the altar. White Eagle and Spike jumped back to avoid becoming new victims. It was clear where things were going.

We need more victims, kill her!

The door exploded, causing everyone to

stagger, but they had a few seconds left. Matrix stepped forward, took out his sword and ran the girl through. Like pinning a butterfly.

"You..." Aini seemed more surprised than scared. "Looks like you've got balls too, huh?"

"To your glory, Great Giz!"

Attention! You have gained 16 SP!

Attention! You have reached Level 3!

Victims: 4/10

Try to send a signal?

Yes/No

Although Matrix couldn't see the enemies, he knew they were here. They were just hiding under *Invisibility* or something similar. They only had a few seconds left...

Attention! Signal has been sent!

The altar lit up and... there was no portal releasing hordes of spiders to help them. Nothing happened!

Attention! Signal is blocked!

Attention! The quest has been updated!

Sacrifice ten victims to open the way for the servants of your Mistress!

Reward: Freedom, and you will be able to leave the goblin world.

Two of his allies were on the ground, knocked down by the players discarding their *Invisibility*. Judging by the *combat forms*, the leaders had come for them. A pity they hadn't mined the room. Actually, no. What's the point of dragging the "good guys" to the grave with you? It's not like collaboration with the arachnids had been even slightly voluntary.

You mustn't fall into their hands alive, the worms reminded him.

"To your glory, Great Giz!"

Turning the sword around, Matrix plunged it into his chest. His allies allowed themselves to be captured, which meant they would face a much slower and more painful death. Idiots.

Attention! You have gained 24 SP!

Attention! You have gained 16 SP!

Attention! You have gained 8 SP!

Attention! You are dead!

Congratulations! Your soul returns to the Altar of the Thousand-Legged Giz!

* * *

"Please, I don't know anything else!" White Eagle howled. "Please don't…"

"That's enough, Sulu," Qing Long said. "We're not here to play games."

Torture wasn't the most reliable way to get information, but if you also had the ability to sense a lie, then learning the truth was a matter of time. Especially when the suspects were ready to talk, and talk, and talk. People willing to betray humanity for their own survival rarely possessed high moral qualities. No matter how they justified it to themselves.

"A-a-a-a!"

"Why did you cut his finger off?"

"I don't like traitors," the African man smiled,

discarding the wire cutters. "Now he won't be able to pick up a sword and stab someone in the back. Although it would be simpler to execute him."

"We promised to spare his life, remember? Don't ruin your reputation. Anyway, I think he'll die of hunger and thirst soon enough."

"You Chinese sure know a lot about torture. But we didn't promise the second one anything, right?"

*　*　*

The discovery of the *Projection of the Altar of the Thousand-Legged Giz* made them focus on uncovering the traitors and interrogating the captives. The city was big and, at first glance, they couldn't prevent the ritual, but the situation wasn't actually so dire. The ritual had to be carried out according to all the rules, and nothing would happen in the absence of communication with the Server. The fortress didn't work—perhaps Quel wasn't the strongest of the gods, but he was quite capable of blocking the signal in the territory he controlled. Even if the cultists had sacrificed the maximum number of victims...

The ritual would come to nothing in most other places. Even if the traitors were lucky and managed to create another *projection*, where would they find ten sentient victims? They would have to sacrifice each other, but slaves had no reason for such self-sacrifice. Loyalty was ensured mainly by threats of a painful death and promises of a generous reward. However, while people believed in the former, no one took the latter seriously. It was an illusion to drown out one's conscience and not go crazy waiting for the inevitable death...

Checking thousands of players took time and a comprehensive approach. Interrogation, list matching, scanning skills. The checks were cross-checked in case there were traitors among the interrogators. It is difficult to catch fish in a leaky net.

Nevertheless, they were slowly catching the "fish" and had managed to find three: a couple of followers of the Ancestor of the Frost Monkeys and one follower of the Ancestor of the Golden Monkeys. The traitors didn't know anything valuable, and their goal was sabotage: pour poison into the common cauldron, arrange an explosion in the arsenal. Moreover, they swore that they weren't planning to do anything like that. They had chosen the fortress in the hope of sitting it out until the mission ended.

Unfortunately, all the people caught were rank and file. They didn't know each other and acted alone. Uncovering the traitors and forcing them to surrender made it possible to catch two more, who tried to escape that night by climbing the wall. Unfortunately, the traitors weren't taken alive, so it was difficult to say which god they served. It didn't look they would get any more useful information from the prisoners. The search continued, but no more results came to light...

INTERLUDE NO. 5
THE OFFENSIVE

THE THOUSAND-STRONG ARMY left the fortress on the fifth day. Not only did this rabble have to be organized and directed, but also supplied with food, water, and other necessities. Fortunately, they had known about the upcoming mission in advance, so preparations had been underway for a long time. Even if there weren't enough *Smuggler's Bags (D)* for everyone, Rank E allowed a person to carry cargo on the way back. Players were supplied with weapons and military equipment first and foremost, but other needs weren't forgotten. Of course, a lot had been lost along with the dead, but a few million didn't matter much when it came to the fate of humanity. One could also transfer items in and out of a personal room even without spatial artifacts. Not to mention the *Slaver's Bags*, which allowed you to transfer goods directly, on an almost industrial scale.

An additional bonus was the food captured in the goblin fortress. Water could be found locally, and decontamination tablets were included in the mandatory kit. Even if the enemy poisoned all the springs, the tanks on the roofs could be cleaned and used to collect rainwater. It was enough for the army to maintain combat capability for an extended period of time—maybe not for the entire 1,000 days of the mission, but for many months. Even if there had been no losses...

The base and supplies left behind were protected by a large unit, in case any goblins appeared, and in case the main plan failed. It was nothing complicated, but then, they couldn't manage anything more complicated. There was no time for additional training, as the case with the traitors had clearly shown.

"Blow it up!" Qing Long ordered, bringing the walkie-talkie to his mouth. He had been given the honor to "cut the red ribbon".

No explosives were spared, and the gate that had been closed for decades shattered into pieces, opening a direct road to the fourth circle. Anything was better than going around, which would have taken two weeks. Or messing around with ropes and pulleys, which may be faster, but was difficult, unreliable, and made it impossible to retreat.

"Get ready!" The Chinese man barked out. "All squads, spread out!"

Although the factions remained competitors, the need for a single leader was unquestioned. His allies wisely shifted responsibility for the inevitable mistakes to the person who wanted it. This played into Qing Long's hands.

The waiting dragged on. They had assumed that the undead would react to what happened, and, this time, they were right. Less than an hour later, a Bone Dragon (C) appeared above them—a monstrous creature as strong as a whole army. Especially if this army didn't have air defense. It was unclear what the goblins and their ballistas had been counting on at all. Magic?

"Attention everyone! Hold and don't shoot before I give the order!"

There were many newcomers among the players, and a shortage of military personnel among the veterans, but serious weaponry had been distributed among the professionals. Nevertheless, someone disobeyed the order and started shooting. Not for long, though, because the commander quickly set him straight.

Even sitting in the shelter, Qing Long saw the monster make several circles, assessing the number of opponents, and then slowly descend.

"Unknown magic attack detected!"

"Fire!"

The city literally exploded with fire, and dozens of rockets shot into the sky. Most modern RPKs responded to various types of radiation, so they weren't suitable for fighting against a sort-of living enemy, but the Bone Dragon was no supersonic fighter plane. A simpler weapon had been chosen for it. The creature was struck by explosions, bones showered down, yet it remained in the sky and even tried to escape, without much success. Another explosion tore its left wing off, and the dragon went into an uncontrollable spin.

"Target is hit!"

"Death not confirmed, stay on your toes! Squad A1—check. Squad A2, A3 and A4—cover them. Any losses? Is there anyone nearby?"

"I'm watching the positions covered by *Breath*. Looks like everyone there is dead, or... No, they're getting up again. But... something is wrong."

"Have they turned into the undead?" Qing Long guessed.

"It looks like it, sir."

"Stay out of the affected area. Surround them and shoot anyone who tries to get out."

Players remaining: 12679/13000.

Judging by the counter, the losses didn't exceed a few dozen players, and if they had taken out one of the strongest enemy pieces, it would be a sin to complain...

"Crash site has been detected. The dragon is alive, it's even moving. Looks like it's calling for reinforcements because skeletons are gathering around it. There are more and more of them, some are even coming out of the ground. Should we wait for reinforcements?"

"No. Use heavy weapons."

They could have gotten a lot of experience for a dragon like this, but the risk of more losses was too great. A gas mask might not protect against

Breath, and only the strongest players could reach its *heart*. Qing Long had no desire to venture there himself, and an attempt to send someone else would arouse suspicion that he was trying to get rid of competitors.

"I know you're in charge, but are you sure?" The Swordsman's voice rang out. A good opportunity, but no...

"We shouldn't be greedy. We have other goals."

They waited for several minutes, which were interrupted by scattered reports. Nothing interesting, nothing important. The building shuddered slightly from fresh explosions.

"Target destroyed."

* * *

The journey to the next wall took a week. The army moved in a wide front and annoyingly slowly, mostly out of caution. The undead had shown that they had magic of mass destruction, so it was necessary to minimize the risks. A compact camp would be an easy target for a night raid by dragons. There weren't many hazmat suits and gas masks in stock, and one still had to put them on before an attack...

There were also problems with reconnaissance, for Bone Birds (F-) appeared regularly in the sky. They were weak, so only a flock of necrobirds could kill a trained player, but the creatures constantly knocked down the drones. Taking advantage of the enemy's blindness, the undead made worrying attacks using small forces, but none were serious.

"Blow it up!" Qing Long ordered again.

They left the gate alone this time, preferring to destroy a section of the wall. It was less effective, but the undead were waiting in another place, which allowed the army to regroup before the enemy attacked again. This was called "rush" in gaming slang. The undead pushed straight ahead, ignoring the hail of bullets, explosions, and snipers. The width of the breach and the remaining stones helped the situation, and the mountain of bones in front of the positions grew rapidly.

"They're here, we need help!"

Qing Long ignored the shouting. Others would deal with tactical issues; he was in charge of overall management. These were the first losses. The undead broke through in places, groups of Bone Chimeras struck from the rear, Bone Birds swooped from above, but so far, it was all within expectations.

"Look! It's rising!"

The Chinese man squinted, activating a skill, and zoomed in on the battlefield. Something abominable was emerging from the dead monsters: the bones were moving, fusing into titanic creatures, and...

Bone Horror, Titan type. Rank: D. Level 1.

The creatures were over five meters in height, which made them dangerous even for the buildings. However…

"Snipers!" Qing Long barked, "Destroy the spheres!"

The order came a little late, bones fusing around the vulnerable points of the newborn undead right before their eyes. While the first bullets disappeared inside the bodies—one chimera actually collapsed—subsequent bullets started to ricochet.

"It's not working! There's too much armor!"

"Bring out the mortars!"

The positions were targeted, and the explosions quickly scattered the monsters that the undead had been counting on. No wonder there were no "command staff" among the attackers, only the bare minimum to coordinate the bone monsters. Five minutes later, the stream of skeletons suddenly dried up, and the battle fizzled out. Victory. But the situation wasn't so rosy—human losses numbered in the hundreds, and how many were wounded?

The army remained there for another three days, collecting bones, and caring for the wounded. Some had to be sent back to the fortress, but those were relatively few. Flocks of chimeras circled around, drawing attention, and the undead continued to rise, but another large-scale attack didn't follow.

The bones were checked over for System items—all skeletons had *bone blades*, but not all of them became *Warrior of Y Swords* or something similar. Most of these natural artifacts simply lost their properties. The remaining useless bones were collected in three *Bottomless bags (F)*—which weren't actually bottomless, despite the name—and then exploded. As practice had shown, with enough damage, the bones remained in subspace, from where they were more difficult to extract.

Two weeks after the start of the expedition, the army entered the third circle. The time had finally come for Hera's squad to act.

CHAPTER 4
THE WAIT

THE ESTATE WAS SURROUNDED by a stone fence and included an impressive four-story house, several outbuildings, and even a scrap of land overgrown with trees twisted by the background magic. Such places were rare. The closer to the city center, the more expensive the land, which meant the buildings were taller and closer together. Ancient cities were usually built chaotically with twisting, narrow streets and randomly positioned houses. However, if the ancient goblin capital hadn't initially been built according to a master plan, it must have been rebuilt later. There weren't many places where the orderly street layout was slightly disrupted for the sake of "private property".

It might have seemed foolish to venture into such a conspicuous place, but this minus had turned into a plus after the city fell: it was assumed that the owners were strong enough to defend themselves, so we hoped that the defense system ignored this place. Unlike some government buildings, which the undead guarded as a "strategic point" and quite likely sent new guards if the old guards were destroyed — or even a reinforced unit to eliminate the intruders.

The owner's coat of arms could be seen on some walls, depicting an ugly ebony tree. Judging by the four goblins hanging from its branches, the founders of this glorious family were not known for their kindness. On the other hand, the estate was located inside the inner circle and outside the paths of the Sacred Goblin Campaigns, so it had barely been touched. However, time was ruthless, and little remained of the former luxury. The most significant find was a library with hundreds of books, mostly applied, historical, religious or entertainment, but I had no doubt that I could find something useful. Especially when I saw several books written in the System language.

"This library belongs to the temple of Hera," Diva declared at once, entering with her entourage. Sure, of course.

"I would say that this library belongs to humanity. As a member of said humanity, I am clearly entitled to a share. Don't you think so?"

"Then let's say the Guild. Would twenty... five percent suit you?"

This was quite generous considering her advantage in numbers, but compared to our main goal, the find was a pleasant trifle, nothing more. And an attempt to probe my position. So, we could bargain.

"Sad to hear how little you value me. Don't forget, I'm not a vassal, but a fully-fledged ally. We'll make copies, and we'll divide the originals fifty-fifty."

"Agreed. I'll assign people to this. We'll count, describe, and photograph them all, then divide them in half and..."

"I don't think that's a good idea. It's much safer to use the *Shard* for storage. Even if our expedition fails, the knowledge won't be lost."

"Alright. Then I'll assign some people once we're done with the rest."

"I'll find someone for this job too," I wasn't far behind. "I'll keep an eye on it myself—I suspect we'll get pretty bored in the coming weeks. By the way, I've been meaning to ask, do you know where Grykh is? I thought the ogre was coming with you?"

"You've met him?"

"We *know* each other. I destroyed his collar on the Outer Battlefield, and we recently crossed paths in Hera's domain."

"I see. Grykh is too big and noticeable to drag around with me. I can summon him using a card if necessary..."

"A slave card?"

"A summoning card."

"That requires connection to the Server, right?"

"Not this time. My card is strong enough to break through the defenses of this world. Not to mention that I can put up a real *beacon*."

"So, you have an escape route?"

"Possibly." The priestess didn't give me a straight answer. "You're not the only one with tricks up your sleeve."

It looked like I wouldn't be able to talk to the ogre. Even if I wanted to continue our acquaintance, there was clearly no point in asking Diva to summon him now. Perhaps I would get a chance in the future?

* * *

The following days were spent on setting up the new base. This time, we didn't shield the walls in only one room, but carefully isolated several. The advantage of this approach was that we could leave several windows looking out into the inner courtyard. The *search wave* spread in a straight line and couldn't pass through them even in theory. We also checked this in practice since several players in the squad had the necessary skill.

We blocked some of the passages with junk, installed concealed cameras along the perimeter, and set up relays and a surveillance station. All this equipment required charging and power, so a small, almost silent generator was installed in the basement. As per local tradition, we found a stone tank with rainwater on the roof. The water was quite drinkable after disinfection. We'd also brought impressive stores in the bags, so there was no need to worry about that.

And then... We waited. I would say the waiting was tedious, but with the library, watching our neighbors, and practicing magic, I had no time to get bored. The situation was less fun for others. Not everyone knew the goblin language, we couldn't leave the building, and the cramped quarters didn't help. The fact that a large proportion of the players were women complicated the situation slightly, while most of the military slept inside the bags. In shifts, since the professionals were responsible for most duties. It would have been more logical to send the players to sleep, but apparently paranoia was becoming our professional disease, and few people voluntarily agreed to such a thing. Maintaining discipline among dozens of young women was a dubious pleasure.

Only the tents gave an illusion of privacy. Even my squad, which occupied a couple of rooms, preferred to put them up as they were made out of shielding material. Although "nothing happened" on the first night, Tatra came to me again on the second night—and this time, she was "of sound mind and body".

"You know that Ryuu likes you, right?"

It wasn't the best topic of conversation with Tatra, however, I wanted to test several things. For example, the limits of her patience.

"I don't remember anyone with that name."

"River Serpent. The Japanese guy who pulled you out of the train."

"He's far away. Even if he's still alive, there's nothing between us. Just like between you and Eva, if I understood your breakup scene correctly."

Tatra didn't go to Tokyo as part of the rescue expedition and had remained in Moscow, so she never got to know Ryuu better. Then she had died and therefore didn't know the news...

"He's a powerful guy. He became a member of the Circle and the Head of the Japanese branch of the Guild."

In other words, he was strong enough to protect her. He also didn't have a patron god, which meant that I could potentially draw him to Heresy. Of course, seducing him with a girl to achieve this wasn't the best idea. Nor was sleeping with her myself.

"In that case, he's already found himself a pretty Japanese girl. Maybe even two."

"The last time I saw him, he asked about you."

"So what? He's cute, of course, but it doesn't make sense to look that far ahead. Perhaps we'll get a chance to get to know each other later. I'm grateful to him for saving me, but that's all."

"Yuki is his sister."

"And? I've never been a dewy-eyed princess, waiting by the window for my handsome prince. Even if we meet up later and he expects me to be faithful, he can take a hike. So can you if you keep this up..."

I felt a slight chill. Having an ice mage in one's bed could be dangerous.

"Oh my!" I chuckled. "Looks like you've completely recovered."

And got mad. A little more, and I might have to turn to the goblin option. There was no ideal solution in this case—even if Tatra needed more support than sex, refusal would inevitably lead to resentment, unease, and other problems.

"You're not attracted to me at all?" Tatra's voice shook slightly. Trying to explain my reasoning would only make things worse.

"To hell with it! Come here," I took her almost icy hand and pulled her towards me. So, so cold…

* * *

In addition to the special forces, several players I knew were also here. I knew some of them from past missions, I'd read the dossiers on most of the others, while Dragonfly actually belonged to the Russian unit. She was here on a divine assignment and spent most of her time with her new allies. One could consider it a betrayal, but I viewed her as a double agent or a goodwill ambassador. At the moment, her loyalty was more to me than to the Diva. It was the same with Spartacus—he was in the fortress and served as my personal source of information. But who knew how things would unfold…

Even Tatra remained a follower of Hera. Quite possibly, she was throwing herself at me not out of a simple desire for protection. However, if that was the case, I had nothing to fear in the near future. Members of my System squad, Yuki, and Dark Steel, were also present. Apart from the leader, the others couldn't choose a *landing point*—their portal was activated only after my decision. In accordance with our agreement, they had entered the portal when the allotted time was about to run out. I wondered what would happen to the squad members if a commander decided to stay in their personal room until the timer ran out. Would they be allowed to cross closer to the deadline? Or would the whole team die? After all, there had been no recorded cases of someone going on a mission, not entering the Summoning Portal, and returning. Not in the history of the Earth, at least...

"Legion, I've been wondering about something for ages. What happens to those who accept the mission but stay in their personal room?"

"I don't know, caw," the raven replied. "Or I don't remember?" The bird closed his eyes for a moment, and I thought that no answer was forthcoming. "Nothing good, I guess."

"Death?"

"Not necessarily, if you believe the legends. The System rarely kills directly, so you might survive if you are strong or lucky enough. There is always or almost always a chance. You can think of it as justice to some extent."

"Justice? Are you saying that everything happening to our world is fair?"

"To some extent. The *Rules* bind us, stopping us from going beyond the set limits. The universe is full of creatures that could easily destroy your world, but where are they? You are fighting, and you still have a chance of winning. Was it an accident that humans appeared on the goblin world? Why are there no other creatures?"

"Chance?" I took out a crystal, twirling it around in my fingers, but the raven ignored the bauble.

"Perhaps, but this does not negate the existence of the *Rules*. They maintain balance, preventing the strong from cutting everyone down and giving hope to the weak. Even if your world falls, some will surely survive. Maybe even escape and settle down somewhere else. Humans are quite a common race and, unlike the goblins, aren't overly oppressed in the System worlds."

"I haven't seen you for a while, El. It is you, isn't it?"

It was a rhetorical question, since the old goblin wasn't trying to hide. Even when I opened my fingers, he glanced at the crystal with an indifferent look.

"That's right. The raven is asleep, and we have a chance to talk. Hard to say if such a chance will come again, for I grow weaker and weaker."

"Then you want to discuss something important?"

"Do you remember when we formed our alliance? I have a favor to ask of you."

*　*　*

One of the few sources of entertainment was radio communication—Hera's supporters in the fortress ensured that we stayed informed of the situation and what our allies were up to. Of course, it was naive to hope that the source of the leak would remain secret for long. As soon as we settled in the new place, Leon let us know that the other leaders wanted to talk to us.

"Did you tell them we kept in touch?" Diva was indignant.

"I denied everything, mistress. However, they don't just suspect, they know. Our position here is quite weak, so it would be wise to clarify the situation."

"What do you say?"

Dmitry shrugged and withdrew, while I nodded—the answer was obvious. Leon was right, it didn't make sense to remain quiet. We would only turn the others against us.

"Fine, you can admit to everything," Diva conceded. "When can you arrange a session? Will five minutes be enough?"

"Mistress, they're not in the room with me. It will take me at least an hour."

"You have two."

*　*　*

"Greetings. Maybe you could share your plans?" The Swordsman's voice rang out. "We're still allies, right?"

"Of course," Diva replied. "Are you alone?"

"No, the others are here too."

"Alexander, can you hear me?"

"Yes," came his voice. "Don't worry, April. I'll take care of your people, as we agreed. Leon will be fine. In exchange for this communication session, he'll even be allowed to remain in the garrison!"

To my surprise, Diva's face remained impassive. If not the most reliable player was in charge of a faction, there was clearly a reason for this. And trying to frame him like that... was poor form.

"Leon, what do you say?"

"I only did what was expected of me. I never planned to stay in the fortress."

"Really?" Alexander chuckled. "But I thought..."

"That's enough!" Qing Long interjected, "We haven't gathered here to waste time."

"I thought we'd agreed that I would speak?"

"Of course, Bill, please continue."

It was a minor squabble, however, it showed that although the Alliance still existed, discontent was slowly brewing. A pity.

"Returning to the main issue," the Swordsman began again. "Why aren't you in the fortress, as we had agreed?"

"Why?" Diva asked. "For the same reason you started mopping up before the appointed time. Each of us uses the resources and opportunities available to them."

"One-one, I admit. But let me guess your plan. You're going to wait for the offensive, and then break through to the temple from a different direction?"

We glanced at each other. Diva shook her head, and I nodded, realizing that I would have the honor of answering. Amazing how informative gestures can be.

"That's right," I agreed. "That's what we're counting on."

"Vasily? I guessed you were there. You shouldn't have picked Hera's side; a woman is not the most reliable ally."

"We'll see," I shrugged. "I've had no cause to complain so far."

"You think you can pull it off?" another familiar voice rang out. "And that we'll obediently play the role of bait?"

"Sulu is a little worked up, but he's right," Saud interjected. "Our army is safe behind the walls. We can stay here forever, unlike you!"

I shook my head. He was bluffing, forever was too long. Even months would be an exaggeration. The undead knew about our arrival, and even if they didn't attack the fortress, the army wouldn't be able to peacefully level up on the skeletons nearby. Followers of outside gods were active in Sar, while infighting between factions would only increase. Not to mention the cramped and unsanitary conditions — the fortress wasn't designed for a garrison of this size. On the other hand, most players weren't eager to fight at all, and the longer they sat in the fortress, the harder it would be to force them to leave its safety. Earth's destruction was a threat so distant and abstract that it was hard to comprehend and believe in. Big words, with no real awareness of the impending catastrophe. If they didn't attack in the near future, it would be difficult, if not impossible, to strike as a united force later.

"We can wait, too," I replied. "As long as it takes. But sooner or later, we'll all have to act. So won't it be better if we work together?"

"You'll most likely die," the Swordsman sighed heavily. "It's a good idea, but you underestimate the undead. The hang gliders all died, none of them even reached the first circle. And they were the best of the best, so it's pointless to send others. Do you know that the undead have aviation?"

"Bone Dragons?"

"Those too, but I'm talking about birds. They're small and weak, but numerous. The air is out of bounds."

"Thanks for the warning."

"You can't get through by force. *Invisibility* won't work either, the undead have artifacts with *True Light*. My friend kept in touch until the last second. The whole first circle is covered in them, even the walls glow."

Sad news, but I didn't really expect to reach the temple this way. Our plan was based on improvisation and the willingness to persist until the end, so that at least one of us reached the goal. It wasn't a great plan, but the chance of success was even lower in the army.

"How did he die?"

"Ethan didn't die, at least, not at once—he ran into a Lich. I suspect that he was taken captive. The last thing he did was destroy the transmitter. However, I can't guarantee that open channels aren't being listened to."

"Thanks for the information."

"I don't want to see you among the undead. Where are you? Let's arrange a meeting, and we can break through together. Even if it takes months, the undead have no divine protection, so we'll succeed."

"How would we divide up the Altar?" Diva snorted. "Toss a coin? Sorry, but it won't work."

Especially if we followed my scheme, where the result was an opportunity to understand our true desires, and not a guide to action. According to the analysts, the probability of success was high if we kept advancing steadily. But it meant big losses and the collapse of our union. Someone would inevitably try to beat the others and get inside the temple first. Someone else would inevitably try to resist, resulting in bloodshed, and...

"Sounds like I won't be able change your mind, huh? Well, I tried."

"And I appreciate it, but we're going to try anyway," I interjected. "We also have something to tell you—one of Izur's followers used my *beacon*. A player named Iris. I only saw her in combat form, and I don't know her level, but she's very, very strong. The System labeled her as an *archon*. She tore off a roof using a skill. She also has scanning abilities and *Invisibility*. That's all I know."

"You fought her?" the Swordsman clarified. "Is she dead?"

"No, I barely escaped with my life. She had a pack of thirty or so creatures with her, mostly high-level *Hellhounds (D)*, but there were two... now just one *Cerberus (C)*."

"So, you managed to do some damage? Where should we look for her?"

The answer to this question could help to pinpoint our landing point, but it was stupid to stop halfway.

"Most likely in the fourth circle. Or in one of the neighboring districts, I can't be more precise than that."

"Where did you see her last?" Qing Long interrupted.

"In the fourth circle. She was heading towards the outer districts."

"Alright," the Chinese man accepted my answer. "This is important information. I'm glad you decided to share it, but a pity that you didn't do it right away. In response, we won't conceal our actions from you, but from now on, you're on your own."

"Agreed."

* * *

When I said that there were looters here, I had every reason to do so. A Wight was found in one of the outbuildings, and its existence indicated that a goblin had died here recently. Quite likely during their last attempt to reach the Altar.

It was hard to miss that most of the undead were skeletons. Yet the *transformation* took a few days at most—not enough time for flesh to fall off the bones. I doubted it had been different in the past. As I understood it, the undead either leveled up, becoming stronger and subsequently evolving into a Death Knight, or stagnating, absorbing the mana spilled in the air and eventually becoming a Bone Warrior. It was difficult to say whether this change was *evolution* or, on the contrary, *degradation*. By discarding the "extra flesh", they lost some of the weight and inherent abilities of the living. Their hearing, for example.

"Grrrr."

Wight Level 1.

Although not much time had passed, the subject was clearly following the second path and, instead of acquiring bone armor and becoming a knight, had started to rot. Having lost its limbs, it was rotting much more quickly.

"Come on, finish it off. You need to get stronger if you want to survive."

"Can't we leave it as camouflage?" Tatra asked.

"There are enough skeletons for camouflage, so this fellow is useless. And it stinks."

I'd found it, so I got to decide how we used the "canned goods". Deprived of its limbs, the enemy didn't pose a threat. Tatra grasped the *Spider Spear (E+)*—it provided an extra experience point for the undead—and struck. Players died quickly or adapted, so she had no fear of killing.

"What did you get?" I asked, collecting my weapon.

"An emptie."

Which is what usually happened. The undead had no magical skills at this rank and level, while the knowledge they had during their lifetime was lost. What could a corpse teach us? How to swipe at someone with claws or rip a victim's throat out?

"Well done. Now take this bag and place the corpse inside."

"What for?"

"It stinks. Can't you smell it?" I would normally suggest digging a grave, but not here. The last thing we needed was for it to be rise again.

"Can you help me?"

She obviously didn't want to mess around with the corpse, but if you dance, you must pay the fiddler.

"No," I bit back, gauging her reaction. "If you can't do it this way, you can hack it into pieces."

"O-okay," she nodded. "And then where do I put it?"

"It can stay in the bag for now, we'll dispose of it later."

I'd probably send the body to the *Shard*, so the scientists could have their fun. They could be bored over there too.

* * *

The situation heated up about a week after we occupied the estate. The undead patrols grew dramatically in size, turning into whole squads, which included Knights (D) and Bone Horrors (D). Bone Birds (F) ceased to be a rarity, but they lacked scanning abilities, so we just had to avoid running into them. *Identification.*

Bone Bird (99%)
Status: *Undead.*
Type: *Silver.*
Creature Rank: *F-.*
Level: *1.*
Danger: *Minor.*
Specifications:
Strength: 1.
Agility: 3.
Durability: 2.
Stamina: 4.
Wisdom: 5.
Perception: 3.
Instinct: 4.
Features:
—Undead — this creature is already dead and was reanimated using magic, with all the consequences.

— Regeneration — this creature's bones can

fuse back together if there is available material.

— System Creature — the creature belongs to the System.

— Magic Flight — the creature can fly.

— Magic Vision — the creature can navigate using magic, which has replaced its traditional sensory organs.

— Information Exchange — the creature is able to transmit obtained data.

Although they were quite weak, they possessed several magical abilities, the most important of which was flight. Clearly, bones couldn't fly by themselves. They would have made dangerous scouts if they had *Search for Life*, but they lacked this key skill. At least, most of them lacked it, we weren't sure if the whole flock was the same. All the creatures looked slightly different and probably hadn't been birds during their lifetime, or even the same creature….

We also didn't observe any intelligence, only its animal replacement — instinct. We could consider them magical data recorders: when they found a target, they returned and passed on the information to someone smarter. Another interesting thing was the mana. The birds didn't have much of it, yet they never seemed fall down or rest. They didn't seem to have any trouble replenishing their energy in this place.

Attention! You have gained 1 SP! (222/460)

The arrow severed the neck, adding this set of bleached bones to my collection. A little risky, but the bird was magical, and could theoretically detect the scan. Better if its mysterious master knew about the disappearance of one of a thousand scouts somewhere inside the third circle than our exact location.

Ideally, I shouldn't have touched it at all, but I was far enough away from our base. Officially, I was looking for a point from where I could access the *Shard.* The flow of undead had almost stopped, having gone to the confront the army, and the area was quiet enough that I had decided to go for a walk. I had always considered myself an introvert, but two weeks of "self-isolation" inside the four walls had left me quite irritable.

The army had reached the third circle, so it didn't make much sense to remain at the base any longer. We had to evacuate anything we didn't need. Diva's card could have simplified the procedure, but it wasn't worth wasting unless absolutely necessary. Even if the *summoning* worked only once, it could briefly create a zone where there was a connection to the Server. It would allow us, if not to evacuate, then to receive reinforcements in an extreme situation.

The destruction of the scout bird didn't elicit a visible reaction, and after another hour, I managed to find a suitable place.

Attention! Connection to the Server is available!

Attention! Summon a goblin?

Yes/No

CHAPTER 5

THE WALL

Recall the goblin?
Yes/No

ULI HANDED ME the heavy bag, bowed, and disappeared. I'd used the opportunity to not only send loot to the other side, but to replenish our reserves as well. Once I was finished, I marked the location where connection to the Server was possible on the System map, and headed back. An additional purpose of the walk was to check the route the main squad would follow.

So far, everything was going better than I'd expected—the number of undead in the area was at an all-time low. There were almost no "officers", and avoiding the occasional patrol was easy thanks to the ghost. On the other hand, I preferred to keep Legion close to me, or even in my bag. The undead were learning, and for the past week, Bone Birds (F-) had been trying to destroy any unidentified flying object, attacking both drones and their living equivalents.

"Caw, caw, caw!" Legion signaled.

A Bone Bird rose from behind the roofs and, spotting the raven, went on the attack. Not the best idea considering the difference in strength, with the undead at a disadvantage. Legion twisted to avoid the enemy, then swooped down from above, striking a blow that threw the fragile skeleton onto the cobblestones. If it had been a real bird, such a collision would have ended in a crash, but the undead flew using magic instead of feathers and traditional laws of nature. So, the fall wasn't as hard, and the bird was even moving. The raven released a jet of flame that swirled around the enemy, and then was sucked inside the eye sockets—its magic heart was located was inside the skull. A second, and the enemy was reduced to a handful of bones.

"Useless! Useless! Useless!" The raven scattered the remains in fury, after checking if they contained nothing interesting. Easy enough to guess what he'd been looking for.

"Impressive," I came up to him. The test had been successful. "How many Bone Birds could you destroy, do you think?"

"There are no crystals in these creatures. They are not afraid and do not feel pain. What's the point of fighting them?"

"But you have a crystal inside you," I retorted.

"And they wouldn't mind taking it."

"Mine!" Legion was indignant. "No one can take my crystals from me! I can kill a million of these birds!"

"A million is too much. What about ten?"

"They don't contain any crystals!"

Technically, Legion wasn't quite correct—the *magic heart* could be considered a kind of crystal or its derivative. But when the monster died, it crumbled to dust instead of coalescing into a stone.

"There don't contain any crystals but what about dust?"

The *heart* particles looked charred after being cooked by the flame but hadn't evaporated completely.

"Not interested." The raven flew up to perch on my shoulder.

"Really? Aren't they similar?"

"Imagine that you like cryst... apples. Yes, you humans like some strange things."

"Apples? Okay."

It wasn't the best example, but the raven had absorbed the memories of dozens of people, and many loved this fruit back on Earth. Starting from the biblical Eve and ending with characters in anime series, like the wolf Holo or the Shinigami Ryuk from Death Note.

"Imagine that your enemy ate an apple."

"Yeah..."

"Sooner or later, the apple will return to this world in the form of droppings. It can be used to fertilize the ground, insult enemies, and a new tree will grow from its seeds, on which apples will someday appear. But is that a reason to love poo?"

Hmm... What a deep philosophy. Not very typical for a raven. Had someone consumed the souls of too many Asian people?

"Are you saying that *hearts* aren't crystals at all, but a product of their processing?"

"Caw! Hearts are hearts, we were talking about the dust."

"Then it's not a good analogy."

"We, golden ravens, are famous for our honesty."

"Is that why so many don't like you all that much?"

"We have too many virtues. Most are simply jealous or afraid of us. You talked to the old man, didn't you? While I was sleeping?"

If not for *Heresy*, I would have said that the change in subject wasn't just unexpected but frightening.

"That's right."

"I don't know what he promised you, but you shouldn't trust him. Whatever he told you, he will certainly betray you."

"Are you saying that I should trust you?"

"I'm saying that you shouldn't trust anyone. Maybe then you'll be able to live a couple of hundred years before somebody eats you."

We had conducted aerial reconnaissance in the first few days after setting up the shelter, outlining possible paths to our goal. The drones didn't reach the temple, of course, they flew up to the second circle at most, but it was better to rely on fresh aerial photographs than on a map from a "century" ago. There were traces of ancient battles in the form of demolished houses and even completely destroyed streets.

A smaller unit like ours could move much faster than the Alliance army. We could have reached the wall by evening if we hurried, but although there were fewer undead around, they hadn't completely disappeared. It meant we were constantly going around them, or, if that wasn't the best option for some reason, fighting our way through.

"On the right!"

There was plenty of low-level undead in the houses, but most couldn't sense our group through the walls. However, our luck couldn't last forever. Six skeleton warriors posed no threat to our group, but their disappearance could draw the attention of the "officers" patrolling the city.

"Damn it," I swore. "Get back! Don't touch them!"

Too late. One had already been eliminated, so there was no point in holding back.

"Counterorder! Destroy them!"

I didn't interfere, letting the others have their fun, and it was over soon. We even gathered the bones, but would it be enough? I could only hope that my suspicions were nothing more than paranoia. After all, the death of "Einstein" didn't trigger a mass hunt, so maybe the same thing would happen here. Or we'd be far away by the time the loss was discovered.

"Over there, boss!" Bri appeared, indicating to the left with its tentacle. Given that most veterans possessed *Magical Ability*, the ghost didn't even try to hide.

"We're turning right," I said. "We'll walk down this street."

The squad kept moving. Everything was going well so far. Bone Birds were infrequent and immediately fell victim to the snipers. Those who managed to dodge were chased and finished off by the raven. He had overwhelming advantage in strength and speed over single targets.

"An unidentified drone is approaching!" said someone's voice in the earpiece.

"Take cover!" Diva ordered.

Activate Invisibility!

I stayed where I was, watching the squad disperse inside neighboring buildings. These security measures might not suffice. Raising my head, I identified a Chinese drone. According to my estimates, the army was quite far away from our current location, so it was strange to see a scout in this area. The drone swayed and made a circle over the street. Had it noticed something? It clearly wasn't planning to go away.

"Son of a..."

Our detection would only cause trouble in the current situation. All the way to an attack by our formal allies.

"Take down the drone!" Dmitry ordered.

"Confirm," Diva's voice rang out. "Shoot in threes."

"Leave it to me," I suggested. "Don't interfere!"

"Wait!" the priestess stopped the snipers.

I'd understood that we had to get rid of the spy even earlier. The raven fell like a stone from the sky, knocking the drone down onto the cobblestones with a well-practiced blow. Unlike the undead, the drone couldn't fly after such a strong blow. However, the cameras might not be out of order and could continue to capture and transmit images. It was a familiar model, so I circled around it, took out one of the captured "swords" and, allowing the *bone blade* to flash in front of the camera, struck the final blow. That's it. And no experience...

"I'm guessing they've spotted us?" Dmitry said.

"It's very likely. However, finding our tracks is not the same as identifying us."

* * *

Actually, the destruction of the drone was a dubious step. That's why I chose to do it myself, without letting my allies interfere. Our Foreign

Ministry was no stranger to complaints — if anything, they would pay compensation. A joke.

It was getting dark, so we had to find a place to sleep. We weren't as fussed this time, occupying the first suitable building, and screening the corridor on the top floor. The windows didn't fill me with confidence, while the basement looked like a classic dead end. There was nowhere to run if something happened.

The night passed without incident, and no one complained about the destroyed drone during the communication session. The army was slowly but steadily moving towards the second circle. There were regular undead attacks, which always ended in the unconditional victory of modern weapons —and significant use of ammunition. Moreover, more and more players dared to fight hand-to-hand with the enemy for the experience points.

The decision not to rush and to spend a day preparing strongpoints was a surprise. There were supposed to be four in total—in case of a magic strike—but I strongly suspected that the number reflected how many large factions there were. It certainly played into our hands, allowing us to better prepare for the breakthrough.

Scouts set out for the wall the next morning. At least five followers of Hera possessed suitable abilities in addition to me. Perhaps there were more, but they had refused to give me a full list of abilities this time.

The wall separating the third circle from the

second was an impressive fifteen meters in height. It had suffered relatively little compared to the external fortifications. The goblin map showed only one gap in the southeast, but we were a very long way from it. Blowing up the wall wasn't an option, so we had to find the best point to get through. We had to cross quickly to the other side and, if possible, without attracting too much attention.

"Go on, Bri."

There was minor damage to the wall here, but this didn't change anything. As soon as the ghost drew too close, the undead standing on the wall turned his head towards it, and several dead birds flew up from their perches.

"Back!"

Defense against *Invisibility* was part of the basic set of measures. It meant we couldn't quietly fly over the wall, transporting everyone else in the bags. The skeletons might ignore such a maneuver, but not the birds or the undead "officers". One of whom suddenly threw a clot of darkness at the ghost. Fortunately, he missed, but it showed that we couldn't continue on like this. To hell with it. We'd have to act by force.

*　*　*

When plans have been made and preparations completed, all that remains is to wait, which is the most stressful of all. But everything comes to an end eventually. I focused on my main target.

Bone Knight. Rank: D. Level 5.

"We're starting," I said. "Legion, distract the birds. Remember, your goal is to get their attention, and then retreat to the ambush site. It will be fine as long as you're fast enough."

The raven wasn't happy about the role he'd been given, but the promise of crystals boosted his fighting spirit. We could have used drones but, unlike a real bird, their appearance couldn't be accidental. Furthermore, Legion was agile enough to appear in several locations and make the search for the main group harder. However, I strongly doubted we'd have an easy time in this instance.

"Crystals!"

The raven's appearance made only three birds take off. Apparently, the Bone Knight responsible for this section of the wall didn't rate Legion's abilities or danger too highly.

"There aren't enough of them, go back," I reminded him, just in case. "Kill them and provoke the others to attack."

Legion turned around and, cawing furiously, crashed into one of his pursuers so hard that only a handful of bones showered down. Was he starting to enjoy this? Two tried to attack him from both sides but were enveloped in flame. It couldn't destroy the birds, but somehow weakened and disoriented them, allowing the raven to barrel into them. Legion began to withdraw with a hoarse croak, faking an injury very convincingly.

"Or is he not faking it?' I muttered, watching his pursuers with some concern. Alas, our communication was one-sided at this distance. "Bri, help him!"

"Boss, maybe I shouldn't? The raven is strong, he can handle them!"

"So, make sure that he does, okay?"

"Yes, boss!"

I threw a couple of capsules into my mouth and, switching to the general channel, announced that I was on my way.

Activate Invisibility!

I left the building, which was far enough away that the knight couldn't spot me ahead of time and ran to the wall. Jump!

Activate Flight!

The mana bar dropped rapidly, but I was almost there.

Blink!

As expected, my appearance didn't go unnoticed. _Invisibility_ only helped on the approach. I swung my sword, and the knight's right arm, with the blade growing out of it, was instantly severed. Good, but not enough.

Pushing off from the wall, I used _Flight_ to leap over the enemy and end up behind him. Just like in real knights, the armor on his back was weaker and more mobile. At least the plates had joints where I could drive the blade in. _Split_! Shards of bone sprayed everywhere, allowing the blade to enter deep into the body. It wasn't enough. I couldn't even see the _heart_ behind the armor. _Shrapnel_!

Attention! You have gained 112 SP!

(334/460)

Attention! The Sword of Heresy has consumed 22 SP!

I didn't bother to maintain *Invisibility* since it wasn't helping anyway. Luckily, it was all over quickly. Not a one-shot, of course, but it took less than five seconds.

"Target destroyed," I said, in case the observers had fallen asleep.

"Copy that," Labbe replied. "The Bone Flock has been destroyed, we're on the way. How are you doing?"

"I'm great," I exhaled, grabbing a card out of the air.

Search for Life (E). Saturation: 34/100.

The mana bar was more than half empty, a dozen skeletons were heading towards me, but I felt calm.

"Left leader destroyed," Diva's voice rang out.

"Right leader destroyed," Dmitry confirmed soon after. "I'm withdrawing..."

Excellent. We'd decided to eliminate three knights at once so we could cross this section of the wall. The others had an even simpler task since they didn't need to clean up the retinue. They had to finish off the leader and retreat so as not to alarm the undead standing further away...

I could have just jumped off the wall too, but by now, ordinary skeletons no longer posed a danger to me. There was always a risk, of course, but it seemed acceptable now.

"Are the snipers in position? Cover me, but

don't interfere unless absolutely necessary."

"Roger that."

It took me a few seconds to assess the situation. The wall was wide enough for the enemy to come at me in pairs—and from both sides at once, so I didn't wait for them to surround me. I could even wield a sword one-handed while in combat form, so a spear appeared in my second hand.

Ten little skeletons went out to dine;

One choked his little self and then there were nine.

Or there will be. It was a stupid rhyme. Maybe the *Skald* skill was working again...

The skeleton swung its blade. Parry, strike the leg, and immediately finish off the fallen undead using the spear. Combining two weapons felt a little strange, but the skill level allowed me to complete the move without any mistakes. "One."

Attention! You have received 5 SP! (339/460)

The sword didn't get anything in this case, but I couldn't be too greedy, right? Or could I? The spear disappeared into the card hidden up my sleeve, and I simply ran the next skeleton through with the sword. The unfinished bone sphere resisted the force for a moment, but then I used *Split.*

Attention! You have gained 15 SP! (354/460)

Attention! The Sword of Heresy has consumed 3 SP!

A few seconds to free the blade, and the next skeleton stumbled, losing most of its skull. Snipers, damn them. "I told you not to interfere!"

However, even with most of its head gone, the skeleton remained on the wall, so finishing him off took but a moment.

Attention! You have gained 10 SP! (364/460)

Attention! The Sword of Heresy has consumed 2 SP!

I was actually enjoying this. I never understood why some people wanted a "fair fight". There was no place for honor in battle, and one could mock a corpse. It wouldn't be offended, but it wouldn't stick a sword in my belly either.

"Take care of the two up ahead!"

"Roger that."

If you thought about it, the control center was inside the *heart*, so they needed the head solely to bite. Well, and to see since their magical eyes were in the usual spot. Unlike their brains, which were long gone...

Attention! You have gained 10 SP! (374/460)

Attention! The Sword of Heresy has consumed 2 SP!

The fourth skeleton fell just as easily, but the fifth one kept its skull integrity and tried to attack me even with a bullet in the temple. It was a reminder to stay on my toes and not be distracted by extraneous thoughts. I jumped back, avoiding a sweeping attack. "Die!"

Attention! You have gained 15 SP! (399/460)

Attention! The Sword of Heresy has consumed 3 SP!

I stopped. There were more skeletons atop the wall up ahead, but they were too far away to sense me, and the leader who could direct them had been eliminated. I cast a sidelong glance at the raven who had landed nearby. He seemed to be fine.

"You owe me two, no, three crystals!" Legion reminded me. He was definitely fine.

"Right, as soon as…"

Five other skeleton warriors were advancing from the left, but they weren't difficult to deal with *(449/460)*. I was much stronger than any of them in combat form. They obediently allowed themselves to be deprived of the semblance of life when they drew closer. I could have cleaned up the wall further, but I didn't want to risk it. I had enough experience as it was, so I needed to collect the loot, help my people up onto the wall, and get the hell out of here.

Players remaining: 10230/13000.

Judging by the losses, the army wasn't doing well.

* * *

"Your goal is to continue attacking the wall. Use rifles and magic, make some noise, and then retreat to the fortress. If it comes to the worst, join the army."

"Of course," Cthulhu nodded. "We'll manage, don't worry."

Our movements and operation had left plenty of tracks, so we needed to cover them somehow. The easiest way to do this was to leave a convoy in the undead's area of interest and blame everything on it. I had first thought to send Legion into the raid, but this was better...

Of course, there was no guarantee that everything would work as it should, and the mission was quite dangerous, but a breakaway group had even higher chances of surviving. The army had drawn most of the enemies towards itself, so if the group didn't make critical errors, it would be able to get out. If not, the undead would finish them off, and calm down. At least, I hoped they would.

Frankly speaking, our plan wasn't the best — this strategy was called "stealth" in games, and "attack with a preliminary distracting blow" in the military. We would take advantage of the undead being distracted by the main force to break through as far as possible. Surely, we weren't the only ones to come up with this strategy. I didn't doubt that the other factions would also send in assault groups. However, time and timing played a key role here. Those who went second would have a much smaller chance.

CHAPTER 6
SPIRITUAL SWORD EMBRYO

"QUICKLY, QUICKLY!"

Although thirty fighters remained on the other side, and a significant number of the remaining soldiers slept inside the bags, there were still too many of us... too many to remain unnoticed for long, yet too few to reach the temple by force.

Now that we were inside Sar's second circle, we needed another hidey-hole to sit out the coming storm. I'd bet anything that the missing wall defenders would soon be discovered and draw undead search parties to the spot. They would be looking for us keenly.

So, our first step was to run. To leave the search area as quickly and as far as possible. The wall wasn't a good neighbor either. Towering over the buildings, it allowed observers to spot our squad from afar. All attempts to choose the optimal path didn't guarantee that the dead eyes of a Bone Knight (D) weren't already watching us. Was I being overly dramatic?

"Air!"

A flock of thirty birds appeared overhead, which even Legion couldn't cope with. We used firearms. Luckily, the *Bone Flock* didn't withdraw, swooping down on our group without hesitation, but only a few managed to reach us. A couple, really.

"No sense of self-preservation," I muttered, batting away the small beast with my spear. How did it target me in this crowd? Finishing blow...

Attention! You have gained 1 SP! (450/460)

No loot either. Or was someone getting a little too greedy?

"Legion!"

The raven sensed my mental order and obediently rushed off in pursuit of the surviving birds. Despite the lack of fear, they possessed some tactics, and part of the flock had hung back to observe. Now they were hightailing it, and in different directions. This was bad since we were unlikely to destroy them all.

"Hurry up, boss, we're almost there!" The ghost waved a tentacle, indicating a safe direction, and immediately flew away to check the road further ahead.

"Turn left here," I translated.

Fifteen minutes later, Legion caught up with

us and landed on my arm. "Caw!" he spread his wings. "I fought like a real raven! I caught up and killed three of them!"

"All three or only three of them?"

"There were four left." The raven turned his head away slightly. "The last one joined some kind of flock, and I couldn't finish it off."

Legion shuffled along my arm and settled on my shoulder. It wouldn't have been very comfortable under normal conditions, but I barely felt his weight in the combat form.

The rest of the trip passed without incident. We successfully avoided patrols and reached the next control point. But I doubted that the undead would limit themselves to formalities. They knew of our existence now and they would search for us until the end.

"You know that's not going to work, right?" Diva came up to me. "We won't be able to sit this out, we need a better plan."

"I suppose you have one?"

"That's right," the priestess nodded. "We'll have to split up temporarily. Send a squad to divert their attention. It should be headed by someone strong and experienced."

"Me, you mean?"

"You, me or Dmitry. Who will manage the best, do you reckon?"

*   *   *

To a certain extent, it was sacrifice. Since the undead knew about a large squad, we had to show them a squad. Draw away most of the search groups, and feed them the bait. Or, according to the official version, "draw the pursuers to a different area, then break away, and proceed to the meeting place."

"Great plan," I nodded. "But, you know, corpses would be more convincing."

I wasn't even joking—faking the second squad's death would protect the remaining players, allowing them to safely make the last dash.

"You don't need to make a monster out of me." Diva grimaced. "I don't wish death on anyone, I'm quite sure that you'll be able to get out. And if not... that's the price. If we fail, billions will die eventually."

Only if we failed the mission, of course. However, we're not the Battlestar Galactica, right? Humanity's last hope and all that?

"How's the army doing?"

"There are too many skellies, and they just keep coming. At this rate, the ammo will run out before the undead."

"It's that bad?"

"Well, it's good for us. It means that the undead have pulled their main forces into that region and we have a good chance of slipping through before they return."

"So we should keep moving?"

"It won't work. We're too far away, and there are probably still undead out there. If we don't throw them a bone, we will be met face-to-face and destroyed on the approach. We need to divert their attention. I'm sure you can handle it."

"I remember our agreement. Shall we decide on a meeting place?"

*　*　*

The discussion didn't take much time, allowing us to settle on a new tactic. We could decide the rest along the way, via radio communication.

"Right, the first and second platoons are coming with me." Alas, I couldn't take everyone for several reasons. "The third one stays with the main squad. I also need volunteers from among the players. They will be Yuki, Steel and... Tatra?"

"Yes?"

"We have a dangerous mission ahead of us," I clarified. "Our squad has to distract the undead. I can't guarantee that everyone will return alive and unharmed. You need to decide if you're going to come with us or if you'd rather stay with the others."

"What's safer?"

"The second option, for sure. You're weak, and I won't be able to always protect you. But if you stay, you won't get any stronger. It's your choice."

"I'll sta... come with you," the girl decided. "Because if I don't get stronger, I'll die again, right?"

"That's right," I nodded.

"Twenty-five people crossed the wall," Diva interjected. "You're one short. It would be better if your group had the same number, in case the undead can count. I have a suitable candidate. You've met Anastasia, right?" Diva indicated Dragonfly.

As befits a good commander, the priestess knew her people not only by their nicknames, but also by their names. I could have taken someone from the third platoon or summoned Armet from his card, but I nodded, accepting the addition.

"We move out in five minutes."

I didn't see a reason to panic. The task seemed somewhat dangerous, but I would have come up with something better if there were no escape routes. Besides, by leaving the main squad, I regained my freedom of movement. There was no certainty that our goals were *truly* the same.

* * *

"What's your plan?" Yuki enquired. "You have a plan, right? Besides gathering all the undead in this part of the city, and then dying heroically in an unequal battle?"

"We'll make a bit of a mess to start with, then move away, and start preparing for a fight."

"And then what?"

"We'll play it by ear," I shrugged my shoulders. "As we always do. Don't worry, I'll get you out. Just don't leave yourself exposed."

The next hour passed the same way, except that we didn't avoid the undead found, but destroyed them diligently. I didn't even have to help. There was no need, and my experience bar was very close to the next level. Levelling up right now would not be a good idea.

Attention! Access to the Server permitted!
Summon a goblin?
Yes/No

"Stop, stop, stop." I looked around. "We'll set up our defense... here."

"Are you sure?" Oleg asked. "This isn't the best place."

"It's no worse than other places," I nodded. "At least there is a connection to the Server here."

"Really?" said Steel, who had been listening in. "I don't feel anything."

"Connection is not access, only the chance to get a reply. Let's hope this "ozone hole" covers the building too."

I wondered if it was possible to isolate a world from the System using such a barrier. To stop the digitization, the missions, the influx of monsters, and creation of new players? I doubted it since the goblins had remained _units_ despite the block. On the other hand, the vast majority of objects around us weren't Systemic. And the animals, such as the horses, hadn't turned into _monsters_.

"Now what?" Oleg inquired once we entered

the building.

"We've drawn enough attention to ourselves, so we can lay low for a while. Screen a couple of rooms and contact the other groups. Learn the news. In addition, I advise everyone to rest and eat while we have the opportunity. We have about three hours. I'm planning to improve a couple of skills."

* * *

Level 23 (450/460).

The question was, what would happen when I reached the twenty-fifth level? Legion struggled to explain—his memories were too scattered, and the specifics depended on the race. There were answers in the vision I saw when I found the *True Heart*, but no matter how hard I tried, I couldn't remember the details. If I had to choose between curiosity and an extra chance of survival, I would prefer the latter.

Attention! Do you want to improve Blink to Level 2? (200 SP)

Yes/No

Rank has increased! Skill strength has been greatly increased!

Choose the development branch:

1) Saving Mana. The energy cost of a jump is significantly reduced.

2) Distance. The maximum distance increases significantly.

3) Flow Control. Allows you to control mana consumption more accurately, depending on the distance and presence of obstacles. The maximum distance varies, but price increases exponentially.

4) Scope of Control. Allows you to specify the landing spot within an area.

5) Expulsion. Any object present at your landing spot is forcefully thrown away.

Initially, I had wanted to reduce the cost or increase the jump distance, however, the first two options didn't provide exact figures.

Mana: 2429/2429.

Blink currently required one thousand units of energy, letting me move within a radius of five meters. Even with my "regeneration pills", I couldn't use it more than three times in one fight. Twice, really, or I didn't have enough mana left for anything else.

Flow Control was a kind of compromise between saving mana and increasing range. There were no numbers again, but compromise options could rarely compete with specialized ones in efficiency. The ability to jump further than the limit was interesting, but I hadn't done so badly in school that I'd forgotten what "exponentially" meant. It'd be good if it meant arithmetic, and not geometric progression. I remembered that, according to the legend, the inventor of chess asked for a "small" reward from his ruler—just a grain of rice on the first chess square. Two grains on the second square, four grains on the third, and so on, doubling the amount each time until all the squares were filled. In the end, there would not have been enough rice in the entire history of mankind to fill the whole chess board. When the wise king discovered that he couldn't keep his promise, he ordered the inventor's head to be cut off—because one shouldn't laugh at those in power. And wrote about a generous reward in the legend. After that trick, the chroniclers weren't inclined to argue with him...

Okay, maybe I'd invented the ending myself, but the legend showed how exponential growth worked in a very clear way. A jump of ten or twenty meters could easily end up draining my reserves, and cause serious magical exhaustion...

The *Scope of Control* was a very interesting option too, both for combat and for escape, but not with my amount of mana.

As for *Expulsion*, it turned the skill into a dangerous weapon. Right now, I would be thrown out of the way if the spot was already occupied, but if it was the opposite, it created some interesting possibilities. Like the ability to teleport to an enemy's exact location or inside the walls, punching holes in them. And yet I was reluctant to select that option.

Attention! (Intuition) Consumes mana, the amount depends on the object's weight and size at the end point.

Right, of course. It had been a while since the System had played such tricks, so I'd grown complacent. If it was all tied to mana, then any serious obstacle at the destination would, at the least, leave me without energy, and, at the most, kill me. It helped when I used my brain once in a while.

Attention! You have chosen Saving Mana! The cost of using the skill has halved!

The clarification made me smile—now I could perform not two, but four jumps. Plus, I'd have a little mana left over for other actions. Of course, the ability to instantly break away from an enemy by twenty meters, ignoring obstacles, could save my life in many situations. Although _Scope of Control_ would have been useful too, by letting me to jump to a precise point. Well, I'd made my choice, and twenty meters was better than ten, no matter how I looked at it. In the end, this ability might allow me to get inside the temple first. Or escape from it... Of course, if there wasn't a block and the walls could be penetrated by this type of skill. This was far from certain, but it was possible. After all, the Great Y had fallen a long time ago, so even if there had been divine protection, it should have faded by now. I couldn't know for sure, but I preferred to consider all options.

Level 23 (250/460).

Despite the Rank E improvement, it didn't take much time—about three minutes, which included me considering all the options.

"Don't approach me and don't get in my way," I ordered, and stepped out into the center of the hall. I wanted to avoid interfering with the screening of the room, so I'd have to put up with the witnesses.

Attention! Do you want to improve Sword Fighting to Level 4? (60 SP)

Yes/No

I actually enjoyed the Sword Dance, and it didn't take long. My high *Intelligence*, along with the other, similar skills, allowed me to absorb new knowledge much faster. It took only twenty-five minutes before I lowered the sword. I wasn't even out of breath.

"Pretty good, pretty good," Yuki clapped her hands. "That was the fourth level, wasn't it?"

"That's right. I'm about take the fifth one."

"I can help you master it if you want. I'm a *Master*, and it's easier to reach your maximum in a fight with someone stronger. Even to surpass them."

"Why not? Let's go!"

Attention! Do you want to improve Sword Fighting to Level 5? (80 SP)

Yes/No

I must admit, unlike most previous fights, the Japanese girl didn't try to overwhelm me, but genuinely helped me to master the strokes. I might have broken through her defenses thanks to my attributes and combat form, but we had a different goal.

"Not bad, you're almost there..."

Minute after minute passed, and I abruptly realized that I was on an equal footing with her, even though the sword was Yuki's top weapon. She no longer treated me gently, and our strikes took on a new strength and fury.

Attention! Your Sword Fighting (F) skill has increased to Sword Master (E).

You must choose a specialization.

"That's enough!"

At my command, the girl jumped back, sheathed her katana and bowed briefly. I had to admit that despite my initial prejudice against this weapon, the System swords were much more advanced than historical ones, and the skill made Yuki truly dangerous.

"Thank you for your help, Master," I bowed in response.

"You're welcome, Vasily-dono."

Yuki smiled, returned to the wall, and took some dry rations from her bag. I was a little hungry myself, but I had to finish what I started, so I went back to the messages.

Attention! You are a follower of the Spear School!

An additional School cannot be selected!

Choose a specialized skill:

— Iron Grip (E-, 1/3). *Only death can make your fingers unclench from around a handle. The hand is covered by a protective field when the skill is activated. Requires Qi.*

— Spiritual Sword Embryo (E+, 1/5). *Places a ghost sword in your dantian.*

Damn it! Out of the whole range of skills, I was offered two that were linked to *Spiritual Strength,* of which I had very little. Moreover, the second one seemed to be rare and valuable, but I wasn't sure why I needed it and what it would bring me.

"Beware of the System bearing gifts..." I muttered.

Attention (Intuition)! If you delay, the skill will be selected automatically based on your attributes and preferences.

Time remaining: 28 minutes and 31 seconds.

Right, as if it could be any other way. The very concept of a weapon embryo raised a lot of questions. However, after checking the match percentage, which was hidden by default, I discovered that it was only 69%. Not enough to try to guess. I approached the other corner, where the raven was preening his feathers. I needed a consultation this time.

"Legion, do you know what a 'Spiritual Sword Embryo' is?"

"I might have heard of something like that. But I can't rem..."

A crystal appeared in my hand, and the bird's eyes lit up with avarice. Legion furiously ruffled his feathers, picked up pace, and crashed into the wall.

"I'll remember, I'll remember! The crystal!"

"Any luck?" I grimaced. Hopefully this method worked.

"I remembered!" Legion suddenly froze. "We three-legged crows never resort to the weapons of the weak. Why have a sword when you have claws, beak, and the divine flame? But I've heard of it!

Some strong practitioners cultivate it inside their dantian."

"Is it bad for you?"

"It's very good for you! However, it's difficult, expensive, and dangerous."

"So, what is it?"

"A scalable weapon that is always with you! Or an ability to strengthen your attacks? *Spiritual Swords* don't appear by themselves, their features depend on who left the legacy. A swordsman who possesses an undeveloped embryo is much stronger than a swordsman who doesn't have one at all. Even the *main disciple* in a sect might not get one!"

"Do spear embryos exist?"

The sword wasn't my top weapon, after all, and I was reluctant to accept a bonus if it stopped me from getting a similar ability for the spear in the future. Although the System rarely imposed direct restrictions, they existed, nevertheless.

"Of course. If you are lucky enough to find such a rarity, you can cultivate it too. It will be even more difficult and dangerous, but possible."

Hmm... I didn't ask what the raven thought of *Iron Grip*. I could see from the number of available levels and the minus that it was a garbage skill from one of the weak schools. I'd seen something similar for the spear when I was going through the options.

Time remaining: 23 minutes and 34 seconds.

"I see, thank you. Is there anything else I

should know?"

"Yes... no. I... don't remember."

I didn't suggest that he bang his head against the wall again. Throwing a crystal to the confused raven—it would come back to me later anyway—I went into another room. I preferred to do this without witnesses. I had complicated feelings about this...

*   *   *

Select Spiritual Sword Embryo!

Receiving the bonus was slightly differently this time: something like a portal appeared above me, and a piece of metal, vaguely reminiscent of a sword, floated down. It wasn't even a card. I'd gotten used to the System providing most bonuses in "standard packaging", but not this time. I opened my mouth, and the *Embryo* flew rapidly inside, dropping into my stomach. I didn't like the beginning...

"I wonder if I can claim a million dollars now?"

Just a joke since this had nothing to do with pregnancy. Despite the similar terminology. According to legends, the dantian wasn't just a reservoir for storing qi, but also a subspace that could hold certain special items. Apparently, that's where the embryo had gone. So, there was no need to be afraid that it would grow into a two-meter-long *Spiritual Sword* and cut its way to freedom one day. I doubted the System would kill me in this way as a reward.

A second later, these idle thoughts went out the window. My *Spiritual Energy* began to move, flowing into the dantian and disappearing without a trace. The bar started crawling to the left, but not for long. The *window* that the *embryo* had fallen out of was still open, and *Qi* flowed profusely from it. The situation stabilized, and the bar crept back to the right, quickly reaching maximum... and then sharply exceeding it.

Qi: 109 units.

I bent over, pressing my hands to my stomach. The bar reflected the processes taking place inside. The *embryo* in the dantian drew in *Spiritual Energy* that my *channels* weren't ready for, and forced them wider, allowing me to grow stronger.

Qi: 132... 133... 134 units.

It... hurt, although not as badly after for the first few seconds. It was quite bearable. Apparently, the creation of this embryo would be quite complicated. Fortunately, the System was doing everything for me, and all I could do was wait and hope there wouldn't be any problems.

Spiritual Strength: + 1 (2).

The message was not unexpected—I'd seen the Qi bar approach 200 units. Despite the training bonus, I could feel that my dantian and channels were at their limit. I'd already undergone Spiritual Deviation once, and it wasn't an experience I wanted to repeat.

"I hate *Spiritual Strength*," I muttered.

But not enough to give it up a second time. Hard work pays off, right? Or is followed by failure and death, but I preferred not to think about that.

Attention! Convert the divine power (Heresy of Cain) into Qi?

Yes/No

Although my *Spiritual Strength* remained at two, the energy bar had increased by 900 units, which had stabilized the situation. Had I done it?

Qi: 1,112 units.

Congratulations! The Spiritual Sword Embryo has formed!

Quality: Very Low.

Attention! (Intuition) The embryo's quality depends on the energy invested in its creation!

A very timely warning, except the portal above my head was rapidly closing, and the full bar trembled and started crawling to the left again. No freebies then?

"Damn it to hell."

Thrusting my hand into the *Ring*, I took out a handful of spirit stones and demonic cores. Although I'd handed over most of the loot to the state, I had kept some of it. Time to spend it. I placed my hand on top, and the energy flowed faster, filling the emptying vessels. It was still dangerous, but now the energy flow was much weaker, so I had greater control over it. There was more energy in the stones, but it was cleaner and more concentrated in the cores.

Attention! The Spiritual Sword Embryo has improved!

Quality: Low.

It wasn't that hard. My stores wouldn't last long, but I knew what to do next.

Summon a goblin!

"I need spirit stones, Uli. A lot of them, right now."

"There aren't much where I am, but *Fifty-Six* should be guarding the main vault today. Everything we've collected since last time is stored there."

Summon a goblin!

Another goblin appeared before me, glancing nervously around him—it seemed he'd left his weapon on the other side. How fortunate that I'd decided to number the Immortals, and then list them according to the gradation.

"My... my Lord."

"Your Lord requires spirit stones," Uli interrupted. "You will return and bring him..."

"A bag," I guessed, in response to the unspoken question. "I'll let you know if I need more."

Speed was more important right now—the stones were crumbling to dust one by one in my hand. It would normally take me hours to absorb one of these.

Recall the goblin!

I tried to draw the energy more slowly, to give my courier time to obtain the cargo. Even holding the bag—a clear sign of my power—he could still run into some problems. I wasn't bothered by the fact that these stones were supposed to be send to

Earth. The *Dungeon* was full of them, so the goblins would collect more, but this chance might not come again soon...

Summon a goblin!

Taking the bag, I emptied its contents on the floor. The bag wasn't that large, but a whole mound of high-quality stones lay before of me. It would last a while. I didn't fall atop the mound but picked the stones up one by one and drained them. The rate of absorption was terrifying and only grew, accompanied by pain in my channels. Or my meridians, to use the correct terminology.

Qi: 1,199 units.

The Qi reached the next limit, but the last unit didn't want to be added. Apparently, I'd hit some kind of obstacle. What if I picked up two large stones? Five seconds later, they crumbled in my hands.

Spiritual Strength: + 1 (3).

Plus two attributes! I had practically gone up a level, thereby justifying my choice. However, if it wasn't for *Cassandra's Whisper*, *Instant Death*, and *Backup*, I wouldn't have dared to continue.

"Have you reached a breakthrough?" The raven cawed. "Congratulations! This is the third layer, if I'm not mistaken? You could even be accepted as an inner disciple in some mediocre sect."

"I'll take that as a compliment. Why didn't you warn me that I'd need stones?"

"I didn't know? Or I forgot, I'm not sure."

"Pfft..."

"Use the demonic cores next time. The Qi in these stones isn't pure enough. You're just lucky that your cultivation is so small."

Attention! The Spiritual Sword Embryo has improved!

Quality: Average.

The Qi bar was growing more slowly now, but the stones were disintegrating by the dozens. Would one bag be enough? I didn't know what kind of object was growing inside me, but it was eating for ten...

"I hope it's worth it."

My greed was to blame for everything—but if not for greed, where would I be now? Rotting in a grave, most likely. I hadn't sent the goblin back for this reason.

"Fifty-sixth! I need more stones, and demonic cores. How many do you have?"

"Another eight bags of stones of varying quality. And one container of rat cores."

"Bring them all. I will return whatever is left over. Tell them that this is my order!"

"Yes, my Lord."

The goblin disappeared, and I focused on embryo improvement. That's what it was called, right? The energy flowing through the channels not only damaged them, but also expanded and strengthened them at the same time. As long as I didn't overdo it.

Activate Great Healing!

Hard to say if it actually helped, but I felt a little better. The goblin returned, emptied a couple of bags of stones before me, and stepped respectfully aside. More, more, more...

Attention! The Spiritual Sword Embryo has improved!

Quality: High.

Was that it? But the flow only intensified, and now I couldn't keep up. Plunging my arms deep into bags of demonic cores, I fell back onto the mountain of stones, feeling myself sink deeper as they crumbled around me. The barrier shuddered and then collapsed, allowing me to reach another peak.

Spiritual Strength: + 1 (4).

"Pour out the stones over me, quickly!"

Luckily, the goblin was smart and didn't argue, but dumped another bag over me. I think that's how a sultan drowned in an old cartoon. Can there ever be too much gold?

Attention! The Spiritual Sword Embryo has improved!

Quality: Very High.

The absorption force increased dramatically, scaring me, and then...

Attention! The Spiritual Sword Embryo has improved!

Quality: Excellent.

For several seconds, the monster inside me tried to demand more food, but there was simply nothing left. Everything the goblin brought had turned to dust. Judging by his baffled expression, this even included the stones in bags that were a few meters away from me.

Congratulations! The Spiritual Sword Embryo (D) has formed!
Qi: 0/1,399 units.

Strangely, I felt only emptiness inside. It was time to get something to eat.

CHAPTER 7
BAIT

Attention! The Spiritual Sword Embryo has reached the first stage!
Transformation completed!
Name has been changed to Spiritual Sword (D)!

NOW WHAT? The thing was inside me, so using *Identification* would be difficult. Closing my eyes, I caught the response of my dantian. Perhaps information about my acquisition will be somewhere in the personal settings?

I was right, and it took me no more than a minute to find the new item. The System viewed the sword as part of my body, to the extent that its outline was displayed on the "self-diagnosis" screen. However, instead of *Vitality*, this limb of mine had *Durability*. I mentally jabbed at the icon.

Spiritual Sword

Type: *System Artifact.*

Rank: *D.*

Development stage: *1/5.*

Quality: *Excellent.*

Element: *Unknown.*

Attributes:

Durability: 64.

Sharpness: 10.

Instincts: 6.

Description:

A spiritual weapon crafted by a Great Master. Contains a piece of his Legacy.

Features:

— System Weapon (D). Enables the owner to absorb 60% of the victim's spirit and life force.

— A semi-material symbiont. The artifact can change its size and density and is stored inside the dantian.

— Spiritual connection. The weapon is bound to its owner's soul, making it easier to control but its destruction will result in severe injuries.

— Scalability. Rank can be upgraded.

— Legacy. Contains the Legacy of an unknown Sword school.

— High quality. The item has high Durability, making it difficult to destroy.

— Hunger (I). The sword requires Qi and Vitality, not only for development but also for its existence. If saturation drops to zero, the user's life will be at risk.

Stage I:

— Overlay. Its semi-material form allows it to strengthen material swords.

— Qi storage. Enables the owner to store spiritual energy inside.

Additional:

*— **Related quest.** Raise the weapon level to five. An additional Sword School will become available as a reward.*

Qi storage (I): 0/1,000.

Saturation: 17,842/1,000,000.

Owner: Vasily.

Well, what could I say? There were a lot of new terms to consider. The benefits of my acquisition weren't completely clear, but I could see the disadvantages. There was a symbiont inside me that had to be fed regularly, otherwise, it was probably devour me. Moreover, it had to be fed not with experience points, which I'd already gotten used to, but with qi. Fortunately, my source was quite capable of maintaining a positive balance without additional injections. At least the reserve was filling up faster than *Saturation* was falling.

Saturation: 17,841/1,000,000.

It was quite impressive. Apparently, this was where the energy reserves absorbed at the end had gone. However, were they supposed to go here from the start? The *Embryo* had gone through six stages of quality evolution before becoming a sword, from *very* low to excellent. Based on my observations, the System had two favorite numbers — five and seven. The sword was supposed to only reach Rank E, however, it had reached Rank D. There was a possibility that this wasn't the limit and there was one more level. Or was the unactivated *Embryo* the first level? Right, what was the use of guessing?

"Legion, did you know that it would take a lot of qi to develop the *Embryo*?"

"No, but I'm not surprised," the raven raised his head. "If it's a *Spiritual Sword*, then it should absorb *Spiritual Strength*, right?"

Was it just me, or was he mocking me a little? It was irritating, but I simply accepted it without complaint. Even if I'd known in advance, I still wouldn't have found enough spiritual stones and demonic cores in time.

"Have you ever heard anything about *Spiritual Sword* quality?"

"Quality?" Legion tilted his head thoughtfully. "No, I don't remember."

I didn't bother taking out more crystals to encourage his memory. Even if there was some Divine quality beyond Excellent, it wouldn't change anything. Perhaps the sword would improve again when it reached the next *stage*, yet I doubted that it was directly related to *quality*. I had been lucky to have such a large supply of spiritual stones at hand. And the awakening process was no simple matter, even though the System had done all the work for me.

Now I just had to obtain a million units of qi to increase the *development stage* of the *Spiritual*

Sword and see what happened next. But even for me, a kind of "spiritual stone mine" owner, the amount seemed too big. Plus, the sword would only consume more after that, right?

While I couldn't take a bite out of *Saturation*, *Qi storage* had, in fact, expanded my personal reserve. Significantly, adding a thousand units in one go. Under normal conditions, I'd have to raise the *Spiritual Strength* attribute to 10 to get that much. It was a real cheat, no matter how I looked at it.

Qi: 16/2,399 units.

The scale had frozen just before the next attribute increase, however, I understood that it would be difficult to take the last step. I need resources...

"Uli!" I remembered about the elder standing by the wall. "We may need reinforcements."

"How many?"

"A few hundred soldiers in heavy gear." I touched my headset. "Oleg, is the list of things we need ready? Can you bring it here?"

A few minutes later, the lieutenant entered the room and handed me a slightly wrinkled notebook. I ran my eyes down the list — it looked like Oleg ought to go to medical school. All the makings were there, although it was still possible to read his handwriting. Uh-huh... I took out a pen and quickly added a few more positions and notes. That's it for now.

"Give the notebook to Khan," I turned to the goblin and passed the bag to him. "You should teleport the weapons immediately, but you have an hour or two to prepare the rest. Best not to delay."

"It will be done, my Lord."

"I also need spiritual stones and demonic cores, so collect everything you can in that time."

"Yes, my Lord," the goblin bowed again. "But there is little time, so I'm afraid that we won't be able to collect much."

"Well, whatever you can. Everything will be paid for, don't worry. You did well too, Fifty-Six."

After giving the goblins instructions, I sent them back home. Well, that was some of the matters resolved. I wasn't planning to spend more stones on improving the *Spiritual Sword* anytime soon, but I felt naked without supplies. With all this theory, I'd almost forgotten about practice.

First, I tried to take the sword out of the dantian, but nothing happened. This could change in the future, but for now, we have what we have.

Taking out the *Sword of Heresy*, I swung it carefully and scoured a line on the stone wall. It was an impossible trick for conventional weapons: the blade would have probably broken instead. Now, let's check the skill.

Activate Overlay!

The sword in my hands was enveloped in a ghostly haze, and there was a waft of ozone. Lightning? Speaking of "unknown element"... I made the second cut parallel to the first, and the scratch was slightly deeper and longer. Not bad. It was hard to measure the improvement, but there was a definite difference. In the cost too — a single blow reduced my *reserve* by 300 units. Well, that was enough experimenting for now.

Attention! Convert divine power (Heresy of Cain) into mana?

Yes/No

I had almost no skills linked to qi, so mana would be more useful right now. And, considering the symbiont and the increase in the attribute, I couldn't complain about a lack of energy.

* * *

If you don't drink and smoke, you'll be healthy when you croak.

I took a bite out of yet another chocolate bar. It was a nasty, high-calorie item, but I wasn't worried about ruining my health with poor nutrition. Even without *Healing*, a player became as healthy as a horse simply by increasing *Vitality*. In theory, those of us whose immunity had surpassed the natural limits could handle even incurable diseases. So, I was simply making up the calorie deficit while doing the rounds at the same time.

I didn't want to waste time on a proper meal. Perhaps I was wrong — the units stationed on the *Shard* had a dining room where I could order something more substantial. But I didn't want to eat too much on the eve of battle, plus I had a lot to do. Medics needed to be on duty too, in addition to equipment and fighters. There was no guarantee that I'd be able to rescue all the wounded since my mana wasn't limitless. Although our goal wasn't to destroy all enemies, but to draw their attention, so cargo was enough for now.

Summon a goblin!

Not the elder this time. Eighteen was playing the role of porter, appointed to this position for his outstanding *Strength*. Goblinoid blood gave him a bonus, so he looked very impressive even at Level 3. For a goblin...

"We have gathered all you asked for, my Lord."

Taking the bag from him, I began pulling out machine guns, ammunition, and explosives. A lot of explosives. It was stupid to spend your own reserves if you didn't know when you could replenish them.

"Oleg, make sure the preparations go smoothly, and take down the screening. Leave it in one room as a last resort. But make it so it can be quickly removed or destroyed."

Our preparations were coming to an end, so there was no point in hiding from the undead any further. On the contrary, our goal was to be discovered as soon as possible.

"Of course."

Recall the goblin!

I had plenty of things to do as well. For example, determine the focal points for the *Temporal Barrier*. Fortunately, I had plenty of experience points for this trick, and *Backup* was ready to go again.

Level 23 (110/460).

* * *

"Sergeant Kozin speaking," I head a sentry's voice in the earpiece. "I've spotted a group of undead. Eleven skeletons, plus... a knight, I think. They're moving along the western street and will be here in about five minutes."

That was it, the lull was coming to an end. Of course, I could still put the squad in the bag and hide under *Invisibility*—or inside the tiny, screened room, but the undead wouldn't rest until they found someone. And if we didn't become that "someone", it would be the main squad. So, the thought was fleeting, on the edge of consciousness. Just an option.

Could it be that I was... nervous? Not enough to activate the *Calculating Mind*, but the jitters were noticeable. Dozens of lives depended on my decisions, and the plan was full of holes and assumptions.

"We wait!" I announced my decision. "Don't shoot, let them spot us first."

Right, the western street. Where the hell was that? He could have just pointed to it, as they say in the joke. With a glance at the compass sewn into my sleeve, I determined the direction, went to the breach, and looked out. The area I could see from this position was clear, but other sentries confirmed the enemy's approach. All we could do was wait.

A couple of minutes later, the undead appeared in sight, and, as always in such situations, I abruptly calmed down. It was as the sergeant had said. I could see, even without *Identification*, that they were higher-level skeletons. Around Level 5, while the commander...

Bone Knight. Rank: D. Level unknown.

Above Level 10, at a guess. In any case, scanning was dangerous since it could be detected. We were pretending to be a squad naively trying to hide in one of the buildings and waiting for the owners of the city to come and kill us all...

"Don't shoot before I give the order!" I reminded everyone. Sometimes, it was better to repeat the obvious than to deal with the results of a mistake.

The undead walked at a leisurely pace, and at some point, goosebumps crawled over my skin. A clear sign of a *Search Wave*. Now?

"Everyone get ready!"

However, the undead didn't behave as expected. They didn't turn and attack but continued to follow their route.

"The enemy is moving at the same speed and in the same direction."

Do we attack? I thought for a moment, but then shook my head — although few people could see the gesture. It was a pity to let such juicy prey get away, but I'd learned to control these impulses long ago.

"Let them go," I declared. "Did anyone feel the

scan?"

"I felt something strange," Yuki replied. "Like a tickle."

"Me too," Dragonfly said. The confessions ended there.

"Steel? Tatra?" I asked.

"Nothing," replied a man's voice.

"I got distracted," Tatra said. "So, nothing for me."

The units were silent for an obvious reason: they didn't have *Wisdom.* However, even the players didn't sound confident. However, I was sure that the knight had scanned the house, which meant he knew of our presence. Yet instead of attacking, he pretended that he hadn't sensed anything. It was the action of an intelligent being who had understood the difference in strength and preferred to retreat.

"The enemy is getting away."

If the Bone Knight had tried to attack or even sped up sharply when he detected us, we would have attacked. The events reminded me of a chess game, but we couldn't let the opponent know that we were playing along. Let him think that he had managed to deceive our vigilance. Our interests aligned for now.

"He spotted us, no doubt," I announced my conclusion. "So, he'll inform the others about us soon and things will get interesting. Prepare for a fight."

* * *

Soon is a relative concept. It took the undead several hours to encircle our shelter. Moreover, they did it sensibly, not lurking in sight, placing sentries along possible escape routes, and massing their forces to crush us for sure.

If it weren't for Bri—whom the undead ignored, if they even noticed the ghost—we wouldn't have realized the full scale of what was happening. But more and more Bone Birds were flitting across the sky, and my scan detected dozens of Bone Chimeras nearby. Spies.

"Undead! Contact!"

The floor in the corner of the room exploded, releasing a Bone Chimera. Like rats, some of them had decided to attack from below. Their position hadn't been a secret for a while, so the creature ran into my blade as soon as it appeared.

Attention! You have gained 1 SP! (111/460)

"Follow the plan!"

If we hadn't been prepared, there might have been turmoil, even panic. It's hard to keep watching the streets when you have dozens of creatures running around behind you. Flimsy creatures, but still capable of inflicting a fatal wound. Only the combat group was fighting the chimeras right now, while the rest of the squad protected the archers and sentries.

Attention! You have gained 1 SP!

(112/460)

Attention! You have gained 1 SP!
(113/460)

Attention! You have gained 1 SP!
(114/460)

Three more chimeras clambered out after the first, and then the flow stopped. The danger then came from the street as dozens of creatures poured in through the doorway. And came across me again.

Attention! You have gained 1 SP!
(115/460)

...

Attention! You have gained 1 SP!
(125/460)

There were a lot of chimeras—as if someone had decided to get rid of old junk—but they were helpless against me. The combat form provided sufficient protection on its own, while the special armor made a death machine out of me. And yet, only eleven frags. No matter how hard I tried, I couldn't finish them all. Assessing the situation at once, the monsters scattered through the building in search of easier targets. They couldn't do something like that without a "puppet master".

"I'm wounded!" someone's voice came through the earpiece. "Cover me!"

I grimaced but didn't move. We had divided the building into zones, with a member of the combat group responsible for each one.

Activate Search for Life!

The wave spread in all directions, allowing me

to assess the situation. Until things got really bad, I'd only help my neighbors, who seemed to be doing fine on their own.

"Damn it," I swore. "I'm reminding you all! Don't shoot unless absolutely necessary!"

Shots rang out more and more often, which was becoming dangerous. Apart from ricocheting, the bullets could easily pierce the old beams and keep going. Given that the chimeras were small and nimble, a lot of bullets were going into the lower floors. The more shooting, the higher the risk of someone getting hurt.

"Birds incoming!" a calm voice announced. "A huge flock is approaching!"

"Destroy it!" I gave the order. "Fire at will."

Not because it was necessary, but because it brought order to the chaos around me. I shifted my grip on the sword and stabbed through the floor. The blade met slight resistance, and...

Attention! You have gained 1 SP! (126/460)

The machine guns roared to life, thinning out the flock I couldn't see, but several creatures still managed to swoop inside. I struck with my gauntlet, knocking down a bird that flew in through the window. Step, punch...

Attention! You have gained 1 SP! (127/460)

"They're retreating!"

So quickly? We'd assumed that skeletons would follow the chimeras, but it seemed that we'd fought too well. I jumped, stepping on a chimera trying to reach the exit, finished it off, and then took out the next one. Another one, and another one... that was it, and when I returned, I stabbed the sword into a wounded creature crawling to a hole.

Attention! You have gained 1 SP! (132/460)

"Not bad, not bad!"

I glanced at Legion perched on an old wardrobe and ignored the praise. The raven had done very little in this battle—the last thing we needed was a fire in here. He was right about one thing: we'd won. It was time to collect the bones and loot, and to count our losses.

CHAPTER 8

THE TRAP

ALTHOUGH THIS WAS NOTHING more than a battle test, we had our first wounded. Six of them, and one had been seriously injured by three Bone Birds attacking at once. By the time his neighbors intervened, it was too late.

"How are you holding up, soldier?" I asked.

Warrant Officer Nosov turned his head towards me and took off his glasses, revealing bloody pits instead of eyes. He'd already been given painkillers, so he was quite calm, almost too much so.

"I can't see anything."

I glanced at Dragonfly, who was looking after him, and the girl shook her head. His weapon had been taken away from him to make sure he couldn't shoot himself.

"Can I take a look?" I touched his forehead,

making the man twitch and activated *Healing*. There was nothing left to save, the eyes had been pecked clean, so I spent the minimum amount of energy. Just to heal the damage slightly. Normal medicine was powerless here, and magic would take a lot of time.

"Can they be saved? I think I can feel my left eye, even though I can't see anything."

"Don't worry, the Department doesn't abandon its people. You know what we can do, right? I'm going to send you to the *Dungeon*, where you will rest, and then the healers will grow you a pair of new eyes."

"I've heard it's possible, but, frankly, I don't quite believe it."

Would you like to place Unnamed Unit inside the Slaver's Bag (C)?

Yes/No

Request sent.

"Don't doubt it. Accept the request, and everything will be fine."

In a sense, the warrant officer had been lucky. He would be safe and unlikely to take part in the upcoming hostilities. He could level up on the rats, I suppose.

"Thank you, Commander."

Request confirmed.

The soldier disappeared a second later, allowing me to take care of the other wounded. Fortunately, the others were doing much better. Their wounds were superficial, so a little magic and a bandage—and the fighter returned to the ranks. There was no point in sending them to the *Dungeon*. We probably didn't need reinforcements just yet.

Summon a goblin!

"Here, my Lord," Uli bowed. "This is all that we managed to collect at short notice."

It wasn't so bad. Spiritual stones were used for lighting, and demonic cores were used as internal currency, so Uli had brought two containers of the first and a container of the second. Although the goblin clearly had to requisition supplies to collect even that much.

"I'm pleased with you, and this will be enough for now. However, I will need new batches in the future, so you should keep going."

Only nine empties had fallen out of the twenty-two chimeras I finished off. It was a below average result, but loot of this kind hadn't excited me in a while. Just an ordinary resource. Taking out ten small cores, I began to absorb energy. Although the *Spiritual Sword* didn't reach the speed that the *Embryo* had demonstrated at the final stages, I replenished my reserve of qi and even used a little for *Saturation* in just ten minutes.

"Shit."

The demonic core melted, and I finally realized what had been bothering me all this time. Even though the undead wasn't attacking us, they were in no hurry to leave, hovering where we could see them. It was a provocation that couldn't be ignored. The next move was up to me.

It was simple. I was pretending to be the leader of a small unit that had infiltrated the undead territory and suddenly learned that they'd been discovered and were being slowly surrounded by enemies. What would I do? I wouldn't consider the option of staying put and hacking away at the enemy until complete and final victory. The undead was sure to win in this situation. Even if this option "suited" me, our "death" had to look as convincing as possible. So, all our preparations had been for nothing. We had only one way out— to leave the building and try to break through. It was very likely that this was what the undead generals were waiting for.

Preparations didn't take much time, although I had to summon the goblins several times to transfer the goods. It was the last opportunity.

"Move out!"

The squad began to move outside and disperse, taking up defensive positions. The undead didn't even try to disrupt our maneuvers. The only hindrance was the Bone Birds circling over the street. They didn't touch the people, but the drone we sent out to check was attacked without the slightest hesitation. Of course, we weren't allowed to scout ahead.

"I hate the undead," I muttered.

"What?" Oleg asked.

"Nothing. Let's go!"

It wasn't hard to choose the direction. Which way would I try to go if this was real? The answer was obvious: back towards the outer wall. Pushing on to the temple would be pure madness. We had to retreat, regroup, and try again in another place. You didn't need to be a genius to figure out this move since the undead were most numerous in that direction. Deeper into the city? As I'd already said, that would be stupid. Even if the barrier was weaker there, the undead would eventually catch up, surround, and destroy us. Well, I wasn't an idiot, was I? I chose the direction perpendicular to these options. A desperate attempt to escape the trap, right? I hoped this is what it looked like.

"Run! If they corner us, we'll all die here!"

The enemy plan was as obvious as my own. The squad picked up pace, switching to a jog, but the undead still had an advantage. Unlike humans, they didn't get tired, so our dash would only have a short-term effect. We had left the shelter, and now we had to make sure the horde didn't attack us en masse. Even hope in vain that we'd break through without a fight.

"Undead!"

Too late. Bri couldn't check the road ahead quickly enough, and the raven kept being attacked by Bone Birds, so he stayed close to me. Turning into another street, we ran into a Bone Horror accompanied by a group of skeletons.

"Stop!" I raised my hand. "Fire!"

Heavy weaponry could have helped, but it was too close for a grenade launcher, and the events unfolded rapidly. The undead rushed at us, and, I had to admit, it was terrifying. I'm sure the thought of running away flashed through many minds, but, thankfully, nobody followed it. Although Tatra almost touched the *Wand of the Fearless Sorceress*, which I'd given her for temporary use.

"Target the leader!"

Activate Search for Life!

Even now, I first checked that we weren't in danger from the flanks. I didn't sense any undead inside the surrounding buildings. I also managed to shoot at the same time.

The Bone Horror was a mature beast: bullets struck the interwoven bones, but didn't break them, ricocheting and spraying shards of bone instead. The *heart* wasn't even visible through the protective sphere, so it was very difficult to hit. I dropped the machine gun, letting the weapon hang on the strap, and a spear appeared in my hand. The sword might not be long enough, and if I stepped aside...

"Legion! Hold the sky!"

"Caw!"

The birds, previously acting as observers, abruptly grew bold and launched an attack. This was not part of my plan, so I had to improvise.

Activate Overclocking?

Yes/No

I was reluctant to waste the skill, but I didn't see any other way to stop this "armored tank".

"Damn it!"

The attack ended as suddenly as it begun when the creature collapsed on the run. The shooters immediately transferred fire to its retinue, and the birds swooping down from above.

"Shoot at the legs!" I considered the situation. "We'll finish them off with System weapons!"

Seeing the death of the Bone Horror and suffering losses from the bullets, the birds scattered again, and now, it was the raven chasing them. The skeletons posed no threat to us without a leader.

"Cease fire! Reload! Finish them off on the go!"

I made sure the order was obeyed—I didn't want to get a bullet in the back—and then I ran, striking the *heart* of one of the three enemies still standing on their feet. *Split!*

Attention! You have gained 20 SP! (152/460)

Bones sprayed in all directions. I turned and, almost without looking, snatched the card out of the air. Steel and Yuki took care of the two remaining skeletons, and the rest dispatched the fallen ones. There was a hiccup when one of the soldiers was stabbed in the leg and, after a quick dressing, moved inside the bag. We had gotten out in time, and the undead had appeared behind us too late. It looked like we broke through this time... but the chase was only beginning.

No one was planning to let us go, and the undead had foreseen such a scenario. The trap had turned into a maw, threatening to swallow us whole. The undead chased us, appearing on the horizon, not letting us rest, and attacking from the air from time to time. Our pace dropped even though there were no serious injuries, and I was promptly treating any "calluses". I could have placed the injured in the bag, but I didn't want to overuse this option. The bait shouldn't shrink too much.

An attempt to turn towards the wall was met by such a horde that only heavy weapons allowed us to retreat. It became clear that running any further was useless. We needed rest, otherwise we would be cornered, and the fiction would become reality. We'd already completed our main task—to draw away as many undead as possible. It was time to find a suitable building and make a heroic stand.

* * *

We ended up in a trap after all, which was another building surrounded by hordes of undead. Just like in the movies, when it's all over and there is no hope left. The undead had stormed the building twice, but we were managing to hold them back. Heavy weaponry was working well, and the enemy leaders remained safe, preferring to litter the approach to the building with the bones of ordinary skeletons. However, this tactic served an additional purpose—if one waited a little, something monstrous was bound to arise from the bones, adding to our problems.

The situation came down to hand-to-hand

combat several times, so there were five dead among the military, and almost half of the others were wounded. Some were quite seriously injured, yet I couldn't send them to the *Shard*. There was no "ozone hole" over our latest fortress. Everyone was absolutely exhausted, bullets were running out, and there was less and less faith in a happy outcome.

"We're going to die here, aren't we?" Tatra asked. There was no fear in her voice this time.

"Not at all, I'll get you out. I promised, remember?"

"Yes, I hope you keep your promise," Dragonfly replied. "I don't want to die like this."

Yuki said nothing. The undead didn't try any tactics this time, but simply piled on. The attack was coming from the ground, air, windows, and roof, and this time, we had no chance of winning.

Level 23 (341/460).

There was no time to spend the points, and I'd already drained the accumulated points into cards several times to stay at the current level. I'd study them later. Preparations were complete, all that remained was to finish the game.

"Do it," I ordered.

Tatra, who had been clutching the staff all the while, nodded, and I felt a wave of confidence. *We will succeed.* The effect of *Battle Aura* was different from *Calculating Mind*, not suppressing emotions but allowing you to maintain control over them. Not only for me, but for everyone nearby, including the woman who had activated the artifact. She looked like a totally different person, with no trace of fear or doubt in her face.

"Retreat!"

We weren't planning to hold our position this time and clambered up quickly. The monsters rushed after us, so everything was going according to plan.

"A-a-a-a!"

"Kozin fell off the roof," someone reported. "The birds knocked him down."

Damn it. I didn't need to guess what happened to a person who fell into a sea of undead. Never mind, we would avenge him soon...

"Five seconds!"

I had reached the control point but decided to wait to give the others a little more time. Any delay right now would be fatal. The last seconds dragged on.

Activate the Temporal Barrier? (100 SP) Yes/No

The world beyond the *barrier* froze, but I deliberately let a few enemies inside—it would be stupid to miss such an opportunity to get stronger. Although we had an hour and a half left for everything.

* * *

To fight back, we just had to control the stairs and, to a lesser extent, the windows. Although dozens of creatures had managed to get inside, destroying them was a matter of time. One of the leaders had also fallen into the trap, so they were quite organized, but the narrow passage and our snipers didn't let them use their numerical advantage.

"They're retreating!"

Activate Search for Life!

The wave covered the entire *barrier*, allowing me to monitor the whole situation. Our enemies had indeed retreated, but this was no reason for celebration. Realizing that they couldn't take us just like that, the leader had decided to withdraw. Damn it. Destroying the *barrier* from the inside wasn't easy, but I couldn't afford to experiment on how *time* would affect those who were, in a sense, immortal. The only question now was which way do we run? Up or down? It was a rhetorical question since nothing was ready yet.

"I'll destroy the leader! Follow the others!"

A few leaps sideways to shorten the distance, and then...

Blink!

The world flashed, and I found myself on the first floor, not far from the Bone Knight. A wave of undead were coming up behind him, so there was no time to wait or hesitate. I had only seconds.

I grabbed my sword, and we faced each other. I crouched down to avoid the blow, then swung my blade, cutting off his legs. The bones were strong, but they couldn't resist the combination of my divine sword and *Overlay*. The knight crashed to the floor, exposing his back, and I instantly struck, finding a vulnerable point with my *Magical Vision. Split!*

Attention! You have gained 180 SP! (441/460)

Attention! The Sword of Heresy has consumed 36 SP!

That was it, right? At least for the leaders—having lost their commander, the remaining undead no longer posed a threat to us. We had to leave a few as bait, in case of scanning.

"Vasily? How did it go?"

"I've destroyed the leader, and I'm fine. We don't have much time, so let's finish up! Don't forget to leave the bait."

It was a pity that I couldn't spend the experience points, but the situation wasn't conducive to it. Meanwhile, the others would deal with the remaining skeletons without me. I needed to restore my spent mana reserves.

* * *

Time remaining: 15 minutes and 59 seconds.

There wasn't much time. The *barrier* would fall, and countless waves of monsters would rush in. I stood on the roof and admired the post-apocalyptic view. Thousands of skeletons were storming the building, their leaders among them. Bone Horrors, Knights... there were no Liches, but when had we ever seen them? Hundreds of birds soared in the sky, which worried me even more. All we needed were some Dragons. "Just freaking great."

When I started it all, I didn't think it would come to this. If there were so many undead here, how many had gone to meet the main army? I touched the bag with all the survivors. It was now up to me whether we would escape or fall into the clutches of the undead. I stepped up to the edge of the roof and tried to find the fallen fighter in this sea... I found him, making sure that "missing in action" didn't apply here. He was dead.

Mana: 2,420/2,430.

My mana bar was almost full. I had to devour the maximum allowed dose of capsules to recover in time. Oh well, it wouldn't kill me.

Activate Invisibility!

Although the skill used up mana, the amount didn't decrease, but the growth rate slowed down slightly. I took a deep breath, enjoying the last moments of peace and safety. Enjoying the feeling of being alive. It would all be decided now.

3...2...1...

The *barrier* disappeared, and the remaining undead continued to storm the building—empty and filled with the bones of their predecessors. And a few surviving skeletons since we were pretending that the undead had been victorious inside the *barrier*. I ran and jumped off the roof. Birds rushed past, almost hitting me in their hurry to reach our flesh. Son of a...

Blink!

Five meters. *Flight* allowed me to hover over the sea of undead, and *Invisibility* stopped me from being detected. A second to get my bearings.

Blink!

Another five meters. Although there were a lot of undead, it took me to the edge of the crowd storming the building.

Blink!

I landed on the roof of the chosen building. Alive. A few undead still remained on the streets below, but I was sure I'd escaped. There wasn't much mana left, so I started walking, hurrying to break the distance, and counting down the seconds. I had a couple of minutes, according to my estimates.

It was time. I slipped under some structure and pressed a button, sending a signal to the detonator. We hadn't spared any explosives, and the debris reached even here, although none fell close enough to disturb my *Kinetic Field*. It worked. The explosion not only destroyed the building, killing hundreds or even thousands of the necrocreatures crammed inside, but also erased all traces of the recent battle. Hopefully, the undead generals would believe that my squad had died. A heroic death, of course.

INTERLUDE NO. 6
DAN

ALTHOUGH KARANDAR, High Priest of the Great Y, was the leader of the Liches, he wasn't the only one. There were six so-called undead generals. Not many, but enough to control the main lines of attack.

Granok, the junior priest, didn't approach the destroyed building—his life was too important for the Goal, so caution had long become his middle name. Once upon a time, his enemies had called him Granok the Coward, but how many of them had lived to see this day? The nickname was slander anyway; a coward would never have reached such heights. Despite everything going wrong: his God falling, Granok losing the status of player, and the world inching towards disaster, he remained strong.

Unfortunately, the rules prevented him from

leveling up by killing his former kin. The rules applied to the leaders, unlike the ordinary undead, so they didn't receive any experience points for killing goblins. Unlike killing humans. Alas, he was too late this time...

Raise the Death Knight!

He required high-quality materials in addition to the skill. Even if the body was seriously damaged and the unit's level was low, the air itself was saturated with magic, and there were plenty of bone dust and fragments lying around. They now enveloped the corpse, encasing it in armor and healing the numerous injuries. Liches didn't often have a hand in creating higher undead.

Attention! The attempt was successful!

The former enemy shuddered and opened his eyes. It remained to be seen how much he remembered about his past life. Even if the resurrected had no soul, some shreds should remain, and the brain stored pieces of information.

"Who are you?"

"My name is... Dan."

CHAPTER 9

A QUIET PLACE

I STARED AT THE GROWING FIRE. Perhaps pouring "gasoline" over everything had been excessive, but there definitely wouldn't be any traces. Moreover, the debris scattered by the explosion would hopefully start several more fires. Just small ones. If it were that simple, the goblins would have burned down the ruins long ago.

I walked to the edge of the roof. I had no desire to go down to street level—too many undead were wandering around—so I'd have travel over the roofs. To do so without insurance would be unwise unless I wanted to end up splattered on the flagstones below.

Mana: 404/2,430.

Hmm... After some hesitation, I popped another handful of capsules into my mouth. Even though I'd escaped the encirclement, I wouldn't get far without extra mana.

"I hate..."

I took a running leap off the roof, only activating *Flight* at the very end to soften my landing. Even after getting rid of all the unnecessary items, I weighed over a hundred kilos in the combat form. The *Slaver's Bag* was empty except for the group members, but it still weighed twenty kilos. Plus the *Ring*, which, although it reduced the weight 300-fold and distributed it around the body, was still packed to the limit. A total of around two hundred kilos. An ordinary person would struggle to stand, but I ran and even jumped, at least for a while.

"Shit!" The next roof wasn't strong enough. Or was I saving too much mana and landed too hard? In any case, it collapsed under me, dragging me down toward new adventures and, quite possibly, multiple fractures.

Blink!

I teleported almost instinctively, to find myself outside the building. I was about three meters away from the roof and ten meters above the ground, but I had to cover the distance in a matter of seconds. *Flight!*

"Bloody hell!" I spun around and landed on my feet. My mana was running out, so it was a hard landing, but with no injuries. Fortunately, *Invisibility* remained active, and there were no undead nearby. To hell with it. I'd gone far enough to take a chance and continue along the ground. I doubted there were trackers among the undead...

Mana: 104/2,431.

The mistake had cost me dearly, so I needed to find a hole to hide in for a while. A short while.

* * *

A tent was a good alternative to proper screening, especially when hiding alone. True, it needed to be kept closed, and the thick walls didn't let in any light, but the ghost was on duty outside and the darkness wasn't a hindrance for meditation. I also had plenty of flashlights. I simply sat there for ten minutes, cradling a crystal in my palms. The capsules continued to work, so...

Mana: 2,143/2,431.

That should be enough. While the dead could wait, the wounded couldn't. At least one needed immediate help.

Retrieve Unnamed Unit (Level 4) from the bag!

I shone a flashlight at the guy lying before me. The bandages applied to him in a hurry were completely soaked with blood in some places. Fractures, cuts, penetrating wounds—that's what happened if you went hand-to-hand with a Bone Horror. He was alive only because the monster's blow had thrown him back. But the situation was critical, and the help he'd received wouldn't last long.

"Sergeant Sychev?" I asked, hearing a groan. "Sergey?"

No response. So much the better. Additional

diagnostic skills might be useful, but *Earth Medicine* was enough to prioritize and find optimal points of application. I'd had the skill since time immemorial, after the first mission. After cutting off the bandages on his chest and placing the "evidence" in the *Spatial Ring*, I lay my hand over the wound. I'd rinsed my hands with hand sanitizer, but these conditions were still completely unsanitary. Never mind.

Healing!

Half my reserve was gone. It felt like fire ran through my veins—a sign of problems to come, but to stop meant letting the man die. Although living processes of those inside the bag slowed down, it was sleep, and not proper stasis. His wounds continued bleeding, so either I stabilized him now, or I'd extract a corpse next time. So, let's shift over here...

Healing!

In addition to treating wounds, magic expelled any poisons from the body, which included medicine. Therefore, I wasn't surprised when the soldier groaned and opened his eyes. I just jabbed his leg with a new dose of painkillers.

"Hush," I reassured him. "It's Vasily. It's okay, we've escaped. I've treated you so you'll survive. Accept the request and get some sleep."

Would you like to place Unnamed Unit inside the Slaver's Bag?

Yes/No

Request sent.

For several seconds, I thought it wouldn't

work, but then the body fell through the opened portal. The mana bar was almost empty again, and I needed to fix that before proceeding further. I took out a couple of crystals, clutched them in my hands, and closed my eyes.

* * *

Of course, I could have set up a temporary base in the vicinity, but it wasn't the best solution. Time was not on our side. Undead from miles around had gathered to destroy our squad, but the pendulum would swing the other way soon. A few hours would pass, and the undead would spread through the streets again. I'd have to be careful, and my speed would inevitably drop.

The city's main defense forces wouldn't remain focused on the army forever. I'd been hearing the occasional thunder coming from the west for the past day, but it had quieted down. Nor were the numbers on the counter very reassuring...

Players: 8,433/13,000.

If this wasn't a resounding defeat, then it certainly looked like heavy losses. Over one and a half thousand players had died in the last day alone! Had we really suffered a major defeat? Were there any internal conflicts? I could only guess and make the most of this opportunity.

I considered getting the motorcycle out of the *Ring*—I could go much faster with its help—but I couldn't hide a moving vehicle under *Invisibility*.

Not for long, at least, and I may not survive another drive hunt.

It began to drizzle after I'd been running for several hours. Not hard, but the clouds promised that this was just the beginning. The rain should remove any traces, but it would leave me vulnerable, reducing the effectiveness of *Invisibility*. Although it was quiet for now, I couldn't forget that I was practically in the heart of the undead's domain. Even if the streets remained empty, Bone Birds regularly flashed across the sky. I doubted they had the concept of zero-zero weather conditions.

"Okay, that's enough," I muttered, stopping.

I realized that I'd reached my limit as soon as I made the decision. It wasn't even my sagging *Stamina*, but the mana channels, which burned more and more with every hour. Although this "training" had a noticeable effect since my storage volume had increased by nineteen units.

Mana: 1,427/2,449.

I hadn't come across any new windows along the way but moving on would be madness. It was strange that I hadn't yet gotten...

Attention! You are magically exhausted! Mana recovery has slowed down.

Magical Exhaustion: 23 hours, 12 minutes, and 56 seconds.

...that. My *Intuition* must have kicked in a little late. I couldn't explain the coincidence any other way.

"And here we are."

It had come out of the blue, but quantity had turned into quality. All the pills I'd swallowed to use the skills almost continuously—this was the result. In addition to a sharp drop in the recovery rate, I could only use magic as a last resort, and I had to forget about doping altogether. Otherwise, minor exhaustion would grow into a moderate one, which might not resolve after a week. A *major* exhaustion would put me out of action for a month, and then came permanent debuffs, loss of the ability, and a quick, but very painful death. However, I didn't even have a week. Well, since there were no enemies behind me, the choice was obvious.

"Bri, check the building."

"Yes, boss." The ghost detached itself from my shoulders and dived inside. The raven was too noticeable and had remained in the bag for most of the journey.

* * *

Deactivate Invisibility!
Deactivate Kinetic Field!
Deactivate the combat form!

As soon as I entered the building, I got rid of everything that used up mana. Perhaps the combat form didn't require much, but now wasn't the time to take risks.

Shit... The loss of some attributes was very noticeable. The pain and fatigue attacked me with new force, and the bag was like a dead weight on my shoulder. It felt like I'd aged ten years in a second. Yet I had no serious wounds, since the pseudoflesh had protected me from bruises and scratches, and the rest would pass.

First of all, I adjusted the straps on my clothes to fit my changed figure in case I needed to fight. Even if the ghost had checked everything, this place couldn't be considered safe until I had shielded myself.

Magical Exhaustion: 23 hours, 36 minutes, and 12 seconds.

While I searched for shelter, my body continued to receive damage, and the counter kept increasing. Now the countdown was finally moving in the right direction. True, it was moving three times slower than normal, but it was a good sign. Although my body continued to receive damage, it was recovering faster than the damage was accumulating. A little longer and the capsules would run out, and the situation would finally return to normal.

Retrieve Oleg the Prophet (Level 4) from the bag?

Yes/No

"So, we got out in the end?" Oleg asked, rubbing his shoulder. "That was dangerous."

"It's still dangerous," I nodded. "Can you take care of shielding this room? It will all be for nothing if we're discovered."

We'd lost six in the last slaughter, while Sychev, Istrin and Vikhrov were wounded and wouldn't be able to fight in the near future. Ideally, I needed to find a *window* and evacuate them to the Shard. Plus Nosov, who'd lost his sight and had already been sent there. Only half of the two platoons that had gone on the mission were still standing.

"We have only one platoon now. You'll take command of the remaining people."

The second platoon commander, "Lieutenant" Kratkov, had been among the losses. A skeleton warrior had driven a blade into his neck. He might have survived if it had been an ordinary wound, but the undead swords were *Systemic,* so the officer was well and truly gone by the time we got his body back. He had lost something important, and even *Healing* couldn't help.

The second platoon's medic Zhmyshenko had fallen defending the wounded from chimeras that had broken through. Losev had been struck by a Bone Knight's magic blow. We managed to get him out, but he became a Wight and caused the death of two more people: Starokorov and Vorontsov. It had been my fault too—if I'd paid more attention, I would have finished him off before he became dangerous. The fact that I'd personally cut off the Wight's head didn't change anything.

I had taken the bodies and put them in the *Ring,* but our sniper's corpse remained with the undead. If we were lucky, he'd been buried under the debris, but if not, Kozin would soon join the enemy ranks. Just like hundreds of other fallen players. Perhaps we would meet some of them in battle. Speaking of which...

"I'm also ordering you to use the backup channels."

"Roger that."

This was an important precaution because we'd previously seen the undead leaders trying to use our weapons and equipment. Bone Knights had been spotted carrying machine guns, and the undead regularly collected loot. Maybe it smacked a little of paranoia, but extra security measures wouldn't hurt.

Retrieve the player Yuki (Level 10) from the bag!

Retrieve the player Tatra (Level 5) from the bag!

Retrieve the player Dark Steel (Level 9) from the bag!

Retrieve the player Dragonfly (Level 8) from the bag!

Incredibly, none of the players were injured. They had actually gotten stronger. The Japanese girl had reached the boundary where she could get a combat form. Unfortunately, she was unlikely to do this without full access to the Server—a simple *window* wasn't enough, she needed her personal room. Which was hardly possible.

Steel had also gone up a level, coming close to this boundary, and Dragonfly wasn't far behind. Tatra had gone up two levels, but this had required significantly fewer experience points. Only the former politician hadn't upped at all... I winced. "Upped". The game terminology sounded kind of fake in the real world. Even inappropriate...

Summon the slave Armet (Level 6)!

"Yuki, you still have mana capsules, right? Recover, and help me with the wounded."

Each veteran had learned an additional skill back in the _Dungeon,_ and Yuki had chosen _Healing._ True, her focus was on treating psychological trauma, but she should be able to manage stab wounds too. Steel had acquired _Stone Armor,_ which had really helped us at critical moments. Dragonfly could fly in addition to _Yellow Noise,_ which was nearly useless against the undead. Not for very long, considering her mana reserves. Funny how her abilities now matched her nickname. Armet had learned to create _mana stones._ There was no way Diamond could meet our needs, and a personal crafter would be useful. If we lived long enough to level him up.

In addition, most veterans had bonus abilities, which were worth keeping in mind. For example, both _Magical Ability_ and _Chakra Circulation System_ provided a bonus ability when going up a rank. Not everyone got something situational, like my _Condensation_ (E-). Even though I hadn't needed to obtain a cup of clean water by literally straining it out of the environment, I wouldn't call the ability garbage.

"What should I do, commander?" Steel came up to me. He'd acquired _Step Technique,_ which allowed him to move more optimally during a fight. It was a useful skill, and E-ranked too. Okay, now wasn't the time to dream.

"Take Anastasia and help the others with the screening. I've got Magical Exhaustion, so we'll have to stay here for about a day."

"Got it," he nodded. "Dragonfly, let's go!"

Retrieve Unnamed Unit (Level 2) from the bag!

Retrieve Unnamed Unit (Level 3) from the bag!

Retrieve Unnamed Unit (Level 2) from the bag!

I started releasing those who weren't badly injured—we needed them to quickly set up the shelter. Each of the survivors had gone up at least one level, some had gone up two, but only one had reached the fourth level. And had nearly died...

The covering squad didn't initially have System weapons, so I gave them some from my own stock. Temporarily, of course: this resource would be in short supply for a long time. Even the crappy blades we'd acquired from the undead were worth a lot on Earth. They were no good for the goblins in the *Dungeon*, since they were a physical analog of the *Monster I* feature. However, the local goblins were units, so the blades were a highly coveted trophy for them.

I didn't scrimp on cards either—there were plenty of empties, and a week of downtime had allowed me to record some useful skills on them. I didn't saturate them, the soldiers did that themselves, so each one now had the necessary System skill. Even if the squad's losses were high, but the survivors had become stronger.

Retrieve Unnamed Unit (Level 2) from the bag!

"Artem, I'm counting on you," I turned to the last medic. "Take care of the dressings, Yuki will help you with the heavy ones. Then we'll return them back to the bag."

"I want to help too," Armet came up to us.

"Okay, help with the dressings. Just don't talk too much, okay?"

"You don't trust me?" The traitor shook his head. "I thought..."

"Yeah, you thought wrong," I cut him off. "Don't piss me off, I'm in a bad mood already."

Difficult to say which one was the bigger reason: the need to keep up a confident appearance, despite the extreme fatigue, pain, and urge to sleep, or because of the losses? It hadn't been a good day.

"Yes, of course. Sorry. I just ***want you to remember that I'm not your enemy***, I..."

A slight chill ran over my body. I stepped forward and punched the bastard in the jaw, silencing him. A spear appeared in my hand. "Did you really think that was going to work?"

"Wait! I wasn't doing anything!"

I smiled wryly—there was no persuasion in his voice this time, only fear. Armet was crawling backwards, staring in horror at the weapon.

"You think denying it will help? Do you take me for a complete idiot?"

"I'm... sorry. I was wrong."

The point of the spear hovered at the traitor's

throat. Most likely, Armet heard about my exhaustion and decided to take advantage of the "gap in my defenses". A few successful suggestions, and who knew how it would end?

"You're not really going to kill him, are you?" Tatra touched my hand. "***He's not our enemy***."

"Seriously?" Now I was keeping everyone else in sight.

"Did he use a skill on us?" Yuki voiced her guess. Steel didn't appear drugged either, unlike the low-level units, who looked at the scene with obvious doubt.

"The *Jedi Mind Trick*," I explained. "The talent of persuasion."

"I see," the Japanese woman nodded. "Traitors shouldn't get a second chance. Kill him."

"I don't think that's wise," Steel objected. I was inclined to agree with...

"***There is no need***," Armet began. I tilted my head slightly, sensing the familiar notes. "I was wrong, I was wrong! Mercy..."

"A slave can't have two masters," I said. "You won't get another chance."

Recall the slave Armet (Level 6)!

* * *

Level 23 (441/460).

I had accumulated enough experience points to spend them on something useful. There were many options to choose from, but my last decision had been correct, so there was no point in changing tactics.

Attention! Do you want to improve Blink to Level 3? (400 SP)

Rank has increased! Skill strength has greatly increased!

Choose the development branch:

1) *Saving Mana II.* The energy cost of the jump is reduced.

2) *Distance.* The maximum distance increases significantly.

3) *Flow Control.* Allows you to control mana consumption more accurately, depending on the distance and presence of obstacles. The maximum distance varies, but the price increases exponentially.

4) *Scope of Control.* Allows you to specify the landing spot within an area.

5) *Expulsion.* Any object present at your landing spot is forcefully thrown away.

I initially wanted to select the first option, but then I saw a slight change in the description—the word "significantly" had disappeared. So, if I chose that one, I wouldn't save as much. Second option it is.

Blink

Rank: *E+.*

Level: *3/5.*

Description:

Allows the user to shift sideways within a certain radius. If the destination is partially occupied, the user will appear a little to the side.

__Features:__
— Activation cost: 500 mana units.
— Maximum range: 10 meters.

* * *

Now that I'd completed my task, I had some freedom of movement. I could take my group beyond the second circle. It wouldn't be hard to break through the wall again, just like escaping pursuit. It was the safest and, at the same time, meaningless option. Is that what I'd risked my life for?

The next option was to try reaching the temple by myself. Of course, the third platoon remained with the main group, basically serving as hostages, but if we didn't get in touch, they would simply write us off. "No survivors". In a way, I had fulfilled my obligations by taking this risk. True, Hera was unlikely to agree with this point of view, but I would cross that bridge when I came to it. The question remained of who would live longer: Hera or me. Although I preferred to avoid the latter, of course.

The last option was to follow the original plan. Contact the main group, report about what has happened, and coordinate further actions... especially since it was the control time already.

"We have communication, commander," said Sergeant Melkov. "I'm switching to a separate channel... encrypted."

"This is Vasily. Do you copy?"

"This is Diva, I copy," came the reply. "I'm glad to hear your voice. How's the situation?"

"Mission completed," I said, omitting the details. "The explosion masked our retreat, so the undead leaders should be convinced that we died. Their activity will subside for a while."

"I knew you could do it."

"We could do it. We did it together. However, I've got Magical Exhaustion, so we have to stay put for the next day."

"Roger that."

"Any information about the army?"

"The Alliance is... retreating. The undead turned out to be stronger than expected. I don't know the details, they're too busy to talk to me right now. But I think you can see the losses yourself."

"Yes, I can."

"Then you know we can't miss this chance. You're coming, aren't you?"

We had discussed the details before, so the question concerned my decision. I wasn't the only one having doubts.

"Of course," I reassured her. "We'll leave in a day."

"Then we'll arrive first and wait for you for thirty hours. If you don't arrive or don't get in touch, we'll proceed alone."

"Roger that. I'll make it. Over and out."

Six hours for any unexpected disasters were more than enough. Except for the fatal ones. I thought for a few seconds, then nodded in response. It would help to check the information directly. I needed to contact Qing Long.

* * *

Now that the main tasks had been completed, the wounded had been helped, and the soldiers had gathered for lunch, I realized that the situation required something more from me. A speech, perhaps?

"Attention, everyone," I began, getting up. "We suffered serious losses today, but you knew what you were signing up for. These days, we don't like pompous speeches, but this mission is extremely important. This isn't about state or individual ambitions, but about the future of humanity!"

Despite the serious losses, no alcohol was allowed. The ones who returned would remember the dead.

"The fallen will not be forgotten, and their families will be taken care of. But will we have a future if the mission fails? As you already know, Shiva was defeated right before our departure. Earth is now protected by only six of those, who call themselves gods, and that is barely enough. One more blow—and it might all collapse! The alien gods will win, humankind's centers of defense and industry will be destroyed, and our cities will be looted. Monsters and players from other worlds will hunt the survivors and their descendants for centuries!"

I took a breath and considered the tired fighters. They were professionals, and they probably didn't need my speech, but it would be wrong to remain silent after everything that had happened. Words were important, but the message itself was much more important. I had said what I thought. What I sincerely believed to be true. I suppose they sensed it.

"You've heard the sounds of battle, right? We thought that we could easily annihilate the undead using modern weapons, but we were wrong. The Alliance army has faced strong resistance and is now retreating. Ammunition is limited, losses are high, and a split is growing among the factions. At the moment, our group has the best chance of success, not for the first or the last time. I won't quote numbers, but the others have an even smaller chance."

Another pause to catch my breath. Perhaps my speech wasn't very rousing, but it didn't trigger any negativity.

"If I can find a *window*, I'll evacuate the wounded and call in reinforcements. If anyone here decides that they can't fight anymore, they can also leave. If not, we'll have to fight to the end! You should use the remaining time to distribute the points received for a new level. Each of you has recommendations from the analysts, but please ask me if you're unsure. I recommend investing in *Stamina*. You have a day to rest. And... bon appetit."

INTERLUDE NO. 7
ESCALATION

ANY BATTLE IS NOT ONLY DEAD, but also wounded. The latter may even be more numerous. They need medical care, protection and, most importantly, to be sent to a safe place. As time went on, the fortress became less and less suitable for this role. There were no trucks, only a few *Slaver's Bags*, and the dozen carts taken from the goblins didn't solve the logistics problem. The wounded were predominantly transported on stretchers, which required two people. Moreover, they couldn't fight at the same time, and required additional cover.

The first major battle resulted in four hundred wounded, and their evacuation required almost a thousand healthy fighters. All this despite the healers sending those who weren't too badly injured back into the fray.

Of course, the problem didn't come as a

surprise—anyone with half a brain could look a few steps ahead. Therefore, the stretcher bearers were met halfway by players from the fortress garrison, so they could promptly return to the main forces. However, this was a one-time solution, and the army needed a new stronghold. Or rather, strongholds...

Once they reached the third circle, the Alliance leaders decided to establish four forts by clearing and equipping suitable areas. The main reasons for splitting up was to reduce risk and gain freedom of movement, but one couldn't forget about the future. The temple was getting closer, the undead were suffering defeat after defeat, so the status of Commander-in-Chief became more and more shaky. Each one was thinking about reaching the Altar first, and Qing Long didn't blame them. It was stupid to blame tigers for wanting meat.

"Shall we just draw lots?" Qing Long glanced at the diagram. The first three forts stood in a curved line, while the fourth one protruded forward. The zone inside the "triangle" could be considered relatively safe.

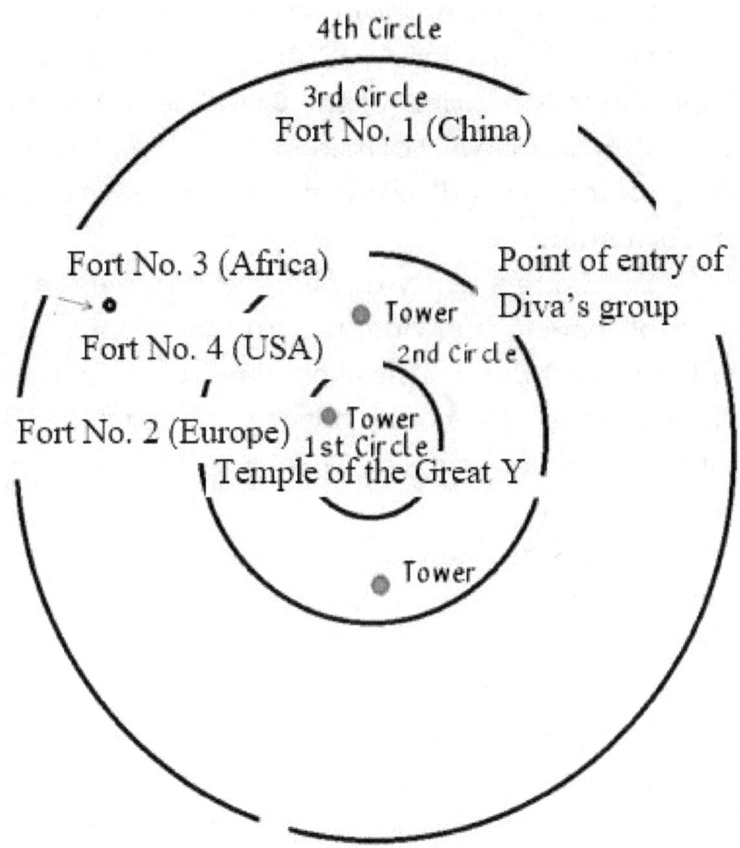

There were no objections. For these elite superheroes, each with their own impressive set of skills, such a game of chance left many opportunities to cheat, but the question wasn't fundamentally important. The strips of paper were placed on the table, and each faction leader picked one up.

"The second fort," Alexander showed his result. He'd gotten the right flank.

"The fourth fort. Did I get lucky?" The Swordsman chuckled. He had scored the main stronghold, where the offensive would launch from. It was an honor the others preferred to avoid.

"The third fort," Sulu grimaced with displeasure. The priest of the Great Seth, and not the Saudi man, was considered the head of the African faction. And he'd gotten the safest spot in the formation.

Qing Long silently turned over the remaining strip of paper, showing the number one. He'd gotten the left flank. This elicited no reaction in the Chinese man. He could have gotten any of the options if he so wished. This one was no worse than any other.

Saud, Ryuu, and Lisa were also present but didn't participate directly in the voting as members of the other factions. The Brahmin remained in the fortress. As for the other three members of the Circle, they were absent for... a good reason. Yet another factor to be considered. The chance that Diva's group would succeed was small, but it was a chance. Although Qing Long would welcome a "joint victory", the others would benefit from it more. However, he'd hedged his bets here too, by easily identifying the weak spot. While he couldn't influence the priestess of Hera, the Russian man, on the other hand... Vasily had demonstrated his talents plenty of times, and there were a few possibilities if he reached the Altar. The Chinese man had done everything he could to convey the idea that Guan Yu could give both the heretic and his homeland a lot more. He had been quite blunt and had even used diplomatic channels. But the others had probably done the same.

"Then it's decided," the Swordsman nodded. "Two hundred and fifty will remain in the garrison, no more than that."

"Isn't that too many?" Sulu snorted. "We'll lose a thousand fighters in one go."

"It's a necessary sacrifice," Qing Long explained patiently, "If we leave fewer people, they won't last long enough when they're attacked."

"Then what's the point of leaving someone at all?" the African man objected again. "Isn't it better to strike a swift blow and defeat the enemy?"

The idea of a blitzkrieg had been floated before, but most leaders preferred to develop the offensive in stages.

"We've already discussed tactics and agreed to minimize the risks," the Swordsman replied. "Hasn't death taught you anything?"

"Sulu was only wounded, but you're right," Saud intervened, casting a warning glance at his partner. "We will proceed cautiously, step by step. As we've agreed..."

* * *

The explosion destroyed a section of the wall, but the undead hardly reacted this time. The snipers took out all sentries, and several reports of skirmishes could be safely ignored. The scouts found no signs of an ambush after crossing to the other side, so the army slowly passed through the breach, taking up defense in the nearby buildings.
Players remaining: 11954/13000.

Less than a month had passed since the start of the mission, yet more than a thousand players were dead. Although this was the total number—less than half of those had been in the army. The rest had disappeared in the city after choosing a random landing point. So, the losses were significant, but not critical. The problem was that the dead were just the tip of the iceberg. There were also the wounded, their escorts, the deserters, the fort garrisons... Ten thousand fighters had left the fortress three weeks ago, but only seven and a half thousand entered the second circle. They had lost a quarter of their personnel.

"Advance!" Came the order, and the player posing as the leader waved his hand. Why become a target yourself?

Qing Long was travelling in a regular second wave squad and looked the same as the other players at first glance. The more noticeable you were, the more likely you were to attract the attention of enemy leaders. A separate 'kamikaze' squad was pretending to be the command team.

The army spread out into a wide front, then slowly moved towards the next wall. They weren't planning to blow it up: the scouts had indicated that it would be easier to use the broken gate. Even if the undead had erected barricades, they would need a lot less explosives.

This battle was completely different to the one before, forcing them to recall modern defense tactics and storming settlements—when any building was a control point, and battles were fought for every street.

The undead had few firearms, but they no longer attacked head on, to be mowed down by machine guns and grenade launchers but took refuge inside buildings. This significantly slowed down the army's progress as they had to spend time mopping up. The advantage of firearms was less impressive under these conditions. At the same time, they couldn't leave the enemy behind them, and risk being stabbed in the back or surrounded.

Qing Long's squad took part in a couple of operations, to avoid standing out to any observers. The Bone Birds didn't only perform reconnaissance but dropped like a brick from the sky every now and then. Considering their speed, collision often ended in mutual death. Or injuries, with all the ensuing consequences.

Collecting the remains also took up a lot of time. Due to the increased necrobackground, leaving the bones behind was just as dangerous as the enemy army.

"No!" someone screamed. "We need help!"

The players refused to die in silence, begging to be saved, blaming the commanders for mistakes, or simply screaming. This had a very dispiriting effect on the personnel.

"Hold on!"

"Argh... no! They're already in the building! We can't hold them back, please!"

Qing Long grimaced, knowing how it would end. Help wouldn't arrive in time—the squad had ventured far too from the main forces. The enemy immediately took advantage of this opportunity, striking a massive blow—not for the first or the last time. The army was frankly lacking cohesion. By the time reinforcements arrived, there would be no one left to save. At best, they could take revenge, but the enemy preferred to withdraw, taking the fresh corpses with them along with their weapons and equipment. This was disturbing, too. Ordinary skeletons couldn't master a machine gun, but a Bone Knight wielding a modern weapon would cause a lot of problems.

There was no doubt that they had seriously underestimated the enemy. Despite the goblin tales and the results of past skirmishes, they didn't have an inkling of the undead's true might. No wonder the mission rank was "A"—it wasn't just about the Altar. Without the advantage in weapons and technology, humans wouldn't have stood a chance of completing the mission. Even now, the future didn't look very rosy...

The fact that the local goblins had reached the steps of the temple could only be explained by one thing: the undead had made it easy for them. Perhaps in the hope that they would succeed, but more likely, to lure in new armies and gather as many victims as possible. If the natives understood the true difference in strength, they wouldn't have continued to beat their head against a stone wall. At the same time, the illusion of a possible victory made them mount Sacred Campaigns again and again, allowing the undead to replenish their ranks. However, the reason wasn't just a love of fresh bones—the undead generals didn't take care of the skeletons at all, allowing the players to rapidly level up.

"Watch out!"

Qing Long spotted the danger and swung his sword, cutting off the clawed hand emerging from the ground. The dead didn't need air, so the skeletons were hiding right under their feet. For much longer than a month, with no outward signs of their presence.

Fortunately, it was just one skeleton, chopped into pieces without his help. It explained why the scouts had missed it: no matter how much they tried, it was impossible to scan every meter of the road. Better buried skeletons than radio-controlled mines.

The unexpected attacks reaped a bloody harvest, and the healers couldn't return the wounded to the ranks quickly enough. Soon they had to organize another field hospital, leaving behind not only those unable to move, but also two hundred guards. It was enough to hold on for a while, but not enough to come back. There were a lot of undead left even in the cleared areas.

Players remaining: 11412/13000.

The total counter wasn't very convenient to refer to but gave you a general idea. So far, the losses were... acceptable.

The undead officers turned out to be quite intelligent and could control the junior creatures, but someone else stood behind them... the ones they called the 'generals'. Liches. The exact number of undead mages was unknown, but according to the goblins, there couldn't be many of them. Fewer than ten. Destroying them would make the task much easier, but so far, intelligence couldn't provide anything concrete. It was useless to launch drones, and enemy leaders wisely stayed away from the front line. It was too naive to hope that mass strikes on suspicious targets would be successful.

"Attention everyone! Don't leave your dead allies unattended!" Qing Long announced. "Dispose of the bodies, otherwise they will turn into wights!"

The closer to the center, the faster the dead rose, attacking their recent comrades at once. Moreover, their fears had been justified—there were instances of the undead using weapons. It was much easier to protect yourself from fangs or claws than from a burst of gunfire in the back. The losses kept growing and, on top of everything else, evening was approaching.

* * *

The night is dark and full of terrors. The undead didn't need to sleep, and were much less reliant on sight, orientating themselves using magic. No matter how much people hurried, it was almost impossible to reach the temple in a day. Therefore, they began to prepare for the night in advance, choosing a city block and clearing it out. They knew the undead's main tricks by now, and the abilities of thousands of players allowed them to find any hidden threats. Basements were cleaned out, bones were dug out and placed in bags, and machine guns were installed on the roofs.

They discarded the idea of a continuous perimeter, so individual buildings served as defense points. Neighbors kept in touch and could cover each other. Numerous bonfires were lit, each soldier had a flashlight, and searchlights were installed in the most dangerous areas.

The flags above the fake headquarters looked a little provocative but made it possible to create a good trap. While the Liches remained unreachable, what about dragons? The enemies should have very few of these creatures.

The undead, of course, didn't take what was happening lying down. Skirmishes occurred almost constantly, but the army lasted until nightfall without any problems. The only question was whether there would be enough ammunition—the seemingly endless supplies were shrinking rapidly.

* * *

The first few hours after sunset passed relatively calmly, although there were frequent shots from all sides. Then the nightmare began. The undead poured in from several directions, machine guns roared, there were explosions, and Bone Birds fell from the sky. "The headquarters are under attack!”

The fake headquarters, of course. As expected, the dragons didn’t stay away, and the building was enveloped in a magical fog. The brave souls in there had received personal protective equipment, but nobody knew if it would work.

“Everyone! Put your masks on!”

Qing Long set an example. The respirators were supposed to help, but most had only cloth masks. However, even they allowed people to escape the affected area and get help from the healers. Or to die outside, at least, where resurrection was possible and hostile magic wouldn’t kill you again. Forever.

Chaos seemed to reign in the camp, but Qing Long was in control of the situation. Air defense was working as it should. The searchlights focused on the dragons, and then the rockets hit, downing two at once. The third one managed to avoid the missile.

“Finish off the dragons!”

“Wait, let me fire an arrow in it!” Lisa’s voice rang out. This was not the time to be greedy…

Once on the ground, the creatures were in no hurry to die, shrouding themselves in black smoke that caused anyone who inhaled it to turn into the undead. This didn’t save them, for the humans didn’t spare any rockets. Yet this was just the beginning. The losses were unlikely to stop the undead, which meant that an attack could come again.

Qing Long glanced at the headquarters

building, and saw several figures stagger out of the fog. One of the players fell, showing that the protective equipment didn't help much. Yet he didn't turn immediately, which is what usually happened.

"Dragons! Three of them! They're attacking... Us..."

Qing Long reacted instantly, breaking the distance. The observer hesitated slightly and was engulfed by the darkness bursting through the window. The mask he'd pulled down to his chin meant he didn't even get a second. However, the masks didn't save everyone who wore them correctly.

"Retreat!" Qing Long raised a hand, "Don't touch the fallen, they're already dead!"

And, more importantly, were in the affected zone. The torches provided little light in the surrounding darkness, so it was hard to tell the boundaries of the fog.

"Michigan! I've been attacked by dragons. Take command!"

"Roger that. Good luck."

The American had grasped the situation at once with no unnecessary questions. Qing Long held the flashlight, illuminating the tentacles of black fog drifting through the windows. One of the first wights rushed at him with a roar, but the Chinese man easily dodged and cut off the former subordinate's head.

Attention! You have gained 10 SP!

"Retreat! Use the flashlights! This is a heavy

gas, so it will sink to the ground soon! We just need to stay out of its way!"

The dragons didn't believe in doing things by halves, so the building was probably engulfed by the cloud. The shooter sitting by the window had turned and was raising his machine gun. Was he being controlled?

"Into the corridor!"

The bodyguards opened fire first, giving the others a chance to leave the room. It was difficult to kill the undead using bullets, but the Wight took a few steps back, and conveniently fell out of the open window.

"Grenade!"

Qing Long was already in the corridor when the explosion hit behind him. He understood from the swearing of his subordinates that the third Wight had decided to use a more "reliable" weapon.

"How did the dragons track us down?" Lee asked, looking around frantically.

An interesting, albeit untimely question. The undead had swallowed the bait the first time, but then attacked one of the real defense centers. It couldn't be a coincidence, but Qing Long would think about that later.

"Over there! Quickly!"

Qing Long's magical abilities allowed him to sense both the survivors and the dead, but he could only identify the black fog visually. Whether they would get out of this ordeal alive depended largely on luck.

"Don't shove, everyone who receives a request, get in the bag!"

Attention! Place the player Jian player in the Slaver's Bag?

Request sent.

It was getting harder to run, but it was the right thing to do. Subordinates who owed their lives to you would always come in useful. Nevertheless, there were more survivors than empty slots, and the cursed fog left less and less room for retreat.

The torchlight danced along the corridor, allowing him to see the darkness creeping out from around the corner. Then came the Wight, raising its machine gun. Qing Long accelerated and took off his head.

Attention! You have gained 50 SP!

"That's it." Lee said again. "We're done for. Unless someone has any suitable abilities, of course."

Their escape routes were blocked, and the fog was approaching from both sides of the corridor. It was a long corridor, but the fog would reach them in minutes. Qing Long raised his sword and, pushing off, jumped and struck the ceiling beam. The ceiling collapsed, opening the way up.

The Chinese man flew through the opening first and helped the others climb up. Despite the panic, no one tried to rush ahead or push away a more successful colleague, so everyone managed to escape.

Qing Long looked down at the black sea

closing over the corridor below. *Dragon Breath* was heavier than air, so the upper floors were clear. Apart from the undead but dealing with the undead was already familiar. Even if half of the group had died, he was alive, so the attempt on his life had failed. But judging from the sound of gunfire, the battle raged on.

* * *

Players remaining: 10230/13000.

By morning, only two-thirds of those who had marched a day ago remained in the ranks. More than a thousand dead, plus wounded. The prospects weren't good.

"We need to move on," Sulu said. "We won't get another chance like this."

"A chance to die a pointless death?" Qing Long disagreed, "We have to retreat."

They didn't gather for this meeting, just allocated a separate communication channel. Talking without seeing the others was awkward, but it was better than giving their enemies a chance to take them all out in one strike.

"Are you serious? Do you think that if we retreat now, we'll do better later?"

"We won't break through to the temple anyway, the undead are too numerous. Only small groups stand a chance, and that's what we should bet on."

"They'll just die," Lisa interrupted.

"Quite possibly," the Chinese man agreed. "But don't forget, we have a backup plan."

"You mean..."

"That's right. This world isn't Earth, so it's not protected by any conventions. Besides, I doubt they'll let us go otherwise."

* * *

Alexander had no intention of leaving. It was true, only small units stood a chance, or individuals. The suit was made of screening fabric and wasn't very comfortable, but it guaranteed that the undead wouldn't spot him. Alexander's skill set gave him hope that he would succeed.

Entering a basement, the priest touched the wall, and the ground parted to let him through. He wasn't going to let that c... take the grand prize. It was victory or death. In the name of Odin!

* * *

People who find themselves in a difficult situation always need a leader. The one who will take responsibility, choose the way, and direct the others. Shiva was dead, but his high priest couldn't afford to appear weak or unsure. Just like he couldn't allow his followers to be weak or unsure. They had a goal, and as for the plans...

He hadn't planned to stay in the fortress, waiting for the outcome of the mission. Perhaps the undead were too dangerous, but there were plenty of traitors and goblins in the ruins. The legitimate prey of the strong, and if he wanted to resurrect his God, then strength was what he needed. In any case, this strength was based on experience. On System Points.

Therefore, as soon as the army moved out, he gathered his own squad and headed in the opposite direction. It probably wasn't a secret for the other leaders, but what could they do? He had left a sufficient garrison, and the rest was a private matter for his faction.

They had finally gone beyond the seemingly endless ruins yesterday, and now they had found their first target. A goblin settlement surrounded by a ridiculous earthen wall, with an even more pathetic gate. The goblins were aware of their arrival, with warriors on the walls, but that made it even more interesting. There were at least a thousand of them. Easy prey...

"Shall we begin, sir? Or shall we send a messenger first?"

"What would be the point? Don't forget why we're here. We don't need prisoners as much as experience. Do you think they'll just let us kill them?"

"What about the women?"

"You don't have enough women?" The Brahmin looked at the officer. "Look around, there are plenty among the players. Or do you prefer goblin women?"

"I have no interest in them myself, but some of the fighters... want something exotic."

"If there are such men, I will personally chop off their heads."

The Brahmin wasn't concerned about the innocence of the 'beautiful goblin women', but he needed an army, not a rabble of bandits. Or would it be more accurate to call it a sect?

"You're right, sir. Do you give the order to commence?"

"I'll do it myself."

The Brahmin jumped off his 'bone horse' and, taking a grenade launcher from one of his subordinates, fired a rocket at the gate. The rocket hit a corner, twisting one side, and causing the other side to collapse. It was more than enough.

"Attack!"

The soldiers attacked, and the priest followed them slowly, surrounded by his bodyguards. The Brahmin wasn't going to waste energy on participating in the massacre himself. The players would give him the excess experience points after battle, allowing him to take another step towards catching up with the other leaders. Perhaps he would become the strongest after all!

* * *

Today was not a good day for the goblins. Far to the northeast, Iris stood in the middle of a small village. The surviving residents had been herded into the square and huddled together, glancing nervously at the *Hellhounds*. Children cried, women begged for mercy, and men cursed through clenched teeth.

The archon felt no pity towards the lowly creatures. She needed sacrificial victims to open the way for the lord's troops. And a little luck...

"In your name, Great Izur! Kill them all!"

*   *   *

Players remaining: 8213/13000.

The retreat went even worse since the wounded slowed them down, yet the army managed to leave the second circle before evening. And stop the enemy at the breach, buying themselves time.

But the Liches clearly weren't going to let their weakened and exhausted opponent go, forcing the Circle to take extreme measures.

"Five for and one against. The decision has been made."

Dozens of titanic explosions shook the ground, turning a large part of the city to rubble and pulverizing hordes of undead. The three Liches commanding the operation ceased to exist. The nuclear mines worked as intended, giving the exhausted people a chance to rest and regroup. As for the radiation... it would be a problem for those who survived until the _return_.

*   *   *

Karandar sat on the temple steps, cleaning the flesh off an enemy's skull. Access to the interface allowed the Lich to track losses in real time, and the instant death of so many friends brought sadness. The enemy had turned out to be much stronger and more deceitful than one could have imagined. Even if the souls returned to the Altar, he couldn't resurrect them.

But this didn't change anything—his duty was to destroy all enemies in the hope that his former kin would take advantage of this last chance.

*　*　*

Far away, an army of goblins was moving along an ancient road. Not as strong as last time, but it included three hundred *Chosen Heroes*, who had believed the words of the dynastic descendant and had joined the Last Campaign. To the battle in which the fate of this world would be decided.

CHAPTER 10
SABOTAGE

IF YOU CONSIDERED what people fear most in our world, nuclear war would be up there. Before the arrival of the System, it was considered the most likely cause of humanity's downfall. The scientists had calculated the end of the world, which was then portrayed by writers and film directors. However, the forecast had improved in recent decades, and instead of the death of all living things, scientists began to say that part of the population would probably survive. A dangerous model that left hope mainly for the top brass. It's much easier to stick to your guns and press the button, knowing that you are guaranteed a spot in the bunker. Or to believe that a cornered opponent won't dare to use the last resort...

"It won't reach us, will it?" Tatra asked.

"Don't worry, we're far enough away," I

smiled. "Besides, it's one of the options. It might not come to that at all."

Empty words. If I understood the situation, the use of nuclear land mines was almost inevitable. Either the Alliance army would find a way to stop the undead following them, or the "tactical retreat" would turn into a "strategic defeat". They could try to hold back the undead in a bottleneck at the wall, but this would only gain a little time. To hope that the undead would stop on their own, without venturing further... was very naive.

"Exactly. They won't dare!"

However, this didn't sound very convincing, considering our movements. As soon as we received the warning, I ordered everyone to move to the basement—the shock wave wouldn't reach us, but I wasn't sure about the radiation. And nobody said that I was being overly cautious.

"We'll wait and see," I sighed, approaching the comms operator. "Have you managed to reach Diva's squad?"

"Not yet," Sergeant Melkov replied. "They seem to be on their way. Perhaps we should cover the station for now? If the explosion goes off now, it could disable the equipment. We might not be able to fix it afterwards."

"All right," I nodded. "It's unlikely to reach us, but let's wrap it up."

If I remembered correctly, the electromagnetic pulse didn't travel far following a nuclear detonation, but why risk it? I recalled the other factors, trying to estimate the size of the affected area. Four land mines, about one kiloton each? I doubted there were more. Each mine was enough to wipe out everything in a radius of eighty meters. It would be very "hot" for another half a kilometer from the epicenter, literally and figuratively. Shrapnel, blast wave, fire and radiation would kill every living thing. And the undead too. Especially if the charges were laid in different places and blew up at the same time.

The main concern was radiation damage, which was unlikely to affect the undead, but would make life difficult for us. The charges shouldn't be dirty, however, they weren't made specifically for the mission but taken from military warehouses. The weapons were intended for sabotage in our world. If I wasn't mistaken, they should have been destroyed as part of an agreement. Nevertheless, as practice had shown, some were hidden, someone didn't sign the agreement, and someone honestly disposed of old land mines, but promptly made new ones. I considered the worst possible situation: radiation spreading for hundreds of kilometers, depending on the direction and strength of the wind.

I went up to the window. Unfortunately, there was a chance that this suburb would be affected. Given the distance, we were unlikely to receive much radiation. Cancer in the distant future wasn't something to fear in our situation. The group would either die from simpler things like physical injuries, or our healers would eliminate the consequences. I had nothing to fear at all, but it'd be stupid not to take safety measures when they cost me nothing. Or not to do a minor favor for an ally, although Diva's group wasn't in much danger. The main danger for them wouldn't be the radiation, but the reaction of the undead, which would suffer huge losses. If everything went according to plan, of course.

*　*　*

I was left alone with Yuki to witness the consequences of the explosion, while the rest of the group took refuge inside the *Slaver's Bag (C)*. There wasn't much point, since even with magical exhaustion, I could get the others out if there was a problem, but extra caution never hurt. Plus, it was a chance for us to talk. There hadn't been much time recently, even though Yuki was in my cult, which meant she was trustworthy. Much more than most other people around me.

"Are you scared?" I broke the silence.

"Should I be? There is little risk."

"I'm not talking about the land mines, but about the situation in general."

"Maybe I am. But if I didn't know how to deal with my emotions, I'd have died ages ago. Do you want me to tell you a... secret, I guess?"

"Sure."

"You know that the Tokyo Thousand were selected differently from the others, right? It's why the Japanese players are much stronger than

233

ordinary newbies."

"Yes, an elimination tournament. The last surviving candidate became a player."

"That's right, in short. Do you know who my first opponent was?"

"No."

"Shinzo Suga."

Oddly enough, I recognized the name, even though I didn't know many Japanese people.

"The missing Prime Minister?"

"Yes, I recognized him right away. My brother was a player, so I knew what was going on at once. So did Mr. Suga. He said he was getting old and didn't want to kill such a young girl. He asked me to kill him and keep living."

"What a noble man."

"I thought so too, but he struck as soon as I drew close. I think he knew that he couldn't defeat me in an honest fight and resorted to lies. If the System hadn't healed the winner, I would have been left with a scar." Yuki touched her stomach thoughtfully, running her fingers up to her navel. If she was indicating the length of her wound, I wasn't sure how she'd survived at all. The System weapon should have drained her in a matter of seconds...

"Would you still call him a noble man?"

The most obvious step would be to denounce his duplicity, but why should the old man die? Everyone wants to live, and he'd simply tried to use the opportunity.

"What kind of weapon did you have?"

"A sword."

As far as I knew, candidates had been given random weapons during the selection process, and only those who reached the end had received skills. Could I blame the old man for wanting to survive?

"He would have made a strong player. Unlucky for him, he came up against you."

Well, the fate of the missing Prime Minister was now clear. The bodies of those who died in the trials had simply disappeared, leaving behind only equipment. If the people of Japan wanted to bury him with honors, they would have to ask the gods for his corpse.

"Maybe, but I never liked his political views. Suga-san taught me a valuable lesson. My next opponent was a man armed with a spear. I didn't stand a chance in a fair fight. So, I told him a sob story, even cried a little, and when he came closer, I slit open his throat... like this." Yuki drew a hand across her neck. Impressive... add to that a bunch of local missions in the ruins of a flooded city, monstrous Slimes devouring corpses, and no idea what the future holds. Surprising that she hadn't gone crazy.

"Our trials either break us or toughen us up. Does it still bother you?"

"It bothered me until I obtained the right skill. The one you gave me in the *Dungeon*. Now, these are simply memories I can talk about. No more nightmares."

"I appreciate your frankness."

"You know, I actually feel better. I should have shared this with someone a long time ago."

Obviously, the murder of such a prominent figure wasn't something you would discuss with a public psychologist. I didn't promise to keep her secret; it was implied. The world had changed so much that this tale would harm the deceased politician more than the girl, if it ever got out.

"Thank you for listening to me."

"You're welcome. Any time."

The conversation petered out, and we went back to waiting. I was lost in thought, and the explosion came almost as a surprise. Thunder, a slight tremor of the walls, and then silence. That was it. If I didn't know about the cause, I would have assumed that it was a weak earthquake.

"Was that it?"

"I guess so. We'll learn more soon."

The waiting was now filled not only with the occasional sentence, but also with watching the radiation meter. It showed nothing special, as we had expected. The background radiation had been close to zero, and now it crept up until it reached the conditionally safe level. A risk of cancer and mutations in our children, but we weren't going to settle down here for the rest of our lives, were we? But what was the situation outside?

"Bri, check the surface."

"Yes, boss." Released from the bag, the ghost rushed to the stairs. One of the meters had been left outside, and Bri didn't fear radiation. I could have gone up there myself, but I was too lazy to get up.

My scout returned after a couple of minutes with a report. As expected, the situation outside was worse, but only slightly. The pouring rain had gotten worse, so I could assume that the fires wouldn't spread far. The important thing was for the precipitation not to turn out to be radioactive. There were no surprises so far.

I was much more concerned about the strategic consequences. What came next? The Alliance army would probably spend the next few days regrouping, resting, and scouting ahead. Traveling through the radioactive zone would be madness, since there wasn't enough protective equipment for everyone. At the moment, only elite detachments could try to reach the temple, but even this was highly unlikely. As a matter of fact, I had a radiation suit, but I couldn't see a use for it so far. Even moving in it was difficult, let alone fighting.

Right, I could guess what our competitors would do. But what tactics would the undead use? I could imagine several possible scenarios, depending on the available forces and resources. They had two main goals: protecting the temple and destroying the army, but did they have enough strength to do both? If not, all their forces would be concentrated in the center, which didn't make my task any easier. Well, to hell with it...

Retrieve Oleg the Prophet (Level 4) from the bag?

Yes/No

"Did everything go well?"

"In a manner of speaking. The wind has carried the radiation to us, but the level is relatively safe in our area. Just use the counters and remain underground for the next few hours."

It only took me ten seconds to let all my allies out—there weren't that many of us left.

"What are we going to do next?"

"Try to contact the main forces, and check that their plan worked as intended. Personally, I'm going to bed. Tatra, do you want to keep me company?"

* * *

Nothing interesting happened until morning. By this time, everyone had distributed their attribute points and were busy exploring their new skills. What one normally achieved through years of hard training, the System gave immediately. The soldiers already possessed the training, so many had reached the first limit, although units didn't get a bonus for reaching 10 in an attribute. Unlike players and even heroes. It made sense to bestow the hero status on them, especially since some had free experience, but...

Attention! Do you want to give this creature a Name? (10 SP, 150 mana units)

Yes/No

In addition to picking a nickname and spending experience points, it required mana, so I wasn't going to bother. Another time, perhaps. We were already wasting time, waiting for my reserve to be replenished.

Since there wasn't much to do, I spent some time conversing with the slave who had made a mistake.

"Do you understand what you did wrong, Armet?"

"Yes." The politician looked away. Wasn't this a sign of lying? Or was it fear?

"Which is what?"

"I shouldn't have tried to... take control of you."

I nodded—he was right overall, he shouldn't have tried. Either you succeed or you face the consequences. However, since I still planned to use him, I wasn't going to share this revelation with him.

"That's right. You won't get another chance. If you try to do something like that again, our contract will be void. Do you understand?"

"Yes, I understand."

Somehow, I doubted it. The main problem was that neither of us took his slave status seriously. Nor was he a slave in the legal sense.

"Alright. Then get to work creating crystals. As small as possible."

Legion usually didn't stipulate the size of the bribe, so I decided to make small crystals, use them when his appetite grew excessive. It was a pity that Armet's reserve was tiny, and you couldn't create stones smaller than 10-20 units, since they simply crumbled to dust.

"And I forbid you from talking to other people.

Do you understand?"

"What if I get... thirsty?"

Going to the toilet, walking, and eating were the most convenient moments to do something stupid. I hoped he was smart enough to refrain from that.

"You'll be looked after. If you need anything, raise your hand, and they'll summon me."

*　*　*

Then we waited again. The communication session with the army was on time, although they didn't tell us anything new, only confirming the success of the trap. The undead offensive had stopped, and the forts weren't exposed to radiation due to a "lucky wind". Diva's group finally answered in the afternoon, when I was becoming seriously worried.

"Do you read me?"

"We're here," came the voice of the priestess. "There were no losses."

"Did you know about the nuclear strike?"

"No. I can't believe none of them warned us! If my hair starts to fall out, I... it doesn't matter."

I didn't think it was done maliciously—rather, the leaders had decided not to notify the majority of the players about this plan, and ordinary informants weren't in the inner circle. Well, and they didn't inform us personally because they were busy with more important things. Or they didn't consider it important enough since the explosions didn't pose a direct threat to our group.

"Is it that bad?"

"No, not really. We got caught in a black rain, so had to wait for several hours. We got exposed to some radiation, but nothing that our healers couldn't handle. Is our plan still in force?"

"Yes, we'll move out in… An hour and a half."

That's how long was left until my recovery. Having a timer for abnormal states was quite convenient. So, they had been traveling for about a day, and I would have to repeat this feat to catch up with them. I wasn't looking forward to it.

*　*　*

Attention! Minor Magical Exhaustion eliminated!

Evening was approaching, but I was reluctant to wait until morning. Radiation remained at an acceptable level, and the undead was gathering forces for a new strike, according to intelligence. It was hard to say how it would all end, but the reserves had to come from somewhere. A better moment for a dash to the temple may not come again.

Activate combat form!

The returned attributes and layer of armor gave me a soothing sense of safety. There hadn't been any experiments on the topic, but it was possible that the pseudoflesh could provide some protection from radiation. It didn't cover my respiratory system, but _Healing_ meant I wasn't too worried about the effects of radiation. The radiation meter was showing quite low readings, so it didn't even make sense to use a respirator for now. I had a long run ahead of me, so I had no desire to complicate the task.

"Well, I'm off."

There was no trouble at first—I easily managed to avoid the infrequent undead. But then night fell on the city. Unlike in some games, it didn't make the monsters stronger, of course, but it became harder to spot them. I'd never obtained a skill like *Cat's Eye*, but it wouldn't have helped anyway, because it only amplified the available light. The stars were the only source of light, and they were completely blocked by clouds, so absolute darkness reigned. Another eternal fear of humanity.

Fortunately, modern night vision devices use infrared and could work even in such conditions. The world became black and green with a few red heat spots, which barely interfered with movement. Unfortunately, the undead were almost the same temperature as their surroundings, so I had to stay alert and rely on my ghost scout. However, the risk of losing Bri had increased dramatically: it wasn't easy for two invisible beings to find each other, especially in the dark. Thankfully, *Heresy* allowed me to send messages, specifying the meeting points. Still...

"I hate the dark."

I also hated radiation. The counter had started beeping several times, warning me that the level slightly exceeded the norm. But if the wind had been blowing in the opposite direction, this region could have avoided contamination altogether.

After almost eight hours on the road, with infrequent breaks for mana recovery, and feeling pretty exhausted, I welcomed the dawn. A virtual map and a real compass allowed me to estimate the distance I had traveled. Thirty-five kilometers, pretty good.

However, my joy was short-lived. A magical wave, resembling a search wave, passed through me, and then again in the opposite direction. What was that? Were the undead looking for saboteurs? Luckily, *Invisibility* remained active, so I didn't that I had been spotted.

"Bri, where are you? I'm at the intersection."

Alas, the ghost couldn't reply, so I had to rely on its ability to navigate. It was a flaw, no matter how you looked at it. Bri didn't appear after five, then after ten minutes, so I was beset by doubts. And suspicion. Already knowing the answer, I raised my head to the sky.

Blink!

Blink!

Activate Flight!

I paused in midair. There were more and more multi-storey buildings as I drew closer to the center, but I was high enough to look around. Without much surprise, I spotted a familiar tower in the distance.

"A ghost trap, of course. Shit."

Mana: 989/2,450.

A second later, I glided onto the roof of the nearest building. Now I knew where to search for the missing ghost. But should I?

*   *   *

I didn't like complicated moral choices. Did I join the main squad or head to the ghost tower, risking not only my life, but also the success of the mission? Wouldn't it be a huge joke if humanity perished because of my "loyalty"? Or was it my greed? The ghost was a valuable vassal.

In contrast to the outer circles, the strategic point was unlikely to be abandoned. There might even be an owner, in addition to guards. Was I ready to face a lich? No, I was being paranoid. Even if dead mages preferred towers, they was unlikely to be home right now. The mages would be either blocking the army of players or guarding the temple. What would the point in remaining so far from the battlefield?

Okay, why make assumptions when I could go and check? I had a bit of time, and I had to at least try to save the ghost. Especially when I'd know about its death right away.

"Bri, I know you can hear me! Don't panic and try to hold on for... a couple of hours. I'll try to get you out of the tower. If you get caught, don't you dare tell them anything!"

Not that Bri could reveal anything really important. I had never shared my strategic plans with the ghost and didn't discuss them in its presence.

"Legion!" I touched the bag, releasing the raven.

"Yes? Where are we?"

"The same place as before. Ghost towers don't work on you, right?"

"Towers? Yes, that's right."

"Bri has been sucked into one. Can we get it out?"

"Not much has changed since last time. You need to give it a body or destroy the tower formation."

"Like I thought... Okay, get back in the bag for now."

I didn't demand that Legion dug up and destroy the plates himself—and not because he had claws instead of hands. I had to scout out and assess the situation first. If the tower was empty, all I needed to do was step inside and collect Bri. If it hadn't been devoured by its fellow ghosts before then.

*　*　*

My fears were well-founded. I had to make 1.5-hour detour to reach the tower, and this area was much more closely controlled by the undead. I was glad that I hadn't send the raven ahead to investigate. And why hadn't I bought him an *Invisibility* card? So many errors and shortcomings were becoming clear along the way! Apparently, having high *Intelligence* was no magic pill.

My earpiece beeped alarmingly, transmitting another warning.

Radiation: 0.5 Sv/h.

Had this area been struck by black rain? Remaining in this zone for long promised, in addition to the traditional risk of cancer and poor well-being, infertility. If I didn't have *Healing*, the beautiful lady goblins could be waiting in vain...

Another annoying thing I had to consider was that objects tended to accumulate radiation. After a long walk through contaminated territory, my weapons and equipment could start "glowing in the dark." In other words, emit radiation. Carrying them around was a dubious pleasure. The same applied to possible loot, although I'd decide once I got any. The situation was less dire with System items, since they would be cleaned when I brought them into my personal room. This would also eliminate one of the main dangers—radioactive dust, which couldn't be removed from the lungs under normal conditions. It had worked with dust and blood. The main thing was not to put the infected items away in a bag or *Ring*. A pity this wouldn't work with units and heroes.

Activate Healing!

I returned to the roofs as I drew closer to my target, so the view of the tower was quite spectacular. Two Bone Knights stood at the door, and there were plenty of skeleton warriors patrolling the perimeter.

Ancient Bone Knight. Rank D+. Level ???

Wow! I didn't dare to use Identification, but what I could see was enough. The ancient warrior's bones glinted black and were comparable to iron in strength. Yet he wasn't worth any more experience than an ordinary skeleton. One of the Knights turned his head, and his eyes flashed golden.

"Is it some kind of skill?"

This was a valid question—since the sabotage squads had never reached this spot, it meant that the undead had a way of fighting invisible foes. Their leaders could well possess a skill like True Light. On the other hand, he couldn't spot me from this distance, and I had no intention of getting closer. I strongly doubted that one of these fellows was the master of the tower. And if the Knights were standing guard, then who was the master? Was this really a Lich's dwelling?

The skeletons were ancient too. Funny, I'd never seen the intermediate form between Skeleton Warrior (F) and Bone Knight (D). I'd never even heard of such beings. If they were in the same "development line", then where were the Death Squires (E) or something? There were two possibilities: either skeleton evolution was incredibly rare, or they skipped the step somehow. Well, anything was possible since the faction was completely artificial. It wasn't the question I should have been worrying about right now, but it was difficult to control one's stream of thought.

A line of stones near the top of the tower glowed faintly. It wasn't very noticeable in the daytime, but it could be a real *lighthouse* at night. At least if you had *Magical Vision*. Perhaps the first tower also had such protection, but I couldn't see mana flows back then, only sense them.

Frankly, the more I considered the situation, the less I wanted to get involved. Apart from the strange magic, hundreds of Bone Birds nested on the roof. Some of them took off, and some landed. I could call this place a dovecote with a certain degree of irony. But why combine such a place with a ghost tower? I had no definite answer to this question, only theories. For example, this is where Bone Birds were created, using ghosts as a kind of donor. Or they created "coordinators" here, since the leaders of large flocks clearly possessed a consciousness.

A few minutes of passive scanning, and a sign I'd been expecting popped up above one of the creatures.

Bone Leader. Rank E. Level ???

Well, it was nice to see that logic and intuition hadn't let me down this time, but it only made the situation worse. If I didn't do anything, perhaps Bri would eventually turn into such a creature.

"Hmm." Now that my worst suspicions had been proven correct, I had to make a choice. The saddest part was, I knew which decision was the **rational** one.

Attention! Do you wish to kill the hero Bri? (10 SP)
Yes/No

Every member of the *Cult of Heresy* depended

on its leader, and a captured scout posed a threat to our entire mission. Even if the ghost knew very little, it was enough. How could I be sure Bri would remain silent?

And yet... was I going too far by thinking that the future of humanity depended on me? The others would manage even if I died. My death would slightly lower the chance of a successful outcome, no more than that. In that case...

No.

Although Bri had been disloyal in the past, it was now fully aware of its position. Simply out, Bri respected strength. As long as the leash was strong enough, I would remain its boss. The ghost would also perish if I died, so the risk of betrayal was low. Not that I could rely on gratitude—if Bri ever became strong enough to free itself, it may well try to avenge the years of oppression. Here and now, though, this didn't matter.

"I'm close. I'm watching the tower. Wait for my orders and keep your head down."

I sent the message and stayed put, observing the enemy's reaction. As expected, there was none. It wasn't a great loyalty check, but better than nothing. Okay, since I'd made the decision, I had to figure out how to get the princess out of the tower without too much fuss.

*   *   *

"The night, the moon, a shallow dig..." I recalled an old song. It didn't make sense to dig deep, I just had to place another explosive charge and remove the traces. It was a simple task, but very tedious, considering the undead patrols and the commentator perched on my shoulder. Unlike ordinary ravens, whose weight didn't exceed a couple of kilograms, Legion weighed more than five. Unfortunately, I couldn't manage without his hints, so I had to put up with the inconvenience.

I leveled the area, a barely noticeable antenna tendril protruding from it, disguised as a dried-up plant stem, and straightened up. Perhaps removing the formation plates would be more reliable, but since this place had owners, they could spot the interference ahead of time. They were also buried deeper, and the conditions weren't conducive to excavating.

"Yes, that's enough!" Legion croaked. "It should work."

Finally. I had to dig up only seven tablets last time, but I decided to play it safe and destroyed fifteen of them here. Although the raven had an idea of how these formations were created, they could vary slightly, and some of the "key points" were located in overly dangerous places. Even now, I was working ten meters away from a skeleton warrior, and the slightest mistake could set off an alarm.

Fortunately, the *Invisibility* field covered not only me, but also the ground where I was excavating. Nevertheless, working with an enemy sentry lurking behind you was a dubious pleasure. Alas, this was an important spot, unless I wanted to go lay charges in five or six more places.

Even so, I didn't dare do this where the Knights were watching. Since they were familiar with ghosts here, they probably had ways of searching for them. Perhaps Bri was sitting in some kind of cage and couldn't escape at all? I had to accept the risk if I didn't want to openly storm the tower.

"A little more, and you will become a true master of formations under my supervision!"

"How much is a little more?"

"Ten years, at this rate. Just don't forget to pay for the lessons. You promised me three crystals!"

"You don't need to remind me. Have I ever deceived you in the past? You'll get your reward, but let's get out of here first."

* * *

"Bri, can you hear me? The tower formation will be damaged in an hour, and a hole will open on the side of the main entrance. Your goal is to escape and catch up with me."

I described the meeting place as best as I could. Waiting for him by the tower was too risky. The explosions were unlikely to go unnoticed, which meant that they would be looking for me. I preferred to have a significant head start by then.

Having sent Bri the instructions, I started the timer and sped away from there. I planned to run long and hard, using doping. Hopefully, it wouldn't lead to another magical exhaustion.

* * *

An hour later, a familiar wave rolled over me, followed by a gigantic explosion. Turning around, I was prepared to see another mushroom cloud, but I was wrong.

I didn't waste mana on teleportation, but I could see that the ghost tower no longer existed when I climbed up onto the roof.

"Legion, what does this mean?"

"It's... it's not our fault!"

"You mean the tower blew up on its own?"

"We compromised the integrity of the formation when we released the ghosts! Someone probably wanted to recapture them and activated the trap again!"

It made sense. To some extent, everything had gone even better than expected. No witnesses, no traces, just a single question. Did the tower explode before it had recaptured all its fugitives, or after? But I knew how to get an answer to this question.

CHAPTER 11

THE MEETING PLACE

BRI WAS STILL LISTED as a member of the cult, so the ghost had survived despite the dubiousness of my plan and the final glitch. I had no intention of returning to the site of the explosion. Undead from miles around were surely flocking there right now. What would I do there, anyway?

"Find me. I am heading towards the center, and I will leave cues from time to time."

The message was sent. I hoped the ghost would scan the city from above and find me quickly enough, but this didn't happen after an hour or two. I marked a new meeting place and removed *Invisibility* from time to time, but there was no sign of my vassal. I also had no luck with a *window*. I couldn't find a spot with a stable connection to the Server.

Another problem was the lack of sufficient

reconnaissance. To release the raven was to expose him to endless aerial battles. So, I had to rely on more primitive methods: my own vision, hearing, and skills.

Activate Search for Life!

The scan revealed thirteen figures around the corner, and then came a "greeting" in return. The wave that passed through my *Invisibility* field was weak, but I was getting better at sensing such details. This coincidence didn't bode well. I hadn't stumbled across a simple undead patrol, but someone powerful enough to sense my actions. They were unlikely to let me pass just because they couldn't see me.

"Legion, we've been spotted," I said. "Distract the enemies."

"Could this be dangerous?"

"It doesn't matter! Do it, or I won't give you any more crystals!"

"You wouldn't dare!"

Nevertheless, the raven took off from my shoulder as he spoke. Legion flapped his wings several times and landed on a pillar. Just in time. My suspicions were confirmed when a group of Skeleton Warriors rushed out from behind a distant house. They were led by an Ancient Bone Knight.

"Get their attention."

"Caw!"

Legion was enveloped in flames, which made the wood beneath him crumble, and took off. The Knight raised his hand and released a black clot...

This wasn't part of the plan! The flames around the raven thickened to withstand the attack, and the bird crashed into the grass with a plaintive croak.

"I'll pretend to be wounded, and you kill him!" Legion's voice said in my head. We could communicate mentally over short distances, and we were still close to each other.

"Alright."

The Knight didn't rush forward but sent his retinue. I moved slowly forward, stepping to the right and then to the left to avoid a collision. It wasn't hard. In that moment, the Knight 's eyes lit up.

"You will die! You will die!" said the voices in my head, but completely different voices this time.

Blink!

The voices predicting my death abruptly fell silent. I glanced over my shoulder, assessing the situation. The skeletons, who had initially ignored me, were now clustered around the spot I'd left a second ago, slicing the air with their *bone swords*. There was no sign that I'd been spotted until the very end. If not for Cassandra, they might have succeeded. No, they would have definitely succeeded.

Change of plan. A split second later, the skeletons turned in my direction, ignoring the raven completely. Considering the situation didn't stop me from speeding up. I drew closer to my main opponent—the Knight already waiting for me. I had to finish him, and quickly. *Identification.*

"You will die, you will die, you will die!"

Blink!

Overlay!

The black clot missed me and kept flying. Now that I was behind the Knight, I slashed at his neck. More precisely, at the thick bone collar protecting the vulnerable spot. A divine sword was a formidable weapon on its own, and together with the *Spiritual Sword* and the applied force...

Split!

Hell, his armor was as strong as metal! Shards flew in all directions, and the head rolled to the side. I jumped back, narrowly avoiding a retaliatory blow. Even in this state, the Knight continued to function, but then his eye sockets went dark, and he began to move less confidently. As expected, his search ability relied on sight, so I had regained my main advantage. Invisibility. The Knight vigorously waved his sword to stop me from getting any closer to him. I took a moment to pop a capsule into my mouth and glance at the scan results.

Ancient Bone Knight (87%)

Status: *Undead.*

Type: *Silver.*

Creature Rank: *D+.*

Level: *20.*

Danger: *moderate.*

Specifications:

Strength: 25.

Agility: 12.

Intelligence: 7.

Durability: 20.

Stamina: 20.

Wisdom: 20.

Perception: 20.

Instinct: 20.

Features:

— Undead — this creature is already dead and was reanimated using magic.

— Regeneration — this creature's bones can fuse back together, if there is available material.

— Search for Life II — the creature senses living beings within a certain radius.

— System Creature — the creature belongs to the System and is capable of development.

— Pack Leader — the creature can control younger members of its species.

— Dead Man's Gaze — reveals what is hidden when activated.

— Death Arrow — magic that devours life. The dead rise as undead.

— Raising a Skeleton Warrior — allows the creature to create a combat construct. Quality depends on the raw materials.

— Steel Bones III — the creature's bones have tremendous strength.

Son of a... Level 20! I risked a lot by engaging him in close combat. If not for the lack of System skills, the Knight would be superior to me in all aspects. Although Sword Master wasn't on his list of virtues, he handled the weapon with great skill. These thoughts floated in the background, without impeding my actions. I couldn't stop since there was a risk that he would send a message. He might have already sent it. I had left myself exposed, and the only way to minimize the consequences was to destroy all enemies as quickly as possible.

Retrieve the player Yuki (Level 10) from the bag!

Retrieve the player Tatra (Level 5) from the bag!

Retrieve the player Dark Steel (Level 9) from the bag!

Retrieve the player Dragonfly (Level 8) from the bag!

...

Retrieve the Unnamed Unit from the bag (Level 2)!

"I'll deal with the leader! The skeletons are on you!" There was no time to explain the plan. The world had narrowed to the Knight still hacking at the air around him. The downside was that he couldn't see me, so he was expecting an attack from all four sides. But not from above.

Flight!

I jumped and struck downwards, driving the blade in next to his neck. Overlay! There was practically no armor in this spot, and the blade slid in with ease. However, I had to not only shove half a meter of steel inside, but to pierce the *heart*. *Split!*

Attention! You have gained 450 SP! (491/460)

Attention! The Sword of Heresy has

consumed 90 SP!

Attention! You have reached Level 24! (31/480)

It was becoming easier to endure the energy flow, but *Invisibility* disappeared this time. Then came the pain, and my pant leg grew warm with blood. The Knight had managed to get me somehow. The skeletons were drawing closer, and my mana was almost at zero...

"Hold on!" Steel burst forward, taking down the skeleton with a huge shield. The others stood on either side of me. The second half of the squad scattered, covering us with their rifles.

"How are you doing?" Steel asked over his shoulder.

"I'm alright."

The pseudoflesh had softened the blow, and the blood... There wasn't much. I tightened the tourniquet sewn into my clothes, then touched the wound with my fingers. *Healing!* I couldn't spare enough mana for this but, at least, I could move and fight without worrying about collapsing at any moment. It was time to finish the undead.

I stood up and ran, ignoring the pain and the limp. My comrades were well-equipped and trained, but they weren't *Masters*, and there were a lot of skeletons. Well, not all of them.

Yuki and Steel dispatched four on the move, Tatra took on another one, and didn't seem to be losing. The others simply kept our opponents back so they could be fired at. It was difficult to hit the *heart*, but the joints were vulnerable. A dull shot rang out and a skeleton's leg gave way. He collapsed, and no longer posed a danger.

"Watch the sky!" I reminded them. "We can't be spotted!"

However, Legion was already hovering overhead without my warning. We didn't need to worry about the Bone Birds unless a large flock appeared. The buildings provided some cover, and the birds didn't ascend too high for some reason. Otherwise, we would have been spotted for sure.

Attention! You have gained 35 SP! (66/480)

Attention! The Sword of Heresy has consumed 7 SP!

After the last fight, the skeletons felt like a surprisingly weak opponent. My blade entered the armor join between the ribs. It wasn't the easiest blow, but my hand and blade stayed strong, shattering the sphere even without an active skill. The skeletons, although dark with age, hadn't yet reached the "ancient" status.

I didn't take the same risk with the next warrior—I cut off his arms first, and only then stabbed him in the *heart*.

Attention! You have gained 25 SP! (91/480)

Attention! The Sword of Heresy has consumed 5 SP!

The battle was practically over at this point. Several enemies were still moving, but they no longer posed a threat. We just had to finish them off and collect the loot.

"I'll take this one," I said, approaching one of the fallen. "Otherwise, I won't be able to activate the *barrier* at a critical moment."

It probably wasn't very fair since my role in neutralizing this skeleton was minimal, but I had to keep my free experience at a certain level. One hundred and five points, to be exact. For one 100-point skill and Backup. I even kept a small stock of "canned goods" to make sure I had enough for the latter when going up a level. But what I had would be enough for now.

Attention! You have gained 25 SP! (116/480)

Attention! The Sword of Heresy has consumed 5 SP!

How much experience had the blade absorbed in all this time? Frankly, I'd lost count a long time ago. Nor did I have a clue where all those points went. Perhaps the sword would evolve one day? No idea...

"Did you see that? I nearly died!" The raven landed nearby. "You should compensate me for the danger and give me three crystals! No, four crystals!"

"I'll give you a small one. You did well."

"Just one? I narrowly escaped death!"

"One more word and I'll change my mind."

The raven opened his beak indignantly but remained silent. Wow, it had worked. Alright, time to the collect the spoils of war. Simply put, it was looting time.

*   *   *

Healing!

I moved my foot, checking that everything was fine. The pant leg was dirty, but that was a chore for another time. The others had finished cleaning up by this time. The monsters had dropped the standard loot: a bunch of empties from the skeletons and a rather interesting skill from the Knight.

Raising a Skeleton Warrior skill card
Rank: *E.*
Level: *1/5.*
Description:
— Allows you to create a combat necroconstruct. Quality depends on the raw materials.
— Requires mana.
Activation cost: *variable.*
Duration: *variable.*
Saturation:
17/100 SP.

"Interesting... Tatra, do you want to become a necromancer?"

"Sure!" the girl agreed promptly, snatching the card from me. "A skeleton? It could fight in close combat instead of me, right?"

"Then it's yours."

"Thank you!"

It wasn't a cheap gift, but the saturation was

tiny, and a single skeleton would be of no use to me. Unlike Tatra. Besides, I had appropriated another's experience, and although I didn't see any disapproval, a little generosity couldn't hurt. If I wanted to become a necromancer, I could always buy the skill later through the Altar... The idea was right but felt false somehow. As if I was acting on automatic, not really believing in the success of our campaign. It wasn't a good attitude to have.

The Ancient Knight's remains turned out to be heavier and stronger than those of ordinary undead, but they weren't steel. I had to take the bones with me, and not only because I didn't want to leave any traces. The bones were Systemic, which meant that they were a System resource. The fact that they had belonged to sentient beings bothered the players less and less. The swords definitely didn't bother anyone anymore. The Knight's blade turned out to be unexpectedly decent. *Identification.*

Sword of the Knight of Y
Material: *Bone.*
Length: *0.7 m.*
Type: *System weapon.*
Rank: *E-.*
Features:
Enables the owner to absorb 50% of the victim's spirit and life force.
— 10% goes to the patron god.
— 40% goes to the owner.
— Strength I.
Dedication:

This was the first time I'd gotten my hands on one. Not only was its rank higher than that of the traditional Sword of Warrior of Y, but the patron god took half as much. Thanks to the extra *Strength* feature, the blade was better than the standard F-ranked weapon. Except there was no scabbard card, and the weapon was awkward to use since it was fused to the undead and there was no handle. Nor was there a guard... Well, these design flaws were solvable.

The dagger I'd killed the adviser with during the negotiations was also dedicated to the Great Y, but I had received the full sixty percent then. I hadn't personally killed anyone with a *bone blade*. I had learned from the reports that the god took a percentage. Should I check? I had nobody to test it on right now, plus... Why hadn't I tried to remove the dedication until now? After all, it had worked with the *Monster Hammer* dedicated to Izur. Odd that such a straightforward idea only came to me now.

Attention! Do you want to desecrate/remove the dedication from the Sword of the Knigth of Y? (Heresy of Cain)

Yes/No

Attention! Dedication has been removed from the item!

Additional property has been obtained:

— Desecration — the blessing of the gods cannot be placed on this object.

The item's name has been changed to the Knight's Desecrated Sword!

— *50% goes to the owner.*

I didn't receive any bonuses, but I didn't get a penalty from the dead god either. I had basically obtained another source of normal System weapons. Even if the swords often fell apart after the undead were killed, and the units couldn't get such a trophy, we had gathered hundreds of them. Their price would increase significantly once we removed the binding. I could certainly give them to the goblins. I had to wonder if this would backfire though. Besides, if I could pull off something like this, the priests could too. It just depended on how quickly they would figure it out. So, I ought to keep quiet about this ability until I'd bought up as many of these weapons as I could. This only mattered if we completed the mission and returned to Earth.

"We're done," Oleg reported. "What's next?"

"Get back in the bag." I stood up. "We shouldn't stay here."

*   *   *

Oddly, there was no pursuit, so after an hour I found a suitable building and put up a shielded tent inside. I needed to distribute the attribute points for the last level. The goal was getting closer, time was running out, and any boost would help. Some cover wouldn't hurt though.

Retrieve the player Yuki (Level 10) from the bag!

"Can you keep watch? I'm going to distribute the attribute points."

"Of course."

The girl sat down at the entrance, placing the katana beside her. I gazed at her back. Good posture. Her ass wasn't bad either... yet the thought was lackluster, just a statement of fact. I didn't have any plans regarding her. I didn't need a harem—it was a pleasant dream, but too stressful in practical terms.

Attributes:

Strength: 8/10 (100 SP) + 4 =12.

Agility: 11/15 + 2 = 13.

Intelligence: 11/15 + 2 = 13.

Vitality: 12/15 + 1=13.

Stamina: 11/15 + 4 = 15.

Perception: 10/15 + 3 = 13.

Luck: 2/10 (1000 SP).

Race Attribute:

Intuition: 15/15 (300 SP).

Additional Attributes:

Wisdom: 15/15 (300 SP).

Spiritual Energy: 4.

Faith: 0.

Heresy: 9 (Cult of Cain).

Fame: 7.

Deactivate the combat form!

Right, let's start at the start. Only one attribute could be raised to the second limit at present. Although I remained apprehensive, something really bad was unlikely to happen. Except that it would hurt...

Stamina: +1 (12).

I hissed. Funny, I had stayed still and silent, although the procedure hadn't become any more pleasant since the last time. Was I getting used to it? Or was it pride and unwillingness to show weakness?

Transfer the Stamina attribute from the Combat Form to the Main Body?

Yes/No

Another bout of torture, much more painful than last time. Blood trickled from my bitten lip. *Healing!*

Stamina: +1 (13).

I listened to myself, trying to assess the changes. So far, they were positive and I didn't see any warnings. Let's continue.

Stamina: +1 (14).

Something felt wrong this time. Slightly wrong, but enough for me to choose another attribute.

Vitality: +1 (13).

It helped. The imbalance was minimal now, so the body should be able to withstand the change.

Stamina: +1 (15).

Attention! You have reached the Second Limit of Stamina!

Cost of unlocking the limit: 300 SP

As I had suspected, I wasn't the first, since there was no achievement bonus. Only the leader of this race got one. Well, I would try it with *Vitality* next time.

* * *

Problems, problems, problems... The counter beeped occasionally, and Bri never appeared, making me wonder about desertion. Although the ghost probably hadn't received most of my messages. The sending distance was limited, and if Bri had been closer, I would have found it by now. As I drew closer to the meeting place, what *really* started to bother me was that Diva's group had stopped responding. Of course, it could be due to magical interference of some sort, but I had to consider the worst scenario. More chances to stay alive then. If I was wrong, it would be a pleasant surprise, and not another disappointment.

Despite my apprehensions, I didn't consider stopping—too much was at stake to retreat without definite proof. Perhaps I could admit to myself that I was scared, almost nauseated with fear. I could hardly blame the radiation since my health bar was green. Pregnancy could also be excluded. Was it intuition?

I could run for hours thanks to increased *Stamina,* but I didn't risk scanning my surroundings. *Dead Man's Gaze* was an active skill, so I had a good chance of avoiding an Ancient Knight if we ran into each other. Although the fight took less than five minutes and gave me a lot of useful things, it wasn't something I wanted to repeat. Dying, even if you have *Backup,* wasn't a pleasant experience. Painful, I would say. Very painful.

"I'm here. Don't make me wait," I warned Bri again. I still had hope that the ghost would manage its topographic cretinism.

I lowered the binoculars and swore softly. I had arrived at the meeting place late in the afternoon—later than I planned, but within the agreed time limit. Since the situation was worrying me, I decided to conduct some reconnaissance. I couldn't even understand what was bothering me at first, but then I noticed traces of a recent fight. Not a huge one, but the potholes were clearly from bullets, and the dark splotches were dried blood. Judging by the amount, whoever had been bleeding was now dead.

I had to get closer to know how long ago it happened, but did I need such details? Three or five hours—what difference did it make? It was unlikely to be less, otherwise I would have heard the noise. The signs of cleaning up suggested that the players had won, but why were they staying silent? Had they damaged the radio? Uh-huh, and the spare one too. If the fight had been intense, they might have left this spot, even abandoned the camp. Okay, I'd try again.

"This is Vasily. Can you hear me?"

"I can hear you. It's me... Dmitry. What happened?"

"I could ask you the same question. I see evidence of a fight. Why the hell have you been silent for the last couple of hours?"

"Are you close by?" he clarified. "Then come

inside, we'll talk in here."

"Can you send someone out to meet me?"

"You can't find your own way? We're in the basement."

"I've been afraid of unfamiliar places and darkness since childhood. Just send someone out to meet me."

"Alright. Wait on the ground floor, near the entrance."

* * *

Our conversation ended, leaving behind a strange feeling. Everything seemed fine, but I hadn't received an answer to my question, and the spring inside me was still wound up tight. Should I contact them again and persist with my questions? If something was wrong, I shouldn't appear suspicious. That left reconnaissance.

But I didn't have the ghost, and couldn't send Legion, since he was too vulnerable in confined spaces. Should I venture in there myself under *Invisibility*? It was dangerous and what did I expect to find anyway? An undead ambush? Fine.

Summon the slave Armet!

"I have a task for you," I said, handing him a walkie-talkie and a machine gun.

"A dangerous task? I mean, what do I need to do?"

"See that five-story building? Diva's group is down in the basement. You go in there, wait for the guide, and make sure that everything is okay. Stay in touch, don't disconnect."

"You're anticipating problems?"

"I doubt it, I just spoke with Dmitry. We'll consider this... a delay."

"That's it?"

"If one of the units comes out to meet you, *ask* them if everything is fine."

"Ask? You mean my skill? But I can't use it..."

"You can this time. If you think you're in danger, say the code phrase, and I'll get you out. Got it? Off you go. And you know what? Hide your nickname and put on this cloak and mask."

* * *

If I was going to give in to my paranoia, I'd do it properly. Armet stepped out five minutes later, when I'd already shifted to another spot. He crossed the street and ducked inside the building. For a while there was silence, broken only by the sound of footsteps.

"Vasily?"

"No, I'm... don't!"

We had agreed on certain code phrases in case something went wrong, but if my scout had forgotten them all, the situation was even worse than anticipated.

Return the slave Armet to the card? (10 SP)

Yes/No

My intuition was correct, yet I wasn't fast enough. There was a burst of gunfire, and the card

in my hand faded. I was seeing it for the first time,
but I knew what it meant. My slave was dead.

INTERLUDE NO. 8
THE EXTERMINATION

THE BONE DRAGON swooped down from the heavens, releasing the *Breath of Death*. The building was enveloped in a dark cloud, and the sentries were the first to die. After all, they had been watching the streets and didn't expect such a sudden and crushing blow. The bodies collapsed and immediately got up again.

"What's happening?" came a voice from the radio.

Magic had raised them as Wights, so they wouldn't have been able to answer under normal conditions. This time, one hesitantly touched a button.

"Enemy attack," he replied. "The Bone Dragon has released a strange fog. We're retreating inside."

"Put your masks on, everyone! Can you see

anyone else?”

The former French special forces officer turned his head to watch the skeletons rush towards the building through the smoke. The same smoke now enveloped him but didn't interfere at all. On the contrary, it gave him additional strength.

"No," he lied. "The fog is too thick."

* * *

The main group of undead took about twenty seconds to break into the building. The attack came on all fronts, and the land mines only delayed them briefly.

"We can't stay here!" Dmitry shouted. "We have to leave!"

The Wights entered the room unnoticed and raised their machine guns, firing a whole swarm of bullets. However, the elite had gathered here, so they reacted instantly. The first bursts of gunfire cut down several players and units, but then magic shields went up, retaliatory shots were fired, and abilities were used...

"Intelligent undead! Watch out!"

"Help the wounded!" Diva ordered. "Dmitry, how are you?"

The undead were clearly trying to take out the leaders first, so most of the bullets struck them. The combat form went runny and disintegrated.

"Looks like I just died," Dmitry sat down, touching his bloody clothes. "Son of a bitch!"

"Be careful, stay out of sight. Hold the line! Don't let them inside the building!"

Nodding, Dmitry shrouded himself in a cloud of mana, returning to his combat form. The wounded were moaning, but there was no time to help them. The attackers were rapidly advancing. The fog wasn't the only threat, for a crowd of undead swarmed out of it. There were too many enemies. So many that it was pointless to stay and continue the fight.

"We have to leave!"

"You're right, we'll break through!"

"No, April, it won't work. We need to gather the survivors and leave the mission."

"Are you mad? Hera will never forgive us for failure!"

"I don't care, our lives are more important! We're going to die here for no reason!"

"If you want, then leave, but I won't! I'll try to break through!"

The fog, which had been almost motionless before, shrank to enclose the people inside the building. The masks helped, but this was only the beginning. Bone Birds flew through the windows, attacking people, and aiming mainly at the head.

"Don't shoot!" Dmitry shouted. "Use the swords!"

He meant System weapons, but swords was shorter. There were hundreds of birds, so losses were inevitable this time. And each fallen fighter strengthened the enemy... Someone's nerves gave out and they started firing. Or was it the undead shooting? This was the end.

"Those still alive, get back in the bags!" Dmitry ordered and activated *Invisibility*. Unfortunately, he needed to be near and see the person to send them a request.

"There's no time!" Diva responded. "We're leaving the building! Let's go!"

"If we get separated, we'll meet up at the backup point!"

Despite the critical situation, there were still enough players in the ranks. Most veterans had life-saving skills and, even after dying, immediately returned to the ranks. Unfortunately, this only worked once, and success depended on the type of injury. If you were impaled on a *bone blade*, you simply died again after resurrection.

"That's it, I'm going back to Earth!" someone shouted. "There's no point in all of us dying here! What? No! The *return card* isn't working! No, no, no!"

"Don't panic!"

There was no question of organized resistance as the undead poured inside, ignoring any attempts to stop it. Around ten players jumped out of the windows, but most of them met their death on the *bone blades*. Even *Invisibility* didn't help— the Ancient Knights controlled the situation by coordinating the lower undead.

The two were still fighting, but it was hopeless. More and more enemies were drawn to the last pocket of resistance, while they... they couldn't fly.

"April! Do you really want to die here?"

"Wait!"

Summon the hero Grykh (Level 24)!
Attention! The block has been overcome!
The signal has been sent!

The ogre appeared ready for battle in the rays of light and rushed at the crowd of undead with a roar. The hero was strong before, but now, thanks to the acquired skills, had become a real death machine. Clad in armor, with a huge mace, he resembled a combine harvester. He didn't have a mask, but he had divine protection, which filtered these threats just as well.

"This is our chance! Follow him!"

"Diva, no! Use the *return card*!"

"You don't understand! I can't! So either fight or leave!"

"Fine, let's try. You're so stubborn..."

Dmitry stopped, touching his chest, then sank down to one knee. The sniper's second bullet threw him onto his back, and blood gushed from his mouth, filling the respirator. *Regeneration* was working, but its power was insufficient, even at the second level. His consciousness was drifting away... The undead didn't wait for the third bullet but swarmed over the fallen body.

"No! No, no, no! You can't!"

Diva raised her staff and flashes of lightning dispersed the fog, striking the undead and causing them to crumble to dust. But this didn't change anything, and the next bullet hit the priestess. Her protective field worked but her mana, which was already low, dropped to zero. The battle form began to crumble.

"Mistress, we must go. You first, and I'll follow!"

Diva didn't hesitate this time and it saved her life. The bullet chipped pieces off the stones, but the priestess was no longer there. Only a pile of non-System equipment remained, which the card couldn't take to the personal room. The ogre growled and spun around, buying himself a few seconds to touch the *return card*. However, the passage opened by the *call* had already closed.

* * *

Granok approached the ogre leaning on his club. A dozen Bone Horrors, and hundreds of Knights around… The Lich was confident the *hero* couldn't reach him.

"It looks like you were left here to die?"

"Looks like it," the ogre replied hollowly. His incredible strength, divine protection, high-quality armor, and weapons only delayed the inevitable. He would die this time. Even if he reached the next level, which had been his dream for so many years.

"My name is Granok," the dead man

introduced himself. "You don't have a lot to go, do you?"

"Grykh," the ogre introduced himself. "Killing you would be enough."

Also, there was a good chance that the leader's death was his only chance of escaping here alive. Someone had to be blocking the teleportation.

"You know, I admire you," the Lich said, "not many of us goblins ever reach this level. You could become a great hero for our people."

"Yet it looks like I'll just be another skeleton in your army. Or maybe you'll let me go?"

"Are you talking about the block?" The Lich raised a hand. "Of course, I won't remove it. You are an enemy, and I need more than simple admiration to let an enemy go."

"Then why all this talk?"

"I can offer you a better fate than becoming a Wight. If you complete the transformation ritual, you can become a Lich. When the Great Y rises again, he will give us new bodies and real life!"

"The Great Y will never rise again. You are simply prolonging this agony. All you can do is decide which one of your enemies will inherit the Altar. At least people won't exterminate the goblins."

"You believe this nonsense?"

"I saw it with my own eyes! You can trust them! Otherwise, I wouldn't be here."

"You're simply dumb…"

Further conversation was pointless. The ogre

jumped to the closest enemy in a final, desperate attempt. The Bone Horrors ran him through, immobilizing him, and depriving him of any hope. The broken fingers unclenched, and the Knights dragged away his weapon.

"Not bad, you almost made it. A pity you didn't agree right away. Now we'll have to waste a couple of hours torturing you. You will agree to serve our master. No one has refused me yet."

Of course, turning the ogre into a Death Knight was much easier, but it would be a waste. The Liches had suffered heavy losses, and they needed a new "brother". The ogre's high level, and, most importantly, racial rank meant he had a good chance of rebirth.

* * *

"I have come."

"You did well, Dan. You will have new comrades soon. Now we need to determine if there are other groups out there, and how best to meet them."

"It is my duty." Although the Knight still had his skills and fragments of memory, his will was controlled by the Altar. He didn't hesitate as he pulled the trigger. The sergeant had been a good sniper in life and remained a good sniper after his death.

CHAPTER 12
RUNNING MAN

WHAT THE HELL did it mean? Confusion... Resentment... Anger... Fear... The betrayal stirred up a storm of emotions, but I was guided by reason. And instinct, which demanded that I get away from here as quickly as possible.

Activate Invisibility!

"Vasily?" Dmitry said in my earpiece. "Are you still here? Can you hear me?"

I popped a handful of pills into my mouth—I was definitely going to need *mana*—and focused on running. I didn't know the reason, motivation or details, but they weren't really important right now. Our paths had diverged, and I had to make sure that I didn't become the next victim.

"There was an accident. One of the sentries fired by mistake..."

Impossible to believe, considering that Armet

not only had the card, but also the Immortal ability. Had he used it recently and not told me? If so, then I didn't have the words to describe what I thought. However, it was much more likely that his resurrection had been blocked.

"By mistake?" I asked, and kept running. "Can someone from our group confirm that?"

"Of course. Just a second."

Frankly, I was surprised. I'd assumed that if they'd gone that far, then the third squad was dead. I'd chosen people I could trust.

"Captain? This is Lieutenant Sigaev. I confirm that what happened was a tragic accident. Better if I explain it in person. I'll come alone. Where are you now?"

I grabbed the railing to make a rapid turn, but my tricks failed this time—the wood wasn't strong enough, so I tore out a piece and slammed into the wall. The wall held. Damn it.

"Are you all right, Captain?"

"What's wrong with your voice?" I asked abruptly.

"My voice?"

"Nevermind. Before we discuss a meeting, can I have a few words with Diva?"

"She's busy," Dmitry interjected. "Isn't this enough for you?"

"In other words, I can't?"

Nobody replied, and then something clicked. End of communication. What happened over there? A coup? I couldn't put the pieces together, but now wasn't the time for wild guesses. The stairs ended, but I had to get higher. That's how flaws come out. I had prepared for something like this in theory, so I was just being cautious. I had worked out the route as a general concept. Right now, I needed to reach the roof.

There were several ways of reaching it, but I decided on the least noisy one. I jumped out of the window, turned in mid-air, and grabbed the edge of the roof. This trick wouldn't have worked normally, but I had activated *Flight* for a few seconds to adjust the direction and make the final leap easier. This took very little mana since my muscles did most of the work. I took a few seconds to assess the situation. Shit.

It was far worse than I'd thought, although the danger came from where I hadn't been expecting it. Hundreds of Bone Birds hovered in the sky, and players were running towards my building. Or beings who used to be players not long ago…

Death Knight. Level 1.

Six Knights clutching machine guns, hundreds of skeletons, and two dozen Wights in military uniform. Not all the humans had been lucky enough to turn into sentient creatures. Hard to say what I felt in that moment. It was depressing, but at least no one had betrayed me. Yet I felt no joy at the thought.

"I hate…" I muttered, not sure who exactly.

"Are you still here, human?" said an unfamiliar voice in my ear. "Were you the one who destroyed my tower?"

Him, apparently. Based on the wording of the question, I was hearing one of the Liches. It was an interesting opportunity, but I suspected that there wouldn't be any negotiations. It wasn't about the destroyed tower—we'd known for a while that the higher undead were intelligent, but they were restricted by lots of different rules. The main rules demanded the death of anyone who wanted to take the Altar.

"What tower?" I lied automatically.

Ding!

Kinetic Field had kicked in! The blow made me stagger, but it made sense to drop down low. I continued falling, rolled over, and crawled away from the fire. It looked to be a sniper rifle, and *Invisibility* wasn't helping at all.

They couldn't cover the whole roof, so once I was safely away from the edge, I jumped up and ran, staying low. I knew I couldn't stay here. Leap, *Flight*, and I was on another roof. There was an explosion behind me as someone remembered belatedly about the grenade launchers. I knocked down a Bone Bird swooping down on me on pure reflex.

Attention! You have gained 1 SP! (117/480)

The bone fragments weren't dangerous enough for the *Kinetic Field* to react to them, and several hit me in the face. Nothing serious, the pseudoflesh had protected me from worse. I dodged three more creatures, while one bird picked up too much speed and crashed into the roof. This was just the beginning.

"Damn it!"

The flock, which I had considered as more of a background, now targeted me. While I could fight off a dozen or two winged chimeras, escaping from hundreds would be a problem. If I used my legs, and not my brain.

Blink!

Mana: 1,534/2,450.

I appeared inside the building, stumbled, rolled a few meters, and jumped back to my feet. The thought of all those creatures I'd avoided didn't please me as they still had a chance. If my *Invisibility* wasn't working, then only speed would save me.

"Are you still alive?" the Lich's voice came again.

"I am," I answered, looking around. "Can you finally introduce yourself?"

"My name is Granok. I am the Guardian of the Main Temple and Priest of the Great Y. If you surrender voluntarily, you may keep your mind. When our *Master* returns, you will get a chance to come back to life."

"Are you offering me to share Dmitry's fate?"

"Being a Death Knight or a Lich is better than a brainless Wight or a handful of inanimate bones. Give up, you can't escape anyway!"

A meaningless conversation at first glance, but each of us was pursuing our own goals. I was hoping to get some information, while the Lich was probably trying to distract me.

"Did you make the sniper fire at me? How can your birds see me?"

"Because I'm helping them," Granok answered, contrary to my expectations. "If you hope to escape, then your only chance is to come and kill me."

"Where should I look for you?"

"Where you were supposed to have come originally."

"I see, then wait for me there."

Another exchange of lies. Of course, I wasn't going to venture inside the deceased group's base. Even if I let the squad out of the bag, it would be a sophisticated form of suicide. What would be the point, anyway? I didn't believe that the Lich would wait for me at the agreed place. We were enemies, so it made no sense for him to reveal his position, or tell me the truth at all.

Activate Search for Life!
Mana: 1,501/2,450.

There was no point in hiding, so I took the chance to assess the situation. The wave spread out, showing hundreds of figures. Most were in the sky, but there were plenty of undead on the streets. Even underground. Nevertheless, I couldn't stay behind these nominally safe walls, I had to keep moving while I still could.

I passed through the house, jumped out of the next window, and considered my destination when I was already in the air. *Flight!* I had gained a lot of momentum, but still managed to land quite smoothly. At least I didn't injure my legs, and the rest didn't matter.

Skeleton Warrior. Rank F. Level 4.

The nearby skeleton turned and headed in my direction. What the hell? I glanced up—the birds were there, but not many. There must have been some effect from *Invisibility* because the skeleton's attack lacked accuracy. I ducked, sliced off his arm as usual, and then stabbed him in the ribs. *Overlay!*

Attention! You have gained 20 SP! (137/480)

Attention! The Sword of Heresy has consumed 4 SP!

It wasn't my best blow, but the blade's sharpness and my effort was enough to slice him in half. Spectacularly and quickly, but not very effectively. I was getting nervous and making mistakes...

Snatching yet another emptie out of the air, I ran. The problem was that the birds had already spotted me, so it was only a matter of time until they'd catch up to me again. I heard a burst of automatic gunfire, and the bullets came very close, clipping the *Kinetic Field*. Damn it... My mana only dropped a little, but it was extremely dangerous nevertheless. I spun around and spotted the shooter. The Knight stood tall in the window, not even trying to hide. The Knight had probably been a young woman when she was alive, but it was hard to say which one of Hera's followers I was facing.

Blink!

Mana: 1,008/2,450.

I calculated the jump correctly and appeared behind the undead. My first strike damaged the machine gun, determining the outcome of the battle. Discarding the broken weapon, the creature tried to stab me with a *bone blade.* It was a short one, which was an advantage in the cramped space if not for the difference in our skill levels. I not only blocked the blow, but also cut off the creature's arm. A kick in the chest threw her against the wall, giving me a few extra seconds. *Identification!*

Sarah the Death Knight. Player. Rank E. Level 1.

The nickname glowed red, but the fact that she had kept her name and status showed that this wasn't just a body reanimated by magic. Her soul hadn't been drawn to the Altar or destroyed, remaining trapped inside a dead body. Disgusting... and the System agreed with me...

Attention! The player Sarah has broken the Rules!

Reward for murder: 20 SP!

Additional: Change in reputation with the goddess Hera.

The new messages only increased my doubts. Finishing off a vile creature that had once been human was one thing but killing an ally who was a hostage of the situation was another. Even if I didn't know the girl very well, I had learned everyone's name during the journey. She certainly didn't deserve this fate. As long as it wasn't a choice between her life and my life.

Deactivate Invisibility!

"Mercy..." The transformation had distorted her face beyond recognition, just like a combat form, but her voice remained the same. Although she took a breath only when she spoke.

"You're Sarah, right? What's my name?"

Crouching down, I picked up the severed arm. It was cold, yet a little warmer than I'd expected. So, not much time had passed since death?

"Vasily."

I didn't want to get any closer to her, despite the touching recognition. Her nickname remained bright red, so I knew the Knight would go for my throat given half a chance. Okay, we should be close enough now.

Would you like to place the player Sarah in the Slaver's Bag?

Yes/No

Request sent.

"You will die, you will die! Die!"

Cassandra? The Knight's lips moved, as if counting down the seconds... Four, three... Come on!

Request accepted!

The woman disappeared inside the bag, and my gaze snagged on a hand grenade. F-1. Without the pin, of course.

Blink!

Mana: 515/2,450.

The explosion caught me mid-fall, and then came the impact. It hurt! I tried to breathe, but nothing happened. Not because of the fragments since the walls had protected me, but the urgent jump meant that I had fallen from a significant height. I put my hand on my chest. *Healing!* Air entered my crushed lungs, allowing me to speak again.

"I hate..."

I rolled sideways, letting another Bone Bird crash into the pavement. It had braked at the last moment, and was thus still "alive", allowing me to get a little experience.

Attention! You have gained 1 SP! (138/480)

But several more creatures were on the way, and I didn't have time to deal with them, nor mana to continue the fight. It was time to end this...

Retrieve the player Yuki (Level 10) from the bag!

"Yuki, cover me! Shoot down the birds!"

"Hai!" No questions asked. Maybe that was why I'd summoned her in particular?

The Japanese girl raised her machine gun, opening fire on the approaching creatures. Bullets worked well against the birds. Even a weak hit knocked out bones, causing them to fall apart mid-air or crash to the ground. The few who managed to get through met her sword.

I watched all this with half an eye. Mentally touching the *Spatial Ring*, I pulled out my trump card, the motorcycle. No matter how hardy the skeletons were, they couldn't keep up with modern technology. Turn the key... Despite the hurry, I moved slowly and smoothly. The machine responded by starting up on the first attempt.

Just in time. There were Knights a hundred meters away, who had already started shooting. It was like a bad movie, except that a random bullet could well kill the main character here. Or his beautiful companion, who didn't have *Kinetic Field*.

"Get on! Quickly!"

I didn't have to say it twice, and I took off as soon as Yuki was behind me. The streets of Sar were utterly unsuited for racing. There was a lot of garbage and sharp turns, not to mention the undead. Any mistake could end badly. A flock of Bone Birds chased us for a while, with Yuki emptying her clip into them, but the creatures couldn't keep up with us. Now everything depended on my skill, as well as luck.

"I think I saw something similar in Terminator," I exhaled. "Are you hurt?"

"No. They should play Stormtroopers with such talents."

"Ha."

"Listen, did I imagine it or are we being chased by players? What's going on?"

"Not quite. Diva's group has been destroyed, and some of them were turned into the undead."

The girl's hands tightened around my waist.

"I'll tell you the rest if we get out of here. You should go back now; it'll be easier for me on my own."

Would you like to place the player Yuki in

the Slaver's Bag?

Yes/No

Request sent.

"Wait, I'll change the magazine. Good luck."

The bike jerked as the girl behind me disappeared, and I leaned forward, concentrating on the road. Had I succeeded?

* * *

My happiness was short-lived. A crowd of skeletons appeared up ahead, with a Bone Horror towering in the center. The last blockade? Or were they here by chance? It didn't matter, the street was narrow here so I was unlikely to slip through.

Braking sharply, I skidded and turned the motorcycle around. I had passed a turn quite recently, so it was easier to try a different route. The Bone Horror unnerved me by rushing after me, but I managed to gather speed before the monster clamped its teeth around the exhaust pipe. Or whatever else it was trying to clamp its teeth around.

Going back was risky too as I was wasting time. A bullet came from somewhere when I was turning and scratched the motorcycle. It looked like they were shooting at the bike and not at me this time. Luckily, they didn't hit anything important. They didn't, right?

"I'm so sick of all this shi..."

My attempt to avoid a fight wasn't successful—the new street was barricaded, and there were even more skeletons here, and less room to maneuver. The only positive was that instead of a Bone Horror, which could easily sweep away a motorcycle, the commander of the barricade was a Bone Knight. There was no time to look for a third option, I had to find a way through. 'Banzai!' as the Japanese say.

Activate Overclocking!

The world slowed down, significantly improving my chances. Plus, the fact that the skeletons didn't stand in line, but scattered as they ran towards me. The bike swerved to the left and I dodged the first skeleton, but there were too many to pass through them unharmed. I dodged the next one, and then knocked the third one down, barely managing to keep my balance and maintain speed. Right... Left...

A soft pop, and everything went to hell. The motorcycle went into a spin and, no matter how hard I tried, I couldn't keep my balance. I was driving straight into a wall.

Blink!

Alas, I couldn't bring the motorcycle with me, so I landed behind the barricade but on foot. I was doomed for sure.

* * *

Not quite, as it turned out. I never thought that I could run so fast or, more importantly, for so long. It was almost a reason to feel nostalgic. I had run away from goblins an eternity ago, but I ran out of puff much faster back then. The Bone Birds complicated matters as they tried to test my reaction speed now and then, but my breathing remained even and I had a little strength left over for swearing.

"Get lost!" I gasped, knocking down another creature with my spear. Bones sprayed in all directions.

Attention! You have gained 1 SP! (197/480)

A spear was much better suited to fighting an agile opponent than a sword. Maybe a bow would have worked even better, but there were too many birds, and it was stupid to waste arrows on the ones further away. Moreover, even having *Bow Master* didn't mean I could shoot accurately while running and jumping. At least the result wasn't guaranteed.

In addition to running and being constantly on alert, I also had to worry about my mana levels, the direction I was going, and trying to shake off my pursuers. There was no point in hiding. I found out how they kept finding me by using *Identification* on myself.

Death Mark

Rank: E.

Description:

— Allows the owner to determine your location.

— Allows the undead to sense when you are close.

— The skill is active within a certain radius.

Creator: Granok.

Well, at least the Lich hadn't lied about his name. Regarding everything else... "A certain radius" was a very vague concept—*Search for Life* had a radius of about a hundred meters. This skill clearly had more because I couldn't shake off the skeletons since this chase had started. Attempts to remove the mark using *Great Healing* were unsuccessful. Apparently, it wasn't considered a curse or a blessing.

"Damn it!"

It was difficult to move in the chosen direction when I couldn't afford to become involved in lengthy battles. The only place where I could possibly find help was the main army camp, but the contaminated territories lay between us. I'd long stopped paying attention to the occasional beeping of the counter.

Plus, the undead stubbornly prevented me from heading in that direction. I could sustain this pace thanks to my increased Stamina, but sooner or later, I would run myself to death. Literally and figuratively. After all, I hadn't had the most relaxing day before this escape. Although *Second Wind* gave me my strength back, I couldn't keep going forever.

I saw a Bone Dragon in the sky several times and wondered why it hadn't tried to blanket me with its breath. Or simply crush me? I was strong, yes, but I knew my chances if faced with such a creature. Fifty-fifty. "Either I die, or I don't..."

Lame humor to match the situation. Everything was slowly heading towards failure. No, I wasn't planning to die, but I'd have to abandon the mission. I could use the easiest option right now—I had a *return card.* But I was unlikely to return to Sar after the evacuation. At least until the fourth mission, if that ever took place. Today hadn't been easy, and I was looking at the situation pessimistically. I was beginning to suspect that without my involvement, the others would fail, and the world would plunge into the abyss.

I didn't like the idea of running away but dying out of stubbornness wasn't any better. Even if I was resurrected, what about the fighters inside the bag? No, I had to find another way and I could see one, in theory.

"I hate... " the old mantra kindled my anger, giving new strength.

Attention! You have gained 1 SP! (198/480)

I was attacked by three birds at once. I knocked down the first one, and Legion, who was urgently summoned from the bag, helped with the rest.

Attention! You have gained 1 SP! (199/480)

Attention! You have gained 1 SP! (200/480)

The raven could have killed them himself, but delayed, giving me a chance to get closer. Otherwise, the birds could have retreated, which was strange considering that the lower undead had little self-preservation.

Just one emptie, which I picked up mechanically. This kind of loot no longer kindled any emotions.

"Well, how did I do?"

"Well done, now come back!" I ordered, recalling the pet. As practice had shown, it was easier this way.

The bag grew heavier with each passing kilometer, while my desire to get rid of the valuable artifact grew. Or to release the others... however, even Yuki and Steel couldn't keep up with me for long, let alone Tatra, Dragonfly, and the units. Nevertheless, I summoned everyone in turn, outlining the situation and telling them to prepare for battle. My attempt to reach the main army was a cover for my real objective. I was looking for a *window* to provide me with other options.

"I found you, boss!"

Bri's appearance nearly ended badly, because the ghost had been stupid enough to possess one of the Bone Birds. Creatures that I now hated even more than I used to hate the goblins.

"Bri?" I smiled a little. "Can you abandon this body?"

"But... what if I get dragged back to the tower?"

The story of his escape was undoubtedly entertaining, and I would have liked to listen to it at another time, but I didn't have the strength now.

"Leave the body!" I grabbed the bird. "That's an order!"

The undead's status remained green, but I wasn't going to check which was stronger in the long run—the ghost's will or the curse on the body. After all, the Knights hunting me were clearly acting against their will. They were being quite inventive, like the trick with the grenade. I even suspected Sarah had tried to circumvent her orders. Formally, she had tried to kill me, but in reality, she had surrendered. A pity that saving everyone else in this way would be difficult. But I wasn't planning to save everyone, I was mainly interested in Dmitry. I had few friends among the players, and I would try to get him out.

"Yes, boss!"

"Wait, on the count of three. One, two, three..."

The Bone Bird instantly became hostile, but I didn't give it a chance to peck my hand by shoving it inside the bag. In case the ghost needed a physical body. In addition, the undead didn't require air and, therefore, could be considered an object as well as a *passenger*. I wasn't sure if it needed the magical background, but I would cross that bridge when I came to it. Right now, I had to keep running.

"Hey, do me a favor. Can you check my stuff for tracking devices?"

"Of course!"

The method wasn't very pleasant—the ghost enveloped me whole like a second skin, simultaneously studying the equipment.

"Here, here and here."

Of course, Bri had no technical education, so the first two objects turned out to be standard communication devices, but the third one... A hidden beacon lay in one of the card pockets, behind an emptie. Son of a... My first impulse was to throw it out or crush it, but I put it in my bag. I didn't know why, but it could come in useful. Although I didn't think the undead were following the signal, it was more like insurance.

"Onwards! Don't go too far."

Another mana capsule... I strongly suspected that I'd be hit with magical exhaustion sooner or later, but the situation had improved slightly with the return of my scout. At least now I could detect an ambush before I ran into it, and thus avoid it. I was moving slowly but surely in the chosen direction.

Occasionally, I had to fight not only the birds, but also the lower undead, but at least they didn't try to shoot me with a sniper rifle. Unlike one of the Knights following me.

Attention! You have gained 1 SP! (297/480)

Another bird crumbled into pieces, and I actually staggered. Step, step, step... Check...

Attention! Access granted to the Server!

Even having reached the desired point, I only allowed myself to slow down to a walk. I picked up the emptie dropped by the bird and sent a message to the *Shard*.

"Attention! Diva's squad was found on approach to the temple. They suffered losses. Red alert, prepare for battle—we need to destroy the undead army. Bone Dragon attacks are possible. We need air defense and personal protective equipment. Time... at least an hour. One day maximum. There are wounded, medics on standby. And I'll need about four hundred experience points..."

I sent the messages three times, in case the elders were outside the "capital". I hoped it would be enough for reinforcements to arrive in time. Of course, there were emergency groups on duty there, but they wouldn't be enough. The problem was that I wouldn't last this long, there were too many enemies behind me. There wasn't even time to summon a goblin and evacuate the wounded. So, having estimated the size of the *window*, I ran on.

I would have to toy with death for a few more hours before I could circle back. It was hard, but given the System card and the ghost, I knew I could do it. Perhaps I could still turn the situation around.

APPENDIX
FACTIONS AND CHARACTERS

Hera's Faction

Goal: To reach the temple before the army.

April / Diva. Level 10+ — faction leader.

Abilities: Mage, Lightning Staff, High-speed Combat Form, Vampirism.

Fled to Earth.

Dmitry / Lone Swordsman. Level 10+.

Abilities: Sword Master, Invisibility, Regeneration, Immortal.

God: Odin. Turned into a Bone Knight.

Grykh. Level 24.

Ogre, hero, Diva's servant. Captured by the undead when covering Diva's retreat.

Abilities: Crushing weapons, Regeneration, enormous strength.

Leon Villard. Level ??? (3+)

Abilities: Mage.

The formal leader of the main group.

Cthulhu. Level 8.

Abilities: Fire Mage, Sword.

Led the covering squad to the outposts. Joined the army. A contender for leadership.

Dragonfly. Level 8.

Abilities: Spear Master, Sword (2), SMD (1), Yellow Noise, Flight, Immortal, Split.

Came as part of the elite team to increase humanity's chances of winning. Currently with the main character.

Tatra. Level 5.

Abilities: Sword + Spear, Ice Magic.

Was resurrected and forced to go on the mission. Craving Vasily's protection, she followed the *beacon*, but miscalculated. The main character's current lover, desperate to survive.

Roland. Level ???

Abilities: Sword, unknown.

A member of Vasily's first group. Currently with the army.

Mario. Level ??? (5+)

First wave newbie. Part of Marcus' group, most likely dead.

Cleo. Level ??? (5+)

An older blonde woman. Most likely alive, currently with the army.

Elite players — died in a fight with the Lich. Six platoons — all killed/turned into undead. Hundreds of the faction's **ordinary players** are with the army.

Reserve in the Dungeon:
Chemist. Level 7.

Abilities: Sword Master (no school), Pain Deactivation I, Healing, Immortal.

Diamond. Level 7.

Abilities: Spear Master (Seven Stones School), Mana Stone Creation I, Lightning I, Immortal.

Vasily's Faction

Goals: Fulfill the agreement with Hera, and capture the Altar.

Vasily. Level 24.

Legion. Hero. Racial Rank: D+. Level 5.

Golden Raven. An ancient Ghost in the body of a raven. Cannot abandon the body as has fused with it. Strong body and strong Fire Magic.

Bri. Hero. Racial Rank: E. Level 3.

An ancient Ghost who can possess enemies. Invisible. Can become visible and communicate telepathically over short distances.

Armet. Level 6.

Abilities: Axe Master, Jedi Mind Trick I, Mana Stone Creation, Immortal.

Vasily's slave. A follower of Izur. Was killed after landing in a Lich trap, possibly turned into undead.

Yuki. Level 10.

Abilities: Sword Master, Sharpness I, Healing (psychological), Immortal.

One of the Tokyo Thousand. A member of the Cult of Cain and Vasily's System squad.

Oleg the Prophet. Level 3.

Hero and Vasily's adjutant. Head of the reinforcement group. MMD, Ice Arrows.

Three special forces platoons. The third platoon was killed or turned into undead. The first and second platoons suffered losses, so one platoon in total remains active.

Survivors in the first platoon (besides Oleg): Remnev, Solovyov, Dyachenko, Melkov, Pronovich, Vikhrov (wounded), Istrin (wounded).

Survivors in the second platoon: Danilov, Vedun, Kirillov, Nikitin. Nosov (wounded), Sychev (wounded).

Dan. Unit. Sniper. Died and was turned into a Death Knight.

Forces on the Shard. Soldiers from Earth and the ***goblin army***. Elders ***Uli*** and ***Hun***, the ***Immortals Goblin Guard***. Around 25 players without a faction, and many without a patron.

Khan. Level 10.

Abilities: Spear Master, Emotion Control, Invisibility, Backup, Instant Death, Split.

Member of the Cult of Cain. Vasily's deputy and confidant. Leader of the players on the Shard.

The Avenger. Level 2 (???).

A newbie player who went to the fortress. Fate unknown.

The Red Queen. Level 7.

Abilities: Sword Master, Digitization I, Healing, Immortal.

Remained on the Shard, has no patron. A

potential candidate for the cult.

Colonel Zubrov. Level ???

Military commander on the Shard. Unit.

Odin's Faction

Goal: Capture the Altar.

Alexander. Level 10+.

Abilities: Mace Mastery, Stone Armor, Combat Form, Underground Travel, Regeneration, Immortality.

High Priest of Odin. Faction leader, tried to reach the temple alone. Most likely died or left Sar using a return card.

~~**Dmitry / Lone Swordsman.**~~ Level 10.

Part of Hera's faction, but a vassal of Odin.

Siegfried. Level 7.

Abilities: Spear Master, unknown.

A member of Vasily's first group, once in love with Lisa. Member of the European Guild and honored veteran.

Alf / Gandalf. Level 10.

Abilities: Mace Master, Moderate Magical Ability, Qi Circulation System, ???, Biolocation, Backup, Instant Death.

Part of the army, and one of the leaders after Alexander's disappearance.

Rodyakha. Level 8.

Abilities: Axe Master, Moderate Magical Ability, Pink Veil I, Regeneration I, Immortal, Emotion Control I.

Used to be crazy, but Emotion Control brought him back to his senses. Possibly in love with Nata, however, returned to Earth for practical reasons. For them to live happily ever after, needs to complete the mission to capture the Altar.

Joined the faction and is currently in the army. Helping Alf control the faction.

Scout. Level 7.

Abilities: Qi Circulation System (5), Spear Master (Qi), Critical Points I, Biolocation, Immortal, Release Qi I, Qi Claws I.

Part of the Russian unit in the army. Helping Alf.

Shanks. Level 6.

Abilities: Sword Master, Search for the Dead, Control of the Undead, Immortal.

Part of the Russian unit in the army. Helping Alf.

Spartacus. Level 3+.

Died in the mission on the Outer Battlefield, resurrected by Hera at Vasily's request.

Jan / Aitvaras. Level 5.

Abilities: Strong Bones, Sword.

A player who joined the European Guild. Didn't achieve anything special.

Nick. Level ???

Abilities: Sword, unknown.

Member of Vasily's first group, was wounded in the leg and dragged to the fortress. Currently with the army.

Brock. Level ???

A passing character in the second book.

At least **sixty military specialists.** Some died in battles with the undead.

Reserve on the Shard:

Leshy. Level 7.

Abilities: Spear Master, Call of Nature, Healing, Immortal, Release Qi, Qi Claws.

Shiva's Faction

Goals: Strengthen, survive, resurrect their god. Possibly, lose the mission so that their god can capture the Altar later.

Brahmin. Level 8+.

Abilities: Mace Master, Moderate Magical Ability, Necromancy, Immortal, Identification of Deadly Intent, Persuasion.

Faction leader. Twelfth. High Priest of Shiva. Took most of his forces to the outskirts of Sar to farm goblins, and look for traitors and agents of foreign gods.

Sahel. Level 10+.

Abilities: Determining Edibility, Healing, Backup, Instant Death, Qi Claws.

Second priest of Shiva. The Brahmin considers him a comrade and a rival for power. The Brahmin tried to get rid of him previously for these reasons and because of his caste. After he was accepted by Shiva, no one dares to say that he belongs to the *untouchables* and not the priests/*brahmins*. Nevertheless, left in command of the of the fortress garrison, in part because the Brahmin didn't want him to get stronger.

Ilyas. Level 8.

Abilities: Spear Master, Danger Detection I, Blink I, Immortal, Split, SMD.

Remained in the fortress to help an old

comrade.

Owl. Level 8.

Abilities: Spear Master, Moderate Magical Ability, Thermal Vision I, Biolocation, Immortal, Split.

Joined the Brahmin's expedition. Can pass on information to the main character.

Yokai. Level 7+.

Abilities: Sword/Spear/Hand-to-hand Combat, Face Swap.

One of the Tokyo Thousand, disappeared during a mission at the Institute by using the return card. Most likely dead.

The Great Set's Faction

Goal: Capture the Altar at any cost. Use the alliance with Izur to their advantage.

Sulu. Level 10+.

Abilities: Axe Master, Spear Master, Foreboding, Combat Form.

High Priest and leader of the African part of the faction.

Saud. Level 7+.

Abilities: Saber Master, Explosives Neutralization Field, Identification of Poisons, Card Sharp.

Follower of Izur and leader of the Muslim part of the faction. Initially the stronger one in the pair, but his position has become much more precarious.

Kasoy. Level 10+.

Abilities: Spear Master, Qi Circulation System

(5), Metered Acceleration, Cosmetic Healing, Immortal, Release Qi, Qi Claws.

Specializes in Qi. Liked by Sulu due to his strength and is considered an interesting pawn. However, God's will is God's will, and the Somali man is confident in his power and strength. Assigned him to protect Saud and keep an eye on him.

Special forces unit asleep in bags, hundreds of players, mostly from Africa.

Quetzalcoatl's Fraction

Goal: Capture the Altar. One of the main contenders.

Bill Michigan / The Chicago Swordsman. Level 19+.

Abilities: Invisibility, Air Steps, Combat Form, Sword Master, Backup.

Ninth. High Priest and leader of the American faction. One of the strongest players, probably the second strongest overall. In full control of his powers.

At least two bags with elite military specialists from the USA.

Warlock. Level 8.

Abilities: Sword Master, Sense of Smell, Healing, Immortal.

Comms operator, met Vasily during the mission with the Hellhounds.

In reserve on the Shard.

Krist. Level 7.

Abilities: Dagger Master, Obfuscation, Step

into Shadow, Immortal.

In reserve on the Shard.

Japanese Faction:

Goals: Humanity's victory and survival.

Ryuu Kawakami / River Serpent. Level 10+.

Abilities: Combat Form, Sword Fighting, Immortal.

Yuki's younger brother, interested in Tatra, whom he once saved. Many players of the Tokyo Thousand are under his command. Exact number is unknown.

Saiko. Level 8.

Abilities: Spear Master (Seven Stones School), Power Burst I, Biolocation, Immortal, Split.

Follower of Quel, one of the Tokyo Thousand.

Inti's Fraction

Goal: Alliance with Quel. Has little chance of capturing the Altar. Dissatisfied with the situation.

Lisa / El. Level 10+.

Abilities: Teleportation, Bow Master (school), Sword Master, full range of abilities unknown.

Priestess of Inti, very strong. Vasily's ex-girlfriend, there is no animosity between them.

Leeloo. Level 7.

Abilities: Sword Master, Qi Armor, Biolocation, Immortal

Chinese-Russian. Helping Lisa at Vasily's request.

Medusa. Level 8.

Abilities: Rapier/Sword Master, Hair Armor,

Invisibility, Immortal.

Helping Lisa at Vasily's request.

Spider. Level 3+.

Abilities: Daggers, Telekinesis.

Died and was resurrected. Went missing while flying over the sea, theoretically died, but could have been resurrected, or survived and changed his plans. Is with the army or in the fortress in that case.

Thirty military specialists from Britain. Hundreds of players in the army, but few strong ones.

Guan Yu's Faction

Goal: Capture the Altar. One of the main contenders.

Qing Long. Level 11+.

Abilities: Tactics, Sword Master, Combat Form, Backup, Instant Death.

One of the strongest players even though he focused on tactics rather than leveling up. Unofficial Commander-in-Chief of the united army. Smart, wily, made a secret deal with Vasily.

Fairy of the Autumn Forest. Level ???
Abilities: ???
A passing character in the second book.

Chang. Level 9.
Abilities: Unknown.
One of Qing Long's sidekicks. A passing character in the first book. The leader's bodyguard.

Ninety military specialists from China. Hundreds of players, many of them quite strong.

Dark Steel. Level 9.

Abilities: Spear Master (Qi School), Magnetism I, Stone Armor, Immortal, Release Qi I, Qi Claws I, Step Technique.

Follower of Guan Yu. Member of Vasily's System squad. Possible spy/contact of Qing Long in Vasily's squad.

Goblins of Sar

Goals: Resurrect the Great Y, save their world, obtain spoils of war.

1) Dinar — a goblin named by Vasily. One of the commanders of a squad of chosen warriors heading into Sar.

2) Hash — Level 10 hobgoblin. An old *hero* whose life is coming to an end. Possibly in the squad.

3) Fyyr — the goblin king. Fate unknown because the goblins are in revolt. However, the royal name is passed on to the heir along with the crown.

4) Ra — the goblin prince. Hobgoblin, Level 15, hero. One of the squad leaders.

5) Ro — hobgoblin, Level 7, hero. Defeated Sulu in a duel.

6) Rebecca/Reb/Re — a female goblin saved by Vasily.

Faction of the Great Izur (and other outside gods)

Goals: Open portals for additional forces to land on Sar, capture the Altar, and prevent its capture by competitors.

Iris. Level ???

Abilities: Impressive, but not clearly stated. Sure to have the basic set.

Mistress of the Pack, archon and player. Reached Sar in a blind jump by using the beacon of Heresy.

Pack: **Cerberus** (C-) and 28 **Hellhounds** (D).

Aini – a traitor and half-mad follower of the Great Giz. This could be due to the parasitic worms used by the goddess to control her followers. Died trying to open a portal for the Arachnoid troops into the fortress.

Grem – a traitor forced to serve the Great Giz. Dead.

Spike – a traitor forced to serve the Great Giz. Captured by other humans. Most likely executed.

White Eagle – a traitor forced to serve the Great Giz. Captured by other humans. Most likely dead after being tortured. However, his life might have been spared, so there is a small chance that he remains in prison.

Matrix – a traitor forced to serve the Great Giz. Sacrificed himself to avoid being captured, his soul was drawn to the Altar. Has a chance of resurrection. Name: Michael.

Traitors among the players, and agents who managed to reach Sar.

A hidden threat.

The Undead Faction

Goals: Protect the Altar of the Great Y and resurrect their god.

Karandar — High Priest of the Great Y, Head Lich. Guards the temple.

Granok the Cautious / Granok the Coward — second Lich.

Third, fourth and fifth Liches — died when the nuclear land mines exploded.

Sixth Lich — commands the forces fighting the human army. Name unknown.

Dan — raised as a Death Knight. Daniel Kozin when still alive, a sniper and member of the second Russian platoon.

Sarah — a Death Knight and player. Captured by Vasily.

Dmitry / Lone Swordsman — a Death Knight and player. Details unknown.

Other undead players. Some have kept their memories, and some haven't.

Intelligent undead of Sar. Countless hordes of ordinary skeletons. Ein the Bone Horror, killed by the main character.

The Chaos Faction

Chaos monsters that have been living in the goblin world since the invasion. External forces.

Fate unknown (possible reserve)

Bruce Lee, Rain, Viking 2001, Joseph, Nagi (4), Ben (3), Sky (3), Diego (5), Jasmine (2), Leia (3), Void (3).

CHAPTER 13
THE RETURN ATTEMPT

GIVEN THAT THE UNDEAD were tracking my movements, I couldn't reveal my interest in a particular location. I had to do a large circle and leave a margin so that I didn't find the "tail of the snake" chasing me when I returned to the starting point. I wanted to put some distance between us, since the transfer of reinforcements wasn't a quick task. I could only open a proper portal in 54 days. The *beacon* had a shorter cooldown period—seventy days instead of a hundred, but it was six of one and half a dozen of the other. I was no Moses to lead the undead around for so long. Nor was it necessary.

"Let's not shame the family name!" I muttered to myself. Especially my real family name, which was associated with long cross-country trips.

I had a long and tough run ahead of time, and

preferably with a trajectory that couldn't be calculated in advance. Otherwise, I would be met by a welcome committee instead of a tail at the end. Thinking of the hours to come filled me with regret. Perhaps I shouldn't have taken the risk and hoped that there were enough units on duty? I discarded this thought at once. Better to be safe than sorry. I'd managed before and I would do it again.

Attention! You have gained 1 SP! (298/480)

The spear struck from below like an ordinary stick, and another Bone Bird crumbled to pieces. It was dangerous, but it was a familiar and controlled danger. I was much more concerned about the overall size of the flock. It looked like another attempt to overwhelm me with the sheer number. Not for the first time, but I always hoped it would be the last.

The map was good, but still not as good as a GPS. I could neither plot a route, nor calculate the travel time, nor mark any interesting sites. Luckily, I showed up on it myself, but otherwise, I had to rely on memory. Judging by the inactive icons, this would become available at higher levels. Another item in the almost endless list of "what I want to learn". It was greed, calling the player to kill again and again, until he met someone luckier than him. Death awaits us all, basically. This was becoming my new favorite topic of thought—like trying not to think of a white monkey. Oh, now I hated monkeys too...

Less than six months had passed since the System came to Earth, but so much had happened that it would be enough for many lives. Enough for four lives, in my case, since that was how many times I'd died so far. And I strongly suspected that I'd have to die a fifth time soon. Or the sixth time, if I counted the death I experienced in a vision when capturing the *Heart of the Dungeon.*

It was enough to make a small mistake and, for example, take the wrong turn on the way back. The window wasn't very big, and my pursuers were unlikely to let me change direction and search more closely. When hordes of undead surrounded you on all sides, topographical cretinism could be very costly. However, I'd managed in the *Dungeon,* and I would manage here. I had a good memory.

"Boss!" Bri appeared. "Strong enemy up ahead!"

As if waiting for this moment, two dozen Bone Birds lined up to attack. A shield appeared in my left hand and a sword in my right. The spear wasn't suitable for this. The birds swooped down, maintaining distance and even formation, but then turned just before reaching me, and soared back into the sky.

"You bastards..."

The outburst of rage was short, but unexpectedly strong. Glancing at the flock, I stuck my sword into a gap between the rocks and pulled out a bow. The practiced move took only seconds. The arrow flew at the leader, but one of the regular birds got in the way at the last possible moment.

There was no time to correct the mistake because a much more dangerous creature appeared at the end of the street. *Identification.*

Hirah the Ancient Bone Horror. Rank D+. Level 9.

A serious opponent—not only ancient, but with a name as well. A hero. I had only seen this with the recently captured Sarah. Even the dragons, if I wasn't mistaken, were just units. Although the undead should be placed in a separate group, along with monsters. I reached forward and gripped the hilt of my sword. Oddly enough, I couldn't see an entourage. Had the beast decided to capture me on its own? Well, not quite…

The flock was turning to make another attempt, while the Bone Horror kept accelerating towards me. Standing here was suicide, but I knew exactly what I was doing.

Blink!

The birds split up, trying to find me, but I was already on a building's second floor, targeting the creature. The simple and reliable RPG-7. The main thing was to have a few empty meters behind you, otherwise the shooter risked getting fried. There was no time to prepare, so…

Hirah noticed me almost instantly and understood what the tube on my shoulder meant. It changed direction, trying to hide in the nearest building. Fortunately, the entrance was too narrow, and the masonry strong enough to stop it from barging inside. Fire! The kickback was impressive but I didn't wait, jumping out of the window and softening my landing by using *Flight* at the end.

Was I being lucky today? The explosion hit the creature and tossed it aside but, by some miracle, it was still moving. Was it a miracle, though? The *heart* was covered by a thick layer of bone armor and missing half its body was no longer fatal for someone already dead. If I gave it enough time and bones, it would recover. Well, this was like a bad divorce where the winner got everything.

"No!" someone screamed.

Despite the obvious futility, the flock rushed forward, trying to stop me from reaching my defeated enemy. Or couldn't they properly assess the situation? I spun on the spot, protecting myself with the shield and stabbing blindly.

Attention! You have gained 1 SP! (299/480)

Attention! You have gained 1 SP! (300/480)

...

Attention! You have gained 1 SP! (305/480)

Bones crunched underfoot. At first, the birds simply got in each other's way, and then I began to attack more methodically. If I had stopped for a couple of seconds or taken off my armor to make running easier, and if they had ground support, things might have turned out differently. As it was, the remaining flock retreated, leaving me with a few scratches and torn clothing as a souvenir. However, the undead knew no fear, so it was someone's order and not an escape, or part of a behavioral program.

Attention! You have gained 1 SP! (314/480)

Armed with the bow again, I aimed better this time, and the new arrow did what the first one had failed to do. I dispatched the flock leader, buying me a little more time.

"Bri, collect the experience from the arrows!"

"Thank you, boss!"

I could try to send Legion after the remaining creatures, but there was no particular need for this. It was also dangerous for him to go far since he could easily run into an ambush. It was the same with arrows. I had no time to look for them and was unlikely to find later, after I was done with the "main course". Well, bon appetit to me!

"Wait, don't kill it!" my earpiece came to life again.

"Seriously?" I was surprised when I recognized the voice. "Why should I?"

The Lich was not only using our technology and was close enough to communicate, but also had an idea of what was happening. It looked like I hadn't destroyed all observers. Or did the *mark* allow him to monitor the situation around me in some way? This was all so infuriating.

"Just try, and you can forget about immortality! I will destroy your soul!"

"Wrong answer." I circled the mound of

bones, looking closely. "Any other options?"

"Don't kill her, she's sentient," Dmitry spoke this time. As if I hadn't guessed that. Speaking of which...

"So, it's a female? You don't think that'll stop me, do you? You have ten seconds to come up with a better offer."

Attention! The challenge conditions do not allow you to stop the fight before one of the parties is dead!

Would you like to challenge Hirah the Bone Horror to a duel?

Yes/No

The creature's surviving paw darted towards me, trying to impale me on a claw, but it was too slow. Not a bad attempt though. I had done something similar with the female Chaosite once, but I had succeeded.

Challenge declined!

"If you spare her, the master will give you the ogre."

"The ogre?"

"Grykh," Dmitry explained. "You know each other, don't you? Diva managed to escape thanks to him, and he is still alive. Well, what do you say?"

"We'd need to meet to exchange prisoners, and I'm not ready for such close encounters yet. Can your new master swear in the name of the Great Y that you'll let us go afterwards?"

"I swear I'll let you go," Granok replied. "In the name of my lord!"

There was no message of a System oath—not

surprising since this number was temporarily unavailable. Or permanently unavailable…

"I don't believe you."

The Bone Horror was moving, trying to stop me, but it was hopeless in his… her condition. Choosing an attack position, I leaped with the help of *Flight*, and gravity did the rest. *Split*!

Attention! You have gained 270 SP! (584/480)

The Sword of Heresy has consumed 54 SP!

Attention! You have reached Level 25! (104/500)

Attention! You are the first player on Earth to reach the second boundary level!

Attention… Connection to the Server established!

Attention! You receive the scalable Renewal skill (D+)!

Attention! You have received the Leader II achievement! Your Fame is greatly increased!

Fame: +2 (9).

First Rebirth is available!

Analysis cannot be conducted. List of races is unavailable!

Attention! A stable connection with the Server is required!

You have received an additional quest: First Rebirth (F)!

Description: Reach the personal room or temple of your patron god!

Reward: Access to possible rebirth.

Penalty for failure: none.

"Granok?" I asked. "Are you still there?"

The flow of messages had stopped, and the Lich hadn't responded to what had happened. If I hadn't been terrified before, I would have been scared now.

"The master doesn't want to talk to you," Dmitry replied. "You killed his old lover."

"Blood for blood. Tell him that he killed my old friend."

The earpiece clicked, indicating the end of our conversation. Once again, my barb went unanswered. Despite the flow of messages, I felt like shit, but I couldn't have acted otherwise. Even if Dmitry hadn't lied and the ogre was still alive, it wouldn't be easy to save the prisoner. Most likely, they would have just killed me at the meeting place. Undead orders are much stronger than any oaths or honor. Fine.

I considered my gains, picking out the only useful one—the one I could use right now.

Renewal

Rank: D+.

Level: 1/1.

Features:

— Restores health and all types of energy.

— Allows you to reset the cooldown of all skills equal or lower in rank.

— Can be used once per one hundred days.

— Scalability. Skill rank can be upgraded.

Saturation: 0/10,000.

My breath caught in my throat for a second— this clearly wasn't a simple skill. No wonder I'd received it for a unique achievement. I was lucky that no one had beat me to it. I doubted anyone could buy it in the System store. Although I couldn't see such details at my level, it had long been clear to me that there was an additional gradation in strength and rarity. This ability could well be considered "legendary" in the language of games. After all, it reset *all* cooldowns. I didn't have that many of them yet, but what I had was plenty. I doubted that it would work on the *beacon* of Heresy—after all, the cooldown was tied to the weapon, but what about the *Dungeon Portal?* On one hand, it was linked to a C-ranked card, but on the other hand, it was also linked to my Overlord status. More likely "no" than "yes", but I'd have to check.

"Another time."

Using the ability now would be a terrible waste, and my plan didn't require the intervention of deus ex machina. I'd manage with what I had when I came up with it. Saturation was at zero and 10,000 points were required to increase the rank. It was a lot, but it could be very useful in the future.

The translucent card in the air glowed faintly, hinting that it wasn't another emptie. *Identification.*

Bone Transformation
Rank: *D.*
Level: *1/5.*
Features:
— *Makes your bones exceptionally strong.*

***Saturation:** 500/500.*

Full saturation, which was surprising. A useful thing, to be sure, but I probably wouldn't rush to study it. This kind of transformation tended to be incredibly painful, and Sar wasn't the place where I wanted to scream loudly, and then lose consciousness for a long time. I could easily never wake up.

"I'm back, boss!"

I nodded and kept running. Quite a lot of time had passed since the start of the race, but I still had a long way to go.

* * *

Oddly enough, the Lich didn't rush to carry out his threat, and the rest of the trip passed without incident. Rare attacks by solitary birds, undead barricades that I stumbled across just to feign a rapid retreat, and rare groups of skeletons and chimeras that fell under my blows. But there was no more dialogue since no one responded to my attempts at conversation.

***Level:** 25 (132/500).*

Nevertheless, I was relieved to finish my run. Despite all the tricks, the noose was tightening, and I wasn't sure that I could break through again. Stamina, medications, Second Wind—I used them all, but my fatigue grew with every hour. Every stop was a small celebration, which also filled me with vague anxiety. It was hard to get used to the idea that I didn't need to run any further. That's it, I'd reached the finish line...

Attention! Connection to the Server established!

Summon a goblin?

Yes/No

CHAPTER 14
THE PERIMETER

"EVERYTHING IS READY, my Lord," Uli bowed slightly. "May I take the bag?"

"Just a second."

Retrieve the player Yuki (Level 10) from the bag!

Retrieve the player Tatra (Level 6) from the bag!

Retrieve the player Dark Steel (Level 9) from the bag!

Retrieve the player Dragonfly (Level 8) from the bag!

Retrieve the hero Oleg the Prophet (Level 4) from the bag!

...

Retrieve Unnamed Unit (Level 2) from the bag!

Fifteen people—that's how many could still

fight. Five players, including me, a hero, and nine units. One and a half platoons. The rest were wounded, dead, or raised as the undead. Although Cthulhu's unit still remained in the third circle. They got in touch, so there was a high chance that they had escaped. Apparently, Diva had also escaped. This was good because, among other things, the priestess should have nuclear weapons.

"We're here," I said. "Does everyone know what to do?"

"Yes, sir."

"Great, then let's go!"

The squad split into two equal groups, taking up defense in buildings on both sides of the street. Unfortunately, the *window* wasn't very large and hung between them on the sidewalk, not covering either building. The undead now had modern weapons, so trying to gain a foothold at a specific location would be a mistake. A couple of shots from a rocket-propelled flamethrower, and the improvised fortress would turn into a funeral pyre. The survivors would struggle to get out.

"My Lord?"

"Here you go!" I handed the goblin a lighter bag. "First of all, take care of the wounded. Also, remind all the soldiers to wear personal protective equipment. The dragon is somewhere close, and we can't risk it until we've dealt with the creature."

"It will be done."

"There is also a prisoner inside. Restrain and isolate her. Perhaps we'll be able to save her..."

"Wait, my Lord." The elder bowed and handed me a notebook. "Not all the hunting parties are in the village, but every player is accompanied by an Immortal. You can summon them by using this list."

"Good job, but it's more important to teleport the regular squads right now. Ready?"

Recall the goblin!

Continuing the thought: traditional medieval tactics wouldn't work this time. And modern instructions didn't take into account the magic on either side—although the first notes were already available on this topic. But without being tested in practice, they were based on experience and logic, which I had as much of as most strategists in the General Staff. I planned to disperse the troops by creating a perimeter, and support them with strike groups and pocket artillery. There were enough reserve forces on the *Shard* for years of war—the government had been generous in this. Given the risk of defeat, the *Dungeon* might also end up as the main reserve shelter.

"Comms check," came Oleg's voice. "How do you hear me, Captain?"

"Loud and clear," I replied. "Remember to only use a secure backup channel. They might be listening in."

I looked at the notebook in the short pause. Someone had done a lot of work in compiling this report. The *Dungeon* was being constantly explored, so most players weren't at the base and hadn't returned in time. Nevertheless, each one was accompanied by an Immortal, so by knowing their number, they could be teleported from anywhere. Closing my eyes, I sent them a *Warning* to prepare...

I turned the page and ran my eyes over the "news". There was nothing particularly interesting or important. Only the report about losses stood out. Six deaths. Despite the advantage in firepower and System magic, humans and goblins continued to die. From rat claws, under rubble, or as a result of accidents.

Well, my family was fine, and the rest seemed hopelessly far away right now. It was sad, but what could I do?

The third page listed the Immortals, with names and the amount of experience points they could hand over. Some had a dash next to their name since there hadn't been time to interview everyone. In any case, I'd have to milk most of them to get the four hundred points. And there might not be enough time. Hmm.

Summon a goblin!

"My Lord?"

"There's no binding," I waved him away. "Unload everyone yourself so we don't waste my time."

Most people in the *Dungeon* had become a unit by this time, so their transfer wasn't difficult—I didn't have to extract anyone manually.

"Ready?" I asked. Having received confirmation, I recalled the goblin. Now I had to sort out what he'd left me.

The units who arrived looked almost identical thanks to their rubberized raincoats and respirators. I wouldn't have been surprised if the stuff had come from some storehouse where it had been lying around for years in case of another war. There was also an impressive number of weapons, but this was the easiest way to transfer gear, without the bother of loading it into crates. Many had a *Bottomless Bag (F)*.

There were almost no players among the new arrivals—it made no sense to risk valuable personnel when professional soldiers would be much more useful. At least until we deployed our defenses. Once here, the soldiers scattered, taking up defensive positions, and only the commander headed towards me.

Khan. Level 10.

"Hi. This place can be dangerous. You should have stayed in the *Dungeon.*"

"You've seen the report, right?" my deputy shrugged. "Nothing really happens there, and everything will be decided here. How's the situation? It's hard to get a complete picture from your messages via the goblins."

"We're being chased, and we need to fortify our positions. The *window* is in the middle of the street, and we need to build barricades so that I can safely transfer the rest of the troops. I'll summon the goblins, so leave a couple of experts to oversee the situation. And help them set up defenses. We'll try to obliterate their main force, and then break through to the temple. It's not that far."

"Got it."

Summon a goblin! (1 SP)

...

Summon a goblin! (1 SP)

Summoning the Immortals didn't require a bag, so I pulled out almost everyone in twenty seconds. Many had brought along bags of System stones as requested. Most goblins were dressed in altered *player clothing* with rat skin inserts and weren't armed, but, as they say, shovels are easy to find.

"Hun, you're in charge," I gave the second elder a look. "You need to construct fortifications, and the experts will explain how best to do it."

"Yes, my Lord!"

Summon a goblin! (1 SP)

Uli reappeared, unloaded another batch of soldiers, who immediately ran away up the street. Drones were buzzing overhead, and snipers were shooting down Bone Birds. My command wasn't required, I just had to summon the elder and then send him back. I decided to combine business with pleasure and started collecting experience points from my donors.

Attention! You have received 2 SP! (134/500)

The Immortal I'd chosen at random had little to offer, so I decided to change my approach.

"Tell the ones who have more than four experience points to come to me. Three at a time, one group after another. If there aren't enough, we'll reduce the number. Go."

Judging by the expression on the hunter's face, I had set him an almost impossible task, but he managed. A trickle of donors flowed to me.

Attention! You have received 5 SP! (139/500)

...

Attention! You have received 7 SP! (218/500)

The shooting increased sharply, marking the beginning of the offensive, and there were explosions in the distance. The goblins were nervous, but continued to work, although it was becoming unsafe to remain in the middle of the street. It would be stupid to use the Immortals in this battle since they would die in vain. Most had their respirators slung around their necks, and they had almost finished building the barricades. Enough.

"All Immortals—to me!"

I certainly couldn't blame the goblins for lack of diligence. They stopped their work at once and reached the *window* in seconds, thereby allowing the evacuation to begin.

* * *

Recall the goblin!

Just in time. Mines began exploding down the street as soon as I finished. They were still far enough away, and the barricades offered some protection, but something felt wrong…

"You will die, you will die, you will die."

Blink!

My traditional response turned out to be correct. I found myself inside one of the buildings. Fresh mine explosions came from behind the wall—was one of them supposed to get me? I couldn't see any other reason for the warning. Just like I didn't feel anything—not for the first time. Most importantly, the *whisper* had subsided, which meant that the danger had passed. For now.

"Who… Captain?" One of the soldiers turned to me. "Where did you come from?"

"It's magic. I'm going up to the roof."

Based on the shooting, the battle was just beginning. We'd made as many as fifteen trips during this time, transferring 450 soldiers and support personnel. A real army, by the standards of this world. Unfortunately, our opponents weren't goblins or simple skeletons, but a Lich with a group of the resurrected. Nevertheless, our chances were good.

"You will die, you will die, you will die!"

What was it this time? I spun around, trying to understand where the danger was coming from, and a Bone Bird flew in through the window. Seriously? The soldier fired, tearing the creature into pieces, but I managed to notice something suspicious.

"Grenade!"

Blink!

The explosion came from not far below me.

Luckily, I'd remembered to limit the range of the jump, otherwise I would have ended up in the air, in the midst of the attacking birds.

"Help the wounded!" I ordered and gulped down a couple of capsules. I hate...

Judging by the shooting and explosions, there had been more than one kamikaze. It wasn't just me that the flying chimeras were hunting. Thankfully, we were managing quite well so far. The less nimble creatures were shot down on approach, and not all of them had grenades.

"The undead is moving along the ground," I recognized Khan's cold voice. "There are hundreds of them. Fire at will!"

If only the original squad had been here, it would have been enough to crush the resistance, but now, it was only a distracting blow. The undead had good intelligence, so it was unlikely that they didn't know about the reinforcements. What next? There was no point in wading into the fray. I mustn't be late when...

"Dragon!" a watcher reported. "Everyone stop shooting!"

My predictions had been correct and, most likely, the undead had almost no dragons left. Otherwise, why would the Lich take so long? Even if the Alliance wasn't doing too well, the enemies had also suffered irreparable losses. We still had a good chance of reaching the Temple using brute force, as long as there was enough ammunition.

I couldn't see the attack, but the data I received was enough. The shooting subsided but didn't stop completely. Three, two, one...

Activate the Temporal Barrier! (100 SP)
Level: 25 (118/500).

It became noticeably quieter, both on the street and over the comms. For several seconds, I worried that someone would keep firing, but my instructions had paid off.

"Destroy the undead inside the *barrier*!" I ordered. "Remember, don't shoot at the *barrier* and don't touch it!"

Even though I'd obtained enough points from the goblins to errect a new barrier, I didn't want to waste them because of someone's mistake.

"I'll post sentries," Khan replied. "Do you want to see?"

"I'll be there soon."

I reached the roof after a few minutes. The *barrier* wasn't that big, but it had done its job. The dragon hadn't swoop down from above, as we were expecting, but had emerged from behind some buildings at a low height. It had nearly caught us.

"Almost doesn't count."

The creature had lost its main trump cards—speed and surprise—and it now hovered near the *barrier*, the soldiers aiming dozens of guns at it. As soon as the *barrier* was removed, the dragon would have only a few seconds left to live. A pity that the rider on its back wasn't the Lich, as I had hoped, but one of the newly resurrected.

Death Knight. Level 1.

"Like a fly in a spider's web, right?" Khan said over the radio. "What should we do with the rider?"

"Nothing," I shrugged. "We can't save everyone. Full fire at the dragon."

"Got it."

It was hard to say who was sitting there, but rocket-propelled flamethrowers didn't need to be sentimental. I would have preferred to capture the new undead, but if that wasn't possible, we had to destroy them. No matter who they were when alive...

*   *   *

Of course, I didn't remove the *barrier* right away. The battle had been short but fierce, and the birds had left many wounded. Plus, we had to take care of the ones inside the perimeter.

Healing!

"That's it, the rest is up to you." I got up. "I need a break."

"Don't worry, we'll manage," Yuki nodded, wiping blood off her hands. "There aren't any other complex cases."

I looked at the guy who had been struck by five fragments at once. I had to extract them all before I could save his life. Fortunately, I understood a little about surgery, so I didn't go in blind. I had transferred several players at the end, and some of them were healers. Interestingly, of the six veterans who chose to remain on the Shard, four had this particular skill. Only Diamond had chosen *Lightning*, but the raven's favorite had remained on the other side. Together with Krist and the Red Queen. Warlock, Leshy and Chemist were here, but I hadn't had time to talk to anyone. We only exchanged a few words. In any case, they would manage.

In addition, there were enough medics in the military to take care of the little things. The corpses were sealed and placed in a bag—no one was going to leave them on Sar.

"I'll be in touch," I said. "Don't bother me for the next half an hour."

I found a suitable room, released the raven, and closed my eyes for a moment, fighting the urge keep them closed. This wasn't the time for rest, I had distribute the attribute points.

Strength: 8/10 (100 SP) + 4 = 12.
Agility: 11/15 + 2 = 13.
Intelligence: 11/15 + 2 = 13.
Vitality: 13/15 + 1 = 14.
Stamina: 15/15 (300 SP) + 1 = 16.
Perception: 10/15 + 3 = 13.
Luck: 2/10 (1000 SP).
Race Attribute:
Intuition: 15/15 (300 SP).
Additional Attributes:
Wisdom: 15/15 (300 SP).
Spiritual Energy: 4.
Faith: 0.
Heresy: 9 (Cult of Cain).
Fame: 9.

The further I went, the more difficult it was to

make a choice, but trying to get a bonus for *Vitality* made sense. For that, I needed to invest the points in the main body.

Deactivate the combat form!

The pseudoflesh melted, increasing my fatigue, and the clothes hung loose on my frame. As time went on, I wanted to return to my original form less and less. This could become a problem…

Vitality: +1 (14)

I closed my eyes, "enjoying" the changes that were supposed to add decades to my lifespan. Sixty years, considering Elvish Longevity. The excruciating pain no longer seemed like a high price to pay. I wondered how many players across the System worlds died of old age. Not many, at first glance, but skills bestowing relative immortality were rare and not available to everyone. There were not only barriers to improving a skill, the amount of experience required to advance to the next level also kept growing. It might not even be linear. Although there was no official upper limit, even goblin legends didn't mention any creatures who had reached Level 1,000 without rebirth.

Level: 25 (118/500).

I was still far from Level 100, but based on the message I received, I could already be reborn. It would be nice to know some details in advance.

"Legion." I glanced at the bird, its feather ruffled. "What do you know about *rebirth*?"

"Not much. The lower the level and higher the rank, the lower the likelihood of success. The list of options is also limited."

"And more specifically?"

"I'm a three-legged golden crow, not a human! How do I know what the System will offer you?"

"Could I become... an archon?"

Vitality: 14.

The pain faded, and I allowed myself half a minute of respite.

"Quite possibly," raven nodded. "As far as I can tell, one of the outside gods is their patron. Remember that witch who came after us? The one who almost killed me?"

Iris? I would have liked to see her corpse... not only out of revenge, but to see the changes. Her combat form had hidden the details.

"What happens if the evolution fails?"

"Nothing, most likely. Perhaps you'll die? It depends on your luck. The universe contains countless beings, but not everyone can raise their Racial Rank. You players have it relatively easy... Oh, and if you're lucky, you'll find out whose blood sleeps inside you."

"Those three percent, you mean?" I took out a crystal and began slowly absorbing its energy. "Remember you predicted it was goblin blood last time?"

"It was just a joke." The raven's gaze sharpened on my hand. "A joke!"

"Really?" I asked. Alright, time to keep moving.

Vitality: +1 (15).

"Yes, you are actually the Chosen One. The

powers of Ancient Gods lie dormant in you! Or perhaps the Dragons of Chaos!"

"Are you messing with me?" I threw a crystal at him. With a satisfied caw, Legion snatched up the gift. Yeesh. I shouldn't have moved.

"Caw, you should get me a storage Ring!" The fact that the raven's beak was full didn't stop him from communicating with me telepathically. "What a shame that I, your loyal ally, don't have one!"

"Where am I supposed to get a second one?"

"The same place everyone else does. Buy it or, if that's not possible yet, take it off a corpse!"

"My enemies aren't that rich yet."

"You think spatial artifacts are that valuable? Perhaps it's a unique artifact for Earth, but it's just an ordinary trinket for the ancient worlds. Valuable, but certainly not rare. You are now in such a world. I'm sure the undead have collected plenty of curios in their vaults over the years. The goblins probably have some too. You simply need to look harder."

"An interesting thought," I nodded. It looked like the bribe had paid off. "Can you tell me anything else about rebirth?"

"No. When the time comes, you'll see for yourself."

We were silent for a while, and then the pain suddenly disappeared, leaving behind a feeling of lightness.

Vitality: 15.

Attention! You are the first from your world to reach the Second Limit of Vitality.

***Cost of unlocking the limit: 200 SP**
**You have received the skill... ??? Pain
Control** (E, 1/1)!*

Pain Control
Rank: E.
Level: 1/1.
Features:
*— Allows you to eliminate all pain. Other
feelings are preserved in full.*
— Active for five minutes.
Cooldown: *7 days.*

How... suspicious. The ability depended on
the situation, yet it opened up another way. By
activating this skill, I could resist the punishment
for desertion and be transported to the *Minor Altar*.
Five minutes would be enough to buy several
cards. Of course, the punishment would catch up
to me, but the pain was a warning at first, a call to
return to the battlefield, which meant that
connection must remain with the mission. If so,
then by teleporting to my personal room, I'd be
able to use the portal to return to Sar. But if there
was a mistake in my reasoning, then I'd be left
with nothing even after resurrection. And the idea
itself may be a trap.

Moreover, there were question marks in the
logs, hinting that something was off. Hinting at
interference, a malfunction, or another attack of
paranoia...

"Is something wrong?" the raven tilted his

head.

"No. I've finished."

At least with this, there were still things left to do. I pulled out the faded card, with the outline of the person who had been imprisoned there not long ago.

Would you like to cleanse the Slave Card? (10 SP)

Yes/No

Success rate: 50%

Interesting. On one hand, I had no use for it in its current form, and the probability of success was quite high, but on the other, could it be used to resurrect the deceased? What did it mean? Even after agreeing to become a slave, Armet hadn't stopped trying to free himself. People like that don't change, so his life didn't end in the worst way. His family would be taken care of, while he would be remembered as a fallen hero. So...

Attention! Cleansing was successful!

Attention! The success rate of repeated cleansing is much lower!

Level: 25 (108/500).

"By the way, is it possible to resurrect a slave using a card?"

"Caw!" the raven sounded amused. "Don't you think you should have asked that before wiping the card?"

"Just answer the question."

"It's possible, but it's very difficult. Perhaps the gods are capable of such a feat? In any case, that worm wasn't worth it. Traitors are only slightly better than phoenixes. Although even he had his good side."

"Because he knew how to create crystals?"

Under normal conditions, this would have been the mitigating factor, but the raven had noticed the trick with crystal sizes, apparently.

"You should have given that card to me! Not him!"

"And you would create stones day and night, and die of magical exhaustion?"

"Caw!" the raven flapped his wings in indignation.

I snorted and pulled out *Bone Transformation (D)* but didn't rush to study it. The description didn't specify how long it would take, and the *barrier* wouldn't last forever. It would soon collapse. Plus, it was bound to be extremely painful... a good chance to test the new skill. Although I wasn't sure that five minutes of *Pain Control (E)* would be enough. Another time...

Activate combat form!

CHAPTER 15

CHECK

3...2...1...

THE *BARRIER* DISAPPEARED, and the Bone Dragon literally exploded, with barely enough time to twitch. It didn't stand a chance against the rockets and machine guns. Neither it nor its rider. One of his tubes exploded, adding to the fire. It was beautiful, in a way. But there was no question of wounding it, which meant that I couldn't finish off the creature to gain experience points and loot. However, I still sent the ghost to see how things stood.

"You will answer for this, you murderer of women!" the old radio channel came to life. I had kept it open in case the enemies wanted to talk.

"Was this dragon also your favorite concubine? You have some interesting tastes, old man."

My attempt to start a conversation failed. The Lich made another vague threat and fell silent. The attack didn't end with the dragon's death for the undead continued to surge forward. But somehow, I couldn't find anything to do. Dumb for a general to personally lead the troops into battle. Sometimes, it helped to turn the tide, but much more often, it ended with the general's death and utter annihilation. Right now, I was the person holding it all together. My death would leave all these people trapped on an alien world, with almost no chance of escape.

"I hate all this..."

The undead knew no fear, which meant that the attack petered out as soon as the "bones" were turned into dust, and the cleanup teams took to the streets. Leaving the bodies unburied meant an inevitable rebirth. Basic undead tactics, I suspected. Throw a low-level army into battle, and then wait a bit. The dead included those who clearly fought in our ranks not long ago. True, they tended to be Wights rather than Death Knights...

"If any of you can speak, do it now."

I looked at the three bound creatures, growling and straining against their ropes, but showing no signs of intelligence. One of them had even managed to kill someone, it seemed. Or had they been lucky during the rebirth?

Wight. Level 2.

"Or forever hold your peace." Khan added. "I think we should finish them off."

"Then why catch them?"

"We were obeying your order," he shrugged. "Look, medicine is clearly powerless here, and to give them to the scientists... I've seen movies that start that way. I don't want them to bite anyone in the *Dungeon*."

"They're not zombies, a couple of bites won't do anything."

"Depends on where the bite is. They tend to aim for the neck. And look at their teeth..."

"I'll finish them off." I took out a card. "Reward the ones who caught them."

Attention! You have gained 10 SP! (118/500)

I shook off the spear as usual. Why not the *Sword of Heresy*? I didn't know the answer exactly, it just felt right. The blade would drink its share from someone else.

Attention! You have gained 5 SP! (123/500)

Attention! You have gained 5 SP! (128/500)

I looked at the faces of the Wights but couldn't recognize the acquaintances I'd finished off. Judging by their clothes: a couple of Frenchmen plus one of our fighters from the third platoon.

"Check the documents, we need to..."

* * *

"I want to talk to Vasily." Dmitry spoke this time.

"You're still alive, aren't you, woman killer?"

Had Granok come up with a new nickname for me? I recognized the good old goblin traditions. Was this a step forward from "invisible asshole"? Or backward?

"Killer of women, monsters, undead, and goblins," I added to the list. "If you're going to use that tone, then don't belittle my merits. Now that we're done with the greetings, what do you want?"

"We need to meet."

"Really?" I was surprised.

"Yes. Do you refuse?"

It smelled like a trap from a mile away, but I didn't see any other possibility. Even if Dmitry tried to kill me, I was confident in my abilities.

"When and where?"

"I'll come to you. It'll take me about fifteen minutes."

"To kill me?"

"Not right away," Dmitry conceded. "We'll talk first."

"Alright, I'll be waiting."

The communication session ended, but the feeling of impending doom only grew. Was he *really* expecting to kill me? In any case, I wouldn't get a better chance to capture him.

* * *

Clearly, this wasn't Dmitry's initiative. He had been sent here by the Lich. I was probably in for a nasty surprise. But I strongly suspected that this surprise awaited me regardless of my decision. It was better to be in the heart of the storm at such uncertain times. At least I could have an effect there. Pfft... Was I becoming prone to cheap rambling?

"He's approaching. We can grab him..."

"No, let him through. We'll find out why he came at all."

The messenger reached the center of the street and stood ten meters away, his white banner striking the dust. He had no bag or weapon other than a small *bone blade*. He should still have his cards though. It was difficult to discern the original person, and the System sign above his head showed minimum information. *Identification.*

Death Knight. Level 1.

"Dmitry?" I moved towards him. Distance wasn't only safety.

"That was my name once. Or this body? I have no nickname, no abilities, not even free will. Only my mind and my memories. Do you think that's enough?"

Apparently, I wasn't the only one musing today. But despite the ornate words, it was clearly a very important issue for him. A mind trapped inside a dead body.

"Stop! One more step and there will be no dialogue."

I stopped, almost reaching the strike zone. However, I could attack nearly instantly from here.

"You are you. Who are we if not the mind?"

"Our soul?" The Knight replied. "It's quite

possible that mine has been in Odin's altar for a long time. Perhaps the true me has already been reincarnated?"

"Then there are two of you now."

"Or my soul died, and this dead body is all that's left."

"I doubt it. When a strong soul dies, its *fragments* remain. Ghosts."

"That's even worse." Dmitry faltered. "It doesn't matter. From now on, my goal is to serve the Master. Switch to our old communication channel."

This reminded me of bad Hollywood movies. Except...

"You will die, you will die, you will die!"

...the situation was close to the end, which meant that words no longer solved anything.

"You will never reach the Altar!" the Lich informed me. "You will suffer! You will kill your friend with your own hands, and then you will die! Go!"

The last order wasn't directed at me. Dmitry swung his arm, and a vaguely familiar backpack materialized in front of him. A nuclear land mine.

Activate the Temporal Barrier! (100 SP)

"Die!" the whisper wouldn't subside. *"This is the end! The end!"*

Cassandra's Whisper continued, which meant that the Knight had to activate the charge. There was only one way I could stop him. The sword appeared in my hand, and I leaped forward, slicing his chest open. The Knight's blade slid across my armor and cut through my pseudoflesh, but it was hardly comparable to a puncture wound. *Split!*

Attention! You have gained 22 SP! (50/500)

Attention! The Sword of Heresy has consumed 4 SP!

"Die!" the whisper insisted. *"This is the end! The end!"*

I leaped at the bomb, knowing that I was out of time, grabbed it with one hand and threw it inside the *Ring*. The *window* closed, and the voice finally died down.

"Shit!"

Healing!

The pain in my side faded, but I still felt absolutely rotten. Kneeling beside Dmitry's body, I didn't find a detonator. So, the signal had to come from outside? Moreover, I could have sworn that I'd been too late. Ten seconds had already passed by the time I hid the land mine. Too long. Sighing, I took the bomb back out, but the whisper didn't return. I doubted it was because of the *barrier*. From the point of view of an external observer, this hour and a half didn't exist. Cassandra was more likely silent because I wouldn't leave the bomb lying around like this, and the future was not set. Or the two time-based skills were simply conflicting with each other.

"Is that what I think it is?" my earpiece crackled.

"Yes, Khan. It's exactly what you think it is.

Gather everyone who was enclosed by the *barrier* on the first floor."

"What for?"

"If they only had one bomb, do you think they would have sent him here?"

"Got it."

Not a very emotional reaction to news of our imminent death. If I was right, then we wouldn't be allowed to evacuate everyone. I wouldn't be a general for long...

I bit my lip, as if the pain could somehow excuse my mistake. A mistake I couldn't have foreseen, but which I could still try to fix. The knight didn't have a bag before, which meant... Yes, there was a familiar *Ring* on his finger. The one that the raven had begged me for in the past. *Identification.*

Spatial Ring. Rank E. Scalable.
Owner: None.

At first, I thought this was proof that the soul had perished, but then I remembered our conversation. If it had been proof, the Knight would have said otherwise. Why would he lie before death? And, without a name, he probably couldn't bind the *Ring*. It was quite possible that Dmitry had received it from the Lich.

Granok wanted to take revenge on me so badly that he was willing to sacrifice not only a Knight, but an artifact as well? Even assuming that he had several of them, it was so stupid... and human. I somehow expected more pragmatism from the undead, because emotions are based on physiology. Was it all for show? If so, I didn't see a reason for it. I didn't find any clues inside the *Ring* — just the remote detonator. Right, why would a sacrificial pawn need property? Dmitry's pockets were empty too, apart from a crumpled note.

Diva shouldn't blame herself for my death.

Apparently, Dmitry knew how it would end. More proof that, despite *turning*, the Knight had retained a part of himself. Enough to consider him human.

I touched the translucent card hanging in the air, and it solidified, falling into my hand. *Sword Fighting (F, 10/10)*. Quite modest for a Knight, but, at the same time, symbolic. Bending down, I picked up the body and put it into storage. If we succeeded, he would get a grave on Earth, a monument in one of the cities, and a memorial plaque. If Dmitry had been resurrected, then only a grave. Or would it be better to hand his body over to Odin?

Even if we found ourselves in the current situation largely because of the turned. I doubted the Lich could figure out how to use our most formidable weapon. The codes couldn't be hacked just like that.

This whole move with the negotiations seemed odd—they could have detonated the bomb somewhere nearby. It would have been more than enough to destroy our defenses, and the survivors would have been wiped out by the radiation, and not the undead. They wouldn't have even needed to finish us off. The only shortfall of this plan was that I myself had a chance of escaping. So, were we still alive thanks to this tiny chance? And the desire to kill me for sure? If so, then the backup plan would be out into action. I had a pretty good idea of what it was.

Check, but not checkmate yet.

*   *   *

My speech was brief and reserved, and people reacted to the news about emergency evacuation without panic. I didn't hide anything, but to them, "other bombs" were only a theory, while I felt the threat with my very bones. It was only a question of how much the undead would give us. If the bombs were already in place, it would be seconds, and if kamikaze were used — minutes. How many people could I rescue from the goblin world in time?

Level: 25 (367/500).

Collecting experience, which I commenced right after my speech, brought me quite a lot of points. This was enough to ensure my own survival. And to take care of others.

"Tatra, Steel, Yuki, Dragonfly — I need you. I'm on the second floor. Ask someone to escort you up."

All four responded, and I looked around me thoughtfully as I waited for them to appear. This part of the city remained almost untouched, and even time hadn't damaged the solid wood furniture. Laying the cards out on the table, I waited for my guests.

"You're the first," I nodded. "There are no doors, so you don't have to knock. Have a seat, the chairs seem solid."

"Aren't these *return cards*?" Tatra reached out her hand, froze, then hid it behind her back a second later, as if struggling with temptation. "Can I have one?"

She didn't beat around the bush, aware of what the situation meant. There were no complaints about the fact that I didn't give her the card earlier. It was a request, not a demand. Perhaps Tatra wasn't very brave, but she was far from stupid. She was leveling up, and with luck, could become a strong player. And maybe live for another year or two. I was feeling pessimistic again after all that had happened.

"Let's wait for the others."

"I'm here," Steel entered the room. "I won't sit down, if you don't mind. The chair might not handle my bulk."

"Whatever you prefer."

A minute later, Yuki came into the room, followed by the hurrying Dragonfly. It seemed that she had been further away than the others when I summoned them. Steel stepped aside so they could see my deck, and their questions died on their lips.

"You're aware of the situation, and it's much more serious for us. While the units can leave the same way they came, we can't. You know about the experiment Tatra and I performed, right? The punishment almost killed her. We can only leave the *mission* through these cards.

Even they're not failproof, otherwise Dmitry wouldn't have died. However, Diva is apparently alive, and I don't see how else she could have escaped from the trap. So, the cards work, you just need to activate them in time."

"Is it that bad?"

"You heard what I said. Even if there are no land mines, what will you do when the soldiers return to the *Shard*? Sit in the bag while I try to do the impossible and break through hordes of undead?"

"You've done it before."

"I didn't have a Lich's *mark* on me before. I now glow like a Christmas tree for all undead to see. It's time to share the cards."

"Shall we draw lots?" Steel suggested.

"No. Tatra, the first card is yours. You'll return it to me later."

"Of course! Thank you."

Tatra stood up, circled the table, and bent down to kiss me. There was no passion, just gratitude and a reminder of what we had. As long as the *barrier* held, we couldn't escape the mission. There clearly weren't enough cards for everyone, and the easiest way to get what you want was to take it from a weaker opponent. And she was the weakest person in this room...

"Aren't you afraid that Eva will rip your head off?" Yuki spoke up. She clearly wasn't looking at me as she said it.

Tatra snorted and stood behind my shoulder. Yes, it was a little late to be afraid. It was interesting to watch the reaction of those present. Allowing me to better understand their motives. Considering that I was hoping to get all four of them out.

"Yuki. The second card is yours."

"Are you sure? You gave me one before." The Japanese girl lay her hand on top of the card but was in no hurry to take it away. As if letting me change my mind.

"I gave it to your brother, not you. And you paid for it by fulfilling our deal. That's why the card is yours. You don't even have to return it to me."

"Really? Perhaps I should kiss you too, in that case?"

"I don't mind," Tatra said. "She can become our accomplice! We can even have a ménage à trois if there's time!"

"A ménage à trois?" Yuki asked, picking up the card and taking a step. "What's a ménage à trois?"

"Well, it's when..."

Yuki bent down and shut Tatra up with a kiss, pulling away before an icy breeze wafted from the stunned Tatra.

"Hey... you... I was just kidding!"

"So was I," Yuki nodded. "I like men more."

"What do you mean, *more*?"

The Japanese girl remained silent and came to stand behind my left shoulder. I chuckled, deciding to ignore all the hints. The scene eased the tension slightly, but couldn't fix the situation. There was only one card left, and no one doubted who would get it. I wouldn't deprive myself, would I? In that case, their chances of escaping the undead encirclement were zero. Even I didn't really stand a chance. And no one wanted to die.

"You know me," I sighed. "I wouldn't have called you here if I couldn't see a way out of the situation. Steel, the third card is yours. Return it to me if you can."

"What about you, Commander?" he asked, putting the card in his pocket. "Do you have a fourth one?"

No gentlemanly offers of giving it to the remaining woman.

"No. But like I said, I have a plan."

It was a pity to give away my cards, especially the last one, but I didn't think I would need them. I'd be resurrected anyway.

"And I didn't get a card because I came last?" Dragonfly hazarded a guess.

"Not really. Maybe you have your own card?"

"Where would I have gotten it? And I would have said if I did, right?"

So, Hera hadn't considered the girl valuable and trustworthy enough to provide her with a means of escape? Even if the gods could obtain the right cards, there was too much at stake. It was sometimes better to "burn the bridges" than relying on the common sense of the fighters. But the price of this decision was much higher risks. Everyone would die in a desperate situation.

"Then I have another option for you," I placed the *slave card* on the table. "You can choose your master. Even if it doesn't protect you from punishment, the mission will be over in two and a half years. The punishment should be cancelled then..."

"The only question is, which one of you will last that long?"

"You could put it that way."

There was actually a third option—to place her in the bag and leave her there until I returned to Sar. The downside was even more obvious—time kept flowing inside the bag. If I was wrong in my calculations, she would die in thirty days. No matter how you looked at it, the slave card was a simpler and more reliable option.

"I choose... Yuki."

* * *

Activate Renewal?
Yes/No

I confirmed my decision and looked at the list of abilities. Right now, I was most interested in the portal... Alas, my guess had been correct, and the cooldown didn't reset. A wasted trump card. However, when hundreds of lives were at stake, I had to try every option. The only positive was that I abruptly felt much better. Like a new man...

"You'll be in the first group, Khan. This is an order!"

"I'm going to stay here until the end. And I'll leave last."

"I'll be the last to leave. It won't help anyone if you die trying to play the hero. Don't waste our time, alright?"

"Fine."

Fortunately, there were no such problems with the others. Depressing as it was, I intended to save the most valuable members of our army first. Except the ones who were needed to maintain order. If we were lucky, everyone would survive, and if not...

"Get ready! We follow the plan. There's little time left!"

Deactivate the Temporal Barrier!

Tatra, Steel, and Yuki left almost at once, as agreed. If I was right, they might not have time for it later.

Summon a goblin!

"Quickly!"

"I'm ready, my Lord!"

Recall the goblin!

The evacuation process was underway and all I had to do was transfer the "courier". The elder appeared, sent requests to the others, and then disappeared, only to reappear ten seconds later.

There were wounded in the second batch, which was stupid to some degree, but I couldn't abandon the helpless people, and the chance to do it would only shrink in the future. The corpses were evacuated in an ordinary second-level bag. A pity we couldn't do it with the living.

Summon a goblin!

Shots rang somewhere in the distance. The covering force were meant to keep the undead back for as long as possible and would almost certainly die. They could have been crushed, but the undead had clearly used the negotiations to withdraw their troops, which meant the end was nigh...

"We're being attacked!" shouted someone in the earpiece. "A Bone Horror with an entourage, we can manage..."

"*You will die, you will die!*" Cassandra's *Whisper* refuted their words.

"Don't shoot, let him through!" I shouted, trying to gain a few precious seconds. Even if the attack was stopped, it wouldn't change anything. I was right, buying us enough time to send another group across before the *whisper* resumed.

Recall the goblin!

We had managed more than I'd expected, with fewer than a hundred fighters left on this side. More than I wanted, but not as many as could have been. Despite being sure that I was right, I didn't dare run away just because of a suspicion.

Blink!

I found myself ten meters away, but the *whisper* didn't subside, on the contrary, it seemed to grow louder and more insistent.

"*You will die, you will die, you will die!*"

The prophecy could come true this time if I

missed the window as I jumped back. I could only see the walls of a room, so I had to hope that I got the direction right.

Blink!

"Where were you? We thought you'd abandoned us."

"I'm sorry."

Activate Pain Control!

"What do you mean?"

"We're too late. You're all going to die."

Activate transfer to the Personal Room!

Attention! Transfer to the Personal Room is impossible right now!

It seems that the System had foreseen such a trick and blocked it. The last seconds were slipping away. I could see the Bone Horror barreling down the street. An explosion that would shatter his bones into atoms and pulverize an entire block. *Spontaneous Insight*? Or an overly active imagination?

3... 2... 1...

I should have been scared, but I simply activated the second option. The penultimate one. If I had calculated everything correctly, the mission wouldn't end here for me. I'd be able to return, even if I had to choose a different location.

Activate the Transfer to the Altar! (100 SP)
Level: 25 (267/500).

EPILOGUE
CONSEQUENCES

THE LICH, HIS FINGER HOVERING over the button, stopped. He could no longer feel the *mark*. The enemy had escaped, just like the Knight said, so there was no point in wasting a unique and valuable weapon. There had been very few technological artifacts in their vaults before. They would find another use for the people remaining in this world.

"Go and crush them! Don't kill them if possible!"

Even if he hadn't gotten his revenge, today had been another brilliant victory. Now he just had to reap the benefits.

The explosion never occurred.

ADDENDUM

CHARACTER TABLE

Vasily

General/Global ID: 89...83.
Local ID: Z-8.
True Name: Ivan Vladimirovich Susanin (hidden).
Age: 24 years old.
Race: human (97%), unknown (3%).
Race Rank: E+.
Gender: male.
Level: 25 (267/500 **System** Points).
Available: 267 SP.

Attributes:
Strength: 8/10 (100 SP) + 4 = 12.
Agility: 11/15 + 2 = 13.
Intelligence: 11/15 + 2 = 13.

Vitality: 15/15 (200 SP) + 1 = 16.
Stamina: 15/15 (300 SP) + 1 = 16.
Perception: 10/15 + 3 = 13.
Luck: 2/10 (1000 SP).

Race Attribute:
Intuition: 15/15 (300 SP).

Additional Attributes:
Wisdom: 15/15 (300 SP).
Spiritual Energy: 4.
Faith: 0.
Heresy: 9 (Cult of Cain).
Fame: 9.

Resultant Attributes:
Mana: 2,450/2,450.
Qi: 499/499.

System Skills:
— Player (D, 1/1).

Linked System Skills (depending on the player's rank):
— Intuitive Interface (D, 1/1) — convenience, features and adaptability of the interface.
— Help (D, 1/1) — allows one to evaluate System objects.
— System Language (F, 1/1).
— Database Query (hidden).

Combat Skills:

— ~~Spear Fighting (F, 5/5)~~ — Upgraded to Spear Master.

— ~~Archery (F, 5/5)~~ — Upgraded to Bow Master.

— Shield Mastery (F, 1/5).

— ~~Sword Fighting (F, 5/5)~~ — Upgraded to Sword Master.

— Hand-to-hand Combat (F, 2/5).

— Last Touch (F, 1/5).

— Mace Fighting (F, 1/5).

— Dagger Fighting (F, 1/5).

— Axe Fighting (F, 1/5).

Earth Skills:

— Basic Army Training (F, 2/5).

— Sniper Craft (F, 1/4).

— Mine Disposal (F, 1/4).

— Sabotage (F, 2/5).

— Small Unit Tactics (F, 1/5).

— Earth Medicine (F, 1/5).

— Camouflage (F, 1/5).

— Japanese (F, 1/1).

— Chinese (F+, 1/1).

— English (F, 1/1).

— Earth Diplomacy (F, 1/1).

— Geology (F, 1/5).

Goblin Skills:

— Goblin Language (F, 1/1).

— Skald (F, 1/3).

— Tracker (F, 3/3)

— Navigating Caves (F, 1/4).
— Recognizing Odors (F, 1/3).
— Horseback Riding (F, 1/5).

Features:
— ~~*Minor Magical Ability (F, 5/5)*~~ —
upgraded to Moderate Magical Ability.
— *Moderate Magical Ability (E+, 2/5).*
— *Qi Circulation System (F, 1/5).*
— *Spontaneous Insights (E, 1/1).* Your
ability to analyze can lead to an epiphany that
cannot be explained by facts and logic. Bonus for
reaching 15 in Intuition, unique.
— *Innate Mana Control (E-, 1/1)* — allows
you to better sense and control the flow of energy
inside you. Bonus ability.
— *Death Mark (E)* — placed by Granok the
Lich. Allows the owner to determine your location.
Allows the undead to sense when you are close.
The skill is active within a certain radius.

Rank E Skills:
— *Invisibility (E, 3/5)* — creates a cloaking
field around the player.
Improvements:
1)   *Eli*
mination of Shortcomings. The field does a
much better job at hiding everything inside.
2)   *Op*
timization. Allows better control of mana
consumption, increasing duration of the skill.
— *Duelist (E, 1/5)* — allows one to conduct a

duel according to certain rules.

— ***Calculating Mind (E, 1/5)*** — removes emotions, increases rationality.

— ***Spear Master (E, 2/5). The Seven Stones School.***

— ***Split Stone (E, 1/5)*** aka **'Split'**.

— ***Shattered Stone (E, 1/5)*** aka **Shrapnel** — a powerful explosion producing a large number of fragments. The sector where the blow came from is unaffected.

— ***Great Healing (E, 2/5).***

— ***Universal Combat Form No. 417 (E).***

— ***Defense Against Scanning.***

— ***Search for Life (E, 1/5)*** — allows one to sense living beings within a certain radius.

— ***Backup (E+, 1/5)*** — Time magic. In instances of death, automatically returns the owner's body to the state in which it was five seconds earlier. **Cost:** 5 SP. **Cooldown:** 24 hours.

— ***The Taking Hand (E-, 1/1)*** — enables one to take free experience points from other sentient beings.

— ***Bow Master (E, 1/5).***

— ***Spiritual Thread (E, 1/5).*** Creates a connection between the user and the arrow. Allows you to remotely absorb experience, and later on, partially control the flight of the projectile.

— ***Sword Master (E, 1/5).***

— ***Flight (E, 1/5)*** — enables one to fly. Consumes a lot of mana.

— ***Blink (E+, 3/5)*** — teleportation within a certain radius.

Improvements:

1)   *Saving Mana.* The energy cost of a jump is significantly reduced (500 mana units).

2)   *Distance.* The maximum distance is significantly increased (0-10 meters).

— *Spiritual Claws (E, 1/5).* Envelops one's fingers in qi to create quite strong claws.

— *Group (E, 1/5).* Combines three players into a squad that arrives on a mission together.

— *Instant Death (E+, 1/1)* — enables you to die voluntarily, increasing the chance of attracting a soul by 30% and the chance of resurrection by 15%. Experience does not fall below the current level limit.

— *Mapmaker (E, 1/5)* — allows you to transfer the surrounding territory to a map. Opens an additional interface tab. A copy of the **Dungeon Card**.

System Bonuses:

— *Identification (E, 2/5)* — allows one to determine the properties of objects.

— *Overclocking (E-, 1/1)* — allows one to significantly speed up one's thinking processes once a day.

— *Mana Sense (E-, 1/1)* — allows one to sense mana flow.

— *True Gaze (E-, 1/1)* — allows one to see the flow of magical energy.

— *Second Wind (E-, 1/1)* — allows fatigue to be reset once a day.

— *Elvish Longevity (E, 1/1)* — slows down

the aging process fivefold.

— **_Water Condensation (E-, 1/1)_** — allows you to condense water from your surroundings to a chosen spot nearby.

— **_Improved Agility (E-, 1/1)_** — ligaments and tendons are much stronger and more flexible than normal.

— **_Emotional Enhancement (E-, 1/1)_** — temporarily strengthens one of your existing emotions.

— **_Pain Control (E, 1/1)_** — allows you to eliminate all pain. **_Duration:_** 5 minutes. **_Cooldown:_** 7 days. Bonus for 15 in Vitality, unique.

Exceeding the Limit:

— **_Cassandra's Whisper (57%) (E+, 1/5)_** — warns of imminent death. Bonus for Intuition.

— **_Meditation (E+, 1/5)_** — mana is restored faster.

— **_Great Regeneration (E+, 1/5)_** — any injury heals over time. Does not require mana.

Rank D Skills:

— **_Kinetic Shield (D, 1/5)_** — creates a passive defense field around the user to deflect fast-flying projectiles.

— **_Temporal Barrier (D+, 1/5)_** — creates a **_Temporal Barrier_** up to 10 meters wide. Time flows much faster inside the barrier, giving the impression that the outside world has frozen. **_Activation cost:_** 100 SP. **_Cooldown:_** 5 minutes.

*— **Spiritual Sword (D)** — a spiritual weapon created by a Great Master. Contains a piece of his Legacy.*

Quality: *Excellent.* **Element:** *Unknown.* **Parameters:** *Strength: 64 Sharpness: 10. Instincts: 6.*

— Hunger (I). The sword requires qi and vitality, not only for development but even for its existence. If saturation drops to zero, then the user's life will be at risk.

Stage I:

— Overlay. Its semi-material form allows it to strengthen material swords.

— Qi Storage (1,000/1,000). Enables the owner to store spiritual energy inside.

*— **Renewal (D+, 1/1)** — restores health and* all types of energy. Allows you to reset the cooldown of all skills equal or lower in rank. **Cooldown:** 100 days. Scalability: (0/10,000).

Achievements and Titles:

— **Eighth (personal, unique)** — sometimes bad luck is so great that great luck passes very close by. Features unknown.

— **Atheist** — reduces the favor of the gods.

— **Heresy of Cain (hidden)** — leader of a heretical cult.

— **Leader I (personal, scalable)** — you are the first to reach Level 10 among the people of your world. This is a significant achievement — Fame is increased (+1). Other effects are hidden. Hidden after receiving Leader II, but the bonus is maintained.

— ***Leader II (personal, scalable)*** — you are the first to reach Level 25 among the people of your world. This is a significant achievement — Fame is increased (+2). Other effects are hidden.

— ***Divine Mark of Enemy of the Golden Monkeys***.

— ***More Than Human*** — you have exceeded the limits for your race.

— ***Representative*** — you are famous enough that your word means something even beyond your home world. For those who can see...

— ***Overlord of the Dungeon (hidden)*** — you are the master of a System Dungeon.

— ***Monster Killer I.*** Fame +1.

Cards and Artifacts:
Rank F:
— A huge number of ***F-ranked weapons***. Exact list is unknown, most are stored at the department base or in the Dungeon.

— ***Junk skill cards (F-)*** — around 15-20. Edible Plants, Hentai, Embroidery, Crafting Stone Arrowheads, Growing Edible Moss, Web Weaving, etc.

— ***Empty skill cards/empties (-)*** — many, exact number is unknown.

— ***Sword of Warrior of Y (F-)*** — loot taken from a skeleton warrior. Basically, part of his arm. Many similar artifacts have been collected.

— ***Bottomless Bag (F, 1/7)*** — many, exact

number is unknown. Most are kept with the goblins or are used by department employees.

— ***Eternal Flask (F+)*** — many. Part of the Player Kit. Converts normal liquids to System ones, keeps them from spoilage.

— ***Qi Circulation System (F)*** — obtained from the Guardian of the Heart in the Goblin Dungeon.

— ***System Arrows (F)*** — many. Hundreds.

— ***Sword Fighting (F, 10/10)*** — obtained from the Death Knight (Dmitry).

Rank E:

— ***Wand of the Fearless Sorceress (E, scalable)*** (0/1,000 SP) — loaned to Tatra before she was sent to Earth; Vasily probably took the artifact back.

— ***Archer's Kit:*** renewable quiver (E), modern bow (-), archer's ring (-), spare bowstring (-).

— ***System Dagger (E)*** — a dagger obtained from the goblin rider during the first mission.

— ***Spear of the Monkey King Killer (E+)*** — increased Durability II. Instills subconscious fear in Golden Monkeys of lower rank.

— ***Monster Hammer (E)*** — poleaxe taken from the Saint. Durability III. Desecration.

— ~~***Soul Piercing Spear (E)***~~ ***/ Spider Spear (E+)*** — deals spiritual damage, reduces the chance of resurrection. Belonged to the Chaosite Laneka. Improved after killing the *Arachnoid Queen,* instills fear in arachnoids of lower rank.

— ***Minor Return Card (E)*** (?/100) x 5 — allows one to leave a mission, avoiding possible penalties. All have now been handed out to allies. One has been lost.

— ***Slave Card (Nata)*** — a card where a player is imprisoned. Placed inside for healing and protection. Not actually a slave. Owner: Vasily.

— ***Slave Card (Eva)*** — a card where a player is imprisoned. Placed inside for healing and protection. Not actually a slave. Owner: Vasily.

— ***Slave Card (Dragonfly)*** — a card where a player is imprisoned. Placed inside for evacuation from Sar. Not actually a slave. Owner: Yuki. Armet used to be kept inside this card.

— ***Backup Key (E)*** x 7 — a card that makes one a contender to the Dungeon. Eva, Nata and Khan have one each. One is kept in reserve. Two were given to unknown veterans in the Dungeon.

— ***Heavy Sword (E)*** — weighs 4 kg, very sharp. Taken from Neuran. Used for farming in the Dungeon.

— ***Round Shield (E)*** — taken from Sangoon.

— ***Axe (E)*** — taken from Sangoon. Loaned to one of the allies.

— ***Insect-Carrying Bag (E)*** — contains venomous spiders. Slots: 9,472/10,000. Related Quest: Maintaining the Natural Balance. Control: 3%

~~***Essence of Golden Monkey Blood (E)***~~ — used by Legion to awaken the Golden Crow Bloodline. Used.

Knight's Desecrated Sword (E-) — taken

from a Death Knight. Desecrated to remove the binding to the Great Y.

Spatial Ring (E) — taken from Dmitry.

Marauder's Bag (E, 1/7) — several, some in the Dungeon, some with veteran players and in the department.

Search for Life (E, 0/100) — a card. Not studied, obtained from a Bone Knight when moving from the beacon's installation point to the temporary shelter.

Search for Life (E, 34/100) — a card. Not studied, obtained from a Bone Knight on the wall.

Skill cards (not studied):

— **Scream to Release Qi (E, 1/5)** — used to stun opponents.

— **Rat Sense of Smell (E-, 1/1) (8/100)** — bestows a rat's sense of smell by rearranging the respiratory organs.

— **Tentacles (E, 1/5) (0/100)** — the ability to grow tentacles.

— **Empty skill card (E, 1/1)** — one was spent on a copy of Healing, but Vasily acquired a new one.

— **Steel Shell (E+, 1/5), (37/100)** — allows one to absorb metals, increasing one's defenses.

— **Acidic Blood (E) (100/100)** — gradually converts one's blood into a weak acid while preserving its former properties.

— **Spider Sense (E) (32/100)** — allows one to sense spiders and identify their location within a significant radius.

— Canine Sense of Smell (E, 1/5) (0/100) — improves one's sense of smell. Limited control over the skill.

— Battle Form (Hellhound) (E, 1/5) (0/100) — allows one to transform into a Hellhound. Requires mana.

— The Great Protector of the Rat Nation (C) — skill card, not yet studied. Saturation: 573/10,000.

— Raising a Skeleton Warrior (E, 1/5) — given to Tatra. Saturation: 17/100.

Rank D:
— Mask of Cain (D, cursed).
Linked Properties:
— Personal Enemy of God II.
— Heretic.
— The Will of Chaos. Slightly improves the regard of **Chaosites**.

— The Eradication of Heresy Quest (deactivated). Reward for the head of the mask owner.

— Smuggler's Bag (D, 1/7) — one, with Vasily having partial rights to it. Belongs to the department.

— Sword of Heresy (D, Cult of Cain) — a divine weapon (Sun Sword, Inti), now defiled by Heresy and Stained with Ancient Blood (Rats, Cerberus).

— Black Sword (D) — Neuran's sword. Weighs 10 kg, self-healing, increased strength. Inconvenient. Vasily kept it but rarely uses it,

preferring the Sword of Heresy.

— *Gate of an Unknown God (D)* — a card to create a gate to an unknown god's domain in one's Personal Room. Most likely leads to Izur. Kept on Earth.

— *Bone Transformation (D, 500/500)* — a modification card, not studied. Makes your bones exceptionally strong.

Rank C:

— *Slaver's Bag (C, 1/7)* — one. No binding, used to transfer troops from the Dungeon.

— *Goblin Caves (C)* — map of the Dungeon.

— *Spatial Ring (C)* — a spatial artifact taken from the Saint and upgraded. Owner: Vasily.

— *The Indulgence of Izur (C) (10,000/10,000)* — a card that can be activated.

— *Essence of Cerberus Blood (C-)* — given to Legion to strengthen his bloodline. Used.

Important:
The Goblin Dungeon:
— *True Heart (MR: 10,000/10,000 SP; AR: ?/1,000,000)*.

— *False Heart.*

— *Golden Monkey Skin Armor.*

— *Minor Altar (Cult of Cain).* Level 1. Reserve: 0/10,000 SP.

Guaranteed Resurrection is active.

— *Destroyed Phylactery* x 4.

— *Mysterious sphere* received from the goblin girl Reb.

— *Insect Bag.* Increased control: 3%.

— *Nuclear land mine (French)* — obtained from Dmitry. Difficulty with access codes.

— *Nuclear land mine (Russian)* — number unknown.

Portal network of the Dungeon:
— *False Heart No. 20* — located at the site of a nest in the ruined goblin village, beside the lake. Third tier, near the passage to the fourth tier. The intended site for a permanent base. Renamed the Safe Zone Stele.

— *False Heart No. 21* — located on the fifth tier.

— *False Heart No. 22* — located on the seventh tier, near the ruins of a town captured by rats.

— *False Heart No. 23* — located on the ninth tier.

— *False Heart No. 24* — located on the thirteenth tier, not far from the opening to the surface.

Other:
— *Damaged Magic Heart (78%)* — natural mana storage, capacity 90 units, leakage 3 units/hour. A rechargeable spiritual stone.

— *Mana Stones* — exact number and size unknown.

— *A set of gear based on the Ratnik 2 M,* modified for players' needs.

— *Bodies and bag contents of four*

Chaosites (Neuran, Estrella, Beza, and Ilmer) and three players (Sangoon + two unknown) who died in the Dungeon.

— *Ilmer's Whip* — a Chaosite artifact. Has magical properties but isn't a System weapon. Can lengthen and emit fire.

— *Neuran's throwing needles x 2* — obtained in a duel.

— *Player Kit* — numerous, in various conditions.

— *Modern Bow (-)* — transformed using the Archer's Kit. There are now several of them, and the card continues to work.

— *Broken Spear (F--)* — the main character's first spear, broken in a battle against the Bone Horror.

— *Faded cards* from studied skills. Can be used as armor, other use unknown.

— *Personal armor (medieval)*, fitted more or less to the figure. Stored in the personal room, no longer relevant.

— *Share of Alliance loot*. A portion of what was found in the fortress, mostly valuable objects. List unknown. Part of it converted into money.

— *Alliance papers.* A list of players, their skills, email addresses, contacts, etc.

— *Dirt from Shiva's domain.*

— *Dirt from Hera's domain.*

— *Seven tablets from the ghost trap tower.*

— *A pile of System weapons rented from the goblins.*

— A pile of System equipment left over after buying Player Kits.

— Captive rats for breeding.

— Great Demonic Core (10,454 SEU) — obtained from the Empress.

— Huge Mana Crystal (25,485 units) — obtained from the Empress.

— Loot from the tens of thousands of rats killed. Cards, hides, meat, bones, demonic cores.

— Library from an estate looted during the third mission to the city of goblins.

— Loot from Sar, obtained during the third mission and transported to the Dungeon.

— Two special suits for Sarah. Lightweight and heavy.

— Motorcycles.

Given to the state:

— Tribute gift from the goblins — demonic cores, spiritual stones, rat skins, etc.

— Golden Monkey corpses — some processed, some in storage.

— Plant seeds and herbs — Vasily took samples of everything that could be useful or interesting. Some samples given to the scientists, some kept at home.

— Non-System weapons and shields from Sar — some left in the personal room, some taken to Earth, some given to the scientists.

— Legacy of the Sorceress — books, treasures, hair, diary, and a letter to her parents. Handed over to the Embassy of Japan, only copies

remain.

— ***Dead Slimes*** — number unknown.

— ***Captured Slimes*** — number unknown.

— ***Samples from the Dungeon*** — moss, dead rats, insects.

— ***Crystal powder*** — dirt mixed with the magic heart dust from the undead.

— ***Loot from the city*** — various objects, books, some silver, gold and jewelry. ***Stool*** left in the personal room to serve as a base for the altar.

— ***Books*** — magic and fiction books which belonged to the goblin shaman at the fortress + other property. Currently being studied. Copies kept by the player.

— ***Arachnoid Head*** — donated to science. Fate unknown after the attack on the Institute.

— ***Set of arrows*** with 1 SP from the rats in the Dungeon — 10.

— ***Experience points from goblins*** — 6 SP and 8 SP.

Companions:

— Legion/L — an ancient ghost/golden raven (D+). Level 5.

— Bri — an ancient Rank E ghost. Level 4.

— Body of the Rat King — left on Earth.

— Body of a Bone Bird — kept in Vasily's ring.

— The Immortals Goblin Guard (100/100):

— Two lieutenants: Uli and Hun. Members of the Cult of Cain.

— Ten sergeants: Mu, Snur, and another eight not named in the text.

— 88 ordinary goblins, most have been given a Name.

— Sergeant Oleg Kotov/Oleg the Prophet — adjutant and bodyguard. Hero. Evacuated to the Shard.

— 10/30 people. A mobile squad inside the bag. Located on the Shard.

— Military base on the Shard.

Rank: Captain of the FSB, Overlord of the Shard (ruler), Head of the Russian branch of the Guild (number: Z-8, rank D-0, member of the Circle), Head of the Cult of Cain.

Awards: Hero of the Russian Federation, Order of Merit for the Fatherland, first class, For Valor medal.

END OF BOOK 6

Want to be the first to know about our latest
LitRPG, sci fi and fantasy titles from your favorite
authors?

Subscribe to our **New Releases** newsletter:
http://eepurl.com/b7niIL

Galactogon
a LitRPG series by Vasily Mahanenko

Invasion
a LitRPG series by Vasily Mahanenko

World of the Changed
a LitRPG series by Vasily Mahanenko

The Bear Clan
a LitRPG series by Vasily Mahanenko

Starting Point
a LitRPG series by Vasily Mahanenko

The Bard from Barliona
a LitRPG series
by Eugenia Dmitrieva and Vasily Mahanenko

**Condemned
(Lord Valevsky: Last of The Line)**
a Progression Fantasy series
by Vasily Mahanenko

Loner
a LitRPG series by Alex Kosh

A Buccaneer's Due
a LitRPG series by Igor Knox

A Student Wants to Live
a LitRPG series by Boris Romanovsky

The Goldenblood Heir
a LitRPG series by Boris Romanovsky

Level Up
a LitRPG series by Dan Sugralinov

Level Up: The Knockout
a LitRPG series by Dan Sugralinov and Max Lagno

Phantom Server
a LitRPG series by Andrei Livadny

Respawn Trials
a LitRPG series by Andrei Livadny

The Expansion (The History of the Galaxy)
a Space Exploration Saga by A. Livadny

The Range
a LitRPG series by Yuri Ulengov

Point Apocalypse
a near-future action thriller by Alex Bobl

Moskau
a dystopian thriller by G. Zotov

El Diablo
a supernatural thriller by G.Zotov

Mirror World
a LitRPG series by Alexey Osadchuk

Underdog
a LitRPG series by Alexey Osadchuk

Last Life
a Progression Fantasy series by Alexey Osadchuk

Alpha Rome
a LitRPG series by Ros Per

An NPC's Path
a LitRPG series by Pavel Kornev

Fantasia
a LitRPG series by Simon Vale

The Sublime Electricity
a steampunk series by Pavel Kornev

In order to have new books of the series translated faster, we need your help and support! Please consider leaving a review or spread the word by recommending *The Return* to your friends and posting the link on social media. The more people buy the book, the sooner we'll be able to make new translations available.

Thank you!

Till next time!